HANNAH AND THE SPRITE

Monica J. Hardie

PublishAmerica
Baltimore

To Haley,
Hope you enjoy it!
Monica Hardie

First printing

At the specific preference of the author, PublishAmerica allowed this work to remain exactly as the author intended, verbatim, without editorial input.

ISBN: 1-4241-3917-1
PUBLISHED BY PUBLISHAMERICA, LLLP
www.publishamerica.com
Baltimore

Printed in the United States of America

This book is dedicated to: Rebecca Noelle Hardie
And Rachel Nicole Hardie
- my very own little sprites!

ACKNOWLEDGEMENTS:

This being the first book I've written, there are quite a few people whom I need to thank for giving me the confidence and encouragement to even attempt this endeavor.

First and foremost, I need to thank the inhabitants of Fairy Town for entrusting their story to me.

Further Thanks:

My husband, Rob, who never seems to be surprised or disappointed by the goals I decide to tackle, but instead is always supportive and encouraging regardless of how much laundry piles up in the hamper, or how much the food supply in our fridge dwindles.

My aunt, Karen Adams, and my grandmother, Vivian Yelliott, for their obvious enthusiasm regarding each chapter, as evidenced by their polite, yet frequent inquiries as to when they would be receiving the next chapter by e-mail.

My young critics who made sure I kept the story exciting and engrossing; my daughters Rebecca and Rachel, my niece Megan Wright, and my nephew Tyler Stevenson Gray – all of whom proclaimed this "the best book ever written."

My dear friend and colleague, Katherine Griffing, who went over the initial draft with an eagle eye and several pencils, and whom I will now always refer to as "The Comma Queen"!

My best friend (B.F.F.) and sister-in-law, Debra Wright, who has been a rock solid supporter of most of my antics for over 20 years now, and who always answers the phone, even when the caller ID says it's me again!

The staff at Sacred Heart – the nurses, therapists, social workers, and fellow docs – who always give me a reason to smile; on the good days and the bad days.

The baristas at my favorite Starbucks for not only knowing my name, but also my usual order of a tall, skinny mocha and a slice of pumpkin bread.

My parents, Bill and Sheli Chandler, and my sister, Tyne Gray, for being their loving, wonderful selves, and for reminding me what else I wanted to be when I grew up. I would have never even started this book without you guys! My mom should get special kudos for having to read this book three times to help me get the final editing done on time – and she even stayed up past her bedtime to do it!

And, finally, I'd like to thank the good Lord for always opening up one door before closing another.

TABLE OF CONTENTS

THE INTRODUCTION

What I am about to tell you is a true story. The characters in this book exist in their proper worlds, and the events recorded in these pages actually took place a fairly short time ago. However, if you were to ask your parents, grandparents, teachers, or anyone of a higher authority (such as your mayor or congressman), they would immediately dismiss this story as a fantasy tale told by someone with an overactive imagination. They would tell you that anyone who attempts to convince you that this story is true, is either stuck in their own fantasy world, or is spouting ridiculous claims which haven't an ounce of truth in them.

However, I would ask you to believe that the contents of this book are as true and accurate as any individual's recollections can be. I have been an actual eyewitness to some of the occurrences in this book, and those that I was not able to observe firsthand were told to me by beings of a most reliable sort. My only regret is that I cannot specifically tell you how I managed to do this, because of my fear that certain powerful individuals would attempt to stop me.

Likewise, I must keep my true identity a secret from the entire world - including you. This must be the case, because there are many people out there who do not want to believe these things exist. They are content with their own orderly world, and do not have either the ability or the desire to believe that there is another world beyond the one in which they exist.

There are also some people, although these are few, who suspect this other world exists, but do not want this suspicion to be shared by others. This may be because of fear, or misunderstanding, or because of a desire to find this world themselves in order to use it for their own selfish reasons. It is because of these potentially dangerous people that I must remain anonymous and in hiding—for revealing my true identity could result in my capture by these desperate individuals, who could then force me to help them gain entrance to this marvelous land. This is a risk I refuse to take, both for my sake and the sake of hundreds of innocent creatures. Thus, I have chosen one of your people to write and circulate this story. A relatively unknown writer, who lives in the state of Washington and who, although at first was understandably surprised and frightened by my existence, has agreed to help me in this endeavor.

But if this story is so dangerous to write, why take the risk at all, you might ask? Well, I am writing this account primarily for you—the young people of this world. This is because I believe that you will recognize this tale for what it is: namely, a fantastical but true account of events which occurred in the life of a young girl named Hannah. I also write this story to make you aware that there are things which exist beyond our usual understanding. These are things which you yourself have probably imagined, and maybe even believed, existed although you have yet to see them with your own eyes.

These things are wonderful and beautiful, and as real as the book you now hold in your hands. It is my hope that this book will touch a place in your heart, and create a small spark of recognition deep inside your brain. As you enjoy your first journey into this incredible realm, I will remain anonymous and in hiding, so that I may continue to observe this world and its activities, and eventually share it with you. I urge you to read this story carefully and completely, and to wait patiently for further writings on this subject, which I will provide for you as quickly as I can in the future.

Thank you,

Your Friend

CHAPTER 1

THE FLANNIGAN FAMILY

Hannah Flannigan looked around in total dismay at the room that had become her prison cell. She wasn't entirely sure how she had ended up here, but she did know that she had never been more frightened in her entire life. The room was about six feet in width and ten feet in length, and the floor and three of the walls were constructed from thick slabs of stone which appeared to be impenetrable. The remaining wall featured iron bars, which were easily as thick as Hannah's wrist, and a cell door which was locked with an intimidating iron padlock. The key to the padlock, a large metal skeleton key, had been tucked securely into the coat pocket of the evil (and most annoying) fairy who had made her his prisoner.

A bare light bulb hung from the ceiling. The only other light in the cell was from the sun's rays, which filtered weakly through a small window in one of the walls. The window also had thick iron bars which had been placed close together, and was too high for Hannah to see out, much less escape through. There wasn't even the barest of comforts in the cell—no food, no water, no blanket or pillow, and most noticeably, no toilet. Water dripped down from the ceiling in several areas and the dank chill brought out goose bumps on Hannah's arms.

Before her captor left, he had first gloated over her capture and then promised that he would make sure she was banished to the realm between the worlds. Hannah had only a vague idea which realm he was referring to, but she had to admit that it certainly didn't sound like a fun trip. She knew that the World of Fairy existed in parallel to her human world, and that magic fairy dust was required to travel between the two worlds. She also realized that another place existed which wasn't part of either of these two worlds, but that was the sum of her knowledge.

As she sat down on the cold stone floor and leaned against a wall, she bit her bottom lip gently and tried not to give in to the tears threatening to spill down her cheeks. Just how had she ended up in this predicament, she wondered to herself; and more importantly, how was she going to get out of it? Before they were led away by their evil fairy captor and his henchman, one of her fairy friends had bravely promised her she would find a way to set her free. However, sitting here scared and lonely in this horrible place, Hannah was beginning to have serious doubts that her friend would be able to save her like she had promised. Furthermore, she knew that she could not count on any assistance from the human world, because no one there even knew she was missing yet, much less where she was.

Because time moved more quickly in the land of fairy, than it did in its human counterpart, it could take hours or even days before anyone in her world realized she was gone—and by that time it would most likely be too late. Besides, no one in her family was even aware that the World of Fairy existed; and although her two best friends, Darlene and Ritchie, knew about it, they certainly didn't know how to get here on their own. No, Hannah sighed, she was pretty much on her own at this point; and she hadn't the foggiest notion how she was going to get out of this mess.

But wait…I'm getting way ahead of myself here. In order for you to completely understand and appreciate the dire mess Hannah is in now, you need to be more informed about those events in Hannah's life which occurred before this. At the very least we need to start at the point where Hannah discovered a little sprite named Fatima. This happened in the meadow by her house on a lovely spring morning which held the promise of summer just around the corner. This meeting resulted in both astonishment and delight for Hannah, and was just the beginning of what would become a genuine friendship between Hannah and the little sprite.

However, before I can tell you about how they met, I must first tell you more about Hannah, and her family and friends. You see, you need to understand what Hannah's life was all about before this fateful encounter, so that you can fully comprehend how events unfolded to result in Hannah's current imprisonment. So, if you'll just bear with me, we'll travel back a little while in time, and start at the point in the story where all good stories must start—namely, the beginning.

Hannah Flannigan was just an average 13-year old girl when our story begins. When I say average, I mean that Hannah considered herself average in just about every aspect of her life. She was average height, average weight, had average looks, had an average family, and lived in an average middle-class neighborhood. Hannah lived with her parents, Tom and Molly, and her older brother, Patrick, in a modest 3 bedroom, 1 bathroom house on Sycamore Street in a small town in Idaho. Her family had moved there when Hannah was just 6 years old, and she felt extremely lucky because her best friend, Darlene, lived directly across the street.

Hannah loved her family very much, although she would readily admit that her 16-year old brother could definitely be the most annoying person on the face of the earth at times. Her dad and mom were really pretty cool (as far as parents go), and Hannah appreciated them the majority of the time.

Tom Flannigan was 44 years old, and worked in the construction business. He had been born in the country of Ireland, and had immigrated to the United States with his parents and two older brothers, Liam and Patrick, when he was 12 years old. They had originally settled in a large Irish neighborhood in Brooklyn, New York, and that was where he had met Molly, whose family had also come to the United States from Ireland when she was just a child. Tom and Molly were high school sweethearts, and they ended up getting married shortly after graduating.

By this time his older brothers, who were already married to nice Irish girls and starting families of their own, had moved to a small town in the state of Idaho named Post Falls. They were in the process of starting up their own construction business, and so Tom and Molly moved there, too, and Tom joined the business with his brothers. By the time Hannah had turned 6, the business was doing well enough that Tom and Molly were able to buy that lovely brick house on Sycamore Street. It was the only home Hannah remembered, and she loved every nook and cranny. She especially loved her bedroom, which she considered to be her own private retreat.

Tom was tall and muscular, with short, curly, black hair, and striking green eyes, which would light up gleefully when he teased his wife or children. Several of Hannah's friends thought her father was quite handsome and, although Hannah pretended to be both annoyed and embarrassed by this fact, she was actually quite proud to have such a good-looking father. However, I doubt she would have admitted to anything of the sort; even while being gruesomely tortured.

Hannah grew up listening to her father tell her and Patrick stories from the Old Country in Ireland, which included tales about leprechauns and other fantasy creatures such as fairies and sprites. When she was younger, she had listened to these stories with wide-open eyes and an expression of awe on her face. As she got older though, she recognized the stories for the fantasy tales that they were, and although she no longer believed them to be true, she could still admit that she thoroughly enjoyed them.

Hannah's mother, Molly, was 42 years old and worked as an artist. Her talents were quite varied, and included painting with oils and watercolors, as well as working with clay and ceramics, which she considered her specialty. She owned a small shop in the downtown area where she exhibited and sold various pieces, and also did a lot of freelance work for an assortment of galleries and private collectors.

Each summer Molly also set up a booth at the Sandpoint art festival, which lasted for an entire week and was located in the small town of Sandpoint, Idaho, which was just 30 miles away. Both Hannah and Patrick thoroughly enjoyed the event, because they were allowed to help their mom by working in her booth and running errands for her. This earned them some extra money in case something caught their eye in one of the other booths. Hannah had quite an assortment of colorful Indian dream-catchers in her room, which she had collected over the past few summers.

Unlike Tom Flannigan, Molly was very petite, standing 5 feet 2 inches tall and weighing only 105 lbs. She had long, wavy, chestnut brown hair, and beautiful hazel eyes, that sparkled whenever she laughed; which was often. Like her husband, she preferred to be very involved in her children's lives, and both Hannah and Patrick thought she was a supportive and understanding mother. However, although usually a good-natured, friendly woman, she had a fiery Irish temper when provoked. Thankfully for Hannah, her brother was more often on the receiving end of that temper than she was, as his mischievous behavior frequently got him into trouble.

Molly's lifelong dream had been to have a whole bunch of children, as she herself was one of eight children, and she had loved being in such a large family while growing up. But during Hannah's birth, she suddenly experienced life-threatening complications, and in order to save her life, the doctors had to perform emergency surgery. The result was that she was no longer able to have any more children.

There were times during her life when Hannah felt unreasonably guilty about this and, when she reached the age of 12, she finally shared this with her mother. In her usual caring manner, Molly explained to Hannah that the two children she had were more than wonderful enough to make up for the fact she couldn't have more. "Besides," she told Hannah, "you two run me so ragged that I can't imagine even having one more of you, much less five or six." In a more serious tone, she added that she was just thankful the doctors had managed to save her life, and make sure she had a beautiful, healthy baby girl. In fact, she had always jokingly told Hannah that she believed it had been a bit of magic from the Old Country that saved her life that day. This always made Hannah and Patrick snicker to each other over their mother's superstition.

Like Hannah, Patrick was totally adored by his mother. He was generally a good kid, but being a 16-year old boy in his first year of high school, he did need an attitude adjustment on occasion; something which his father was more than happy to provide. While Hannah tended to resemble their mother, Patrick was the spitting image of their father with jet black, curly hair; striking green eyes; and several dimples, all of which put him in good standing with the girls at school.

He was a sophomore at Lincoln High School, which was located five or six blocks further than the junior high, but still easily within walking distance from the Flannigan home. Patrick currently had his learner's permit and was itching to get his driver's license so he could drive to school himself. His parents had promised him he could get his license if he made the honor role for spring quarter, as that guaranteed the auto insurance premiums would be more affordable. Patrick was definitely capable of making the honor roll, since he was most likely as smart as Hannah, although she would rather pluck out all of her eyelashes than admit that to anyone.

Patrick's trouble was not his intelligence, but his inability to apply himself to his schoolwork long enough to get those kind of grades. He was very popular at school, so he always had a full social calendar, which included dating several girls in his class. Although there were a number of girls at the high school who had a crush on Patrick, he didn't have a steady girlfriend yet. A natural athlete who was above average at most sports; he played both baseball and football on the high school teams.

He and his best friend, Brian Adams, spent more of their time hanging out at the mall or the Paul Bunyan burger joint downtown, than they did on their homework. But even Hannah had to admit that Patrick had been buckling down more lately, with the promise of the driver's license dangling in front of him like a carrot tied to a stick in front of a donkey's nose.

Hannah loved her older brother, and even genuinely liked him most of the time. Only her mother realized that Hannah also idolized her brother, as this wasn't something that Hannah would ever even admit to herself. Patrick also loved his younger sister very much, and they usually got along with each other fairly well. However, being a boy and a bit on the playful side, there were lots of times when Hannah could recall her brother being an obnoxious pain in the butt.

Like the time he had discovered a shed snake skin in the backyard and put it on Hannah's pillow, so that when she pulled back the covers she screamed so loudly that she almost wet her pants. Or the time he had tested the sharpness of his new jackknife by cutting off all of her Barbie dolls' hair. But the worst thing he had done happened the previous summer, when he had somehow found the key to her journal, and read through almost half of it before Hannah caught him.

She had chased him all over the house, screaming at him and threatening him with serious bodily harm, until their father arrived home early from work and demanded an explanation for their behavior. Patrick had ended up being grounded for two weeks, and Hannah had refused to speak to him the entire time. She finally accepted what must have been his 34th apology, although she warned him that if he ever told anyone a single secret she had written, she would never speak to him again for the rest of her life.

Patrick had agreed to her ultimatum and, as far as Hannah knew, he had never broken his promise. Hannah was immensely relieved, because she knew that Patrick had read at least some of the entries that talked about her crush on Sean Adams, the quarterback of the varsity football team. But Patrick hadn't breathed a word of it to anyone, including his best friend, who was also Sean's older brother. For that show of loyalty alone, Hannah was eternally grateful.

All in all, Hannah was thankful to be surrounded by such a wonderful family, in a house and town which she truly loved with all her heart. In addition to her brother and parents, she also had numerous cousins in town, as her dad's brothers and two of her mother's sisters lived in Post Falls. Between the four of them, they had a total of fifteen children. The Flannigan family seldom had a week go by without some kind of family gathering, even if it was only a barbecue or a birthday party.

The only bummer as far as Hannah was concerned was that all of her cousins attended a private Catholic school on the other side of town. Hannah felt that school would be much easier if she had some of her cousins with her at Roseveldt Junior High. But, unfortunately, that wasn't the case, and Hannah's life at school was nowhere near as perfect as her life at home. In fact, sometimes it was just downright horrible with a capital H!

But, before we venture into the complete misery which Hannah often felt at school, we'll continue to delve a little deeper into the life of a girl named Hannah.

CHAPTER 2

MORE ABOUT HANNAH

Our story truly begins on a beautiful Saturday morning in late March. This Saturday marked the last carefree day of spring break, because Sunday would be spent moping around thinking about going back to school the next day. Hannah had awakened early so she would have a chance to enjoy the entire day. Luckily, the whole week had been filled with gorgeous sunny days; which was a blessing considering the countless rainy days they had before the beginning of spring break.

Today, she was determined not to spend even a single second thinking about going back to school on Monday. Because as soon as Monday came around, she'd be back among the jocks, the cheerleaders, the snobs, the mountains of homework, the ...Oh my gosh, she thought to herself, I'm already thinking about school and I've only been awake for an hour! Hannah's face drew into a scowl, and she puffed a burst of air between her lips up towards her bangs, which fluttered from the breeze. Hannah had a tendency to puff her bangs off of her forehead whenever she was angry or frustrated. Her parents found it endearing, but her brother recognized it as a signal for him to vacate the room quickly.

Hannah walked to the end of her block, and stepped onto a trail which led into a forested area where no houses or apartment complexes had yet been built. It was a large area, and one which Hannah knew quite well. She directed her footsteps to a large, grassy meadow situated in the middle of the wooded glen. Making her way over to a large rock in the center of the clearing, she sat down on the soft grass beside it, leaning back against the warmth of the rock. Besides her bedroom, this was her favorite spot in the entire world. Hannah retreated to this spot whenever the weather allowed, and no matter how blue she was feeling, coming here never failed to make her feel better.

Hannah took off her backpack and began rummaging through it. She removed her journal, several pens and pencils, and the newest fantasy novel by her favorite author. Hannah's literary interests were a combination of her mother's love of reading, and her father's stories about leprechauns and such residing in the Old Country of Ireland. Hannah picked up the book and immediately lost herself in the magical journey.

While Hannah is occupied with her book, let's take a few minutes to examine her life in greater detail. Hannah was born on August 17th, 1993 in the small town of Post Falls, Idaho, and has lived there all of her life. She is of average height and weight with long, wavy chestnut brown hair like her mother, and striking green eyes like her father. Those eyes have been hidden behind glasses since the 6th grade, and Hannah is really hoping that her parents will let her get contacts on her 14th birthday this summer. She also has braces, and freckles on her nose, both of which she hates with a passion. She isn't naturally athletic like her brother, and in fact, is in the middle of a growth spurt, which has made her quite gawky and clumsy.

However, she can take comfort in the fact that there is nothing average about her brain. Hannah is easily one of the smartest kids at Roseveldt Junior High. She has never gotten a grade lower than an A- (and that was only once in a class that bored her to tears), and has always scored in the highest bracket on all of the state's aptitude tests. She is a voracious reader, and especially loves reading books about fantasy and science fiction. She also loves writing, and enters several accounts into her journal daily, as well as writing poetry and short stories. Hannah's favorite classes at school are Art and English Literature, and she also loves being on the Debate Team and in the Chess Club. Besides being fun, the other great thing about those two activities is that her two best friends, Darlene and Ritchie, are also members of both.

Hannah had been best friends with Darlene O'Brien and Ritchie Pearson since they were all 6 years old. Like the Flannigans, the O'Briens were also of Irish origin, but as they had lived in America for 3 generations, they were further removed from their Irish ancestry. Unlike the Flannigans, the O'Briens were quite wealthy. Mr. O'Brien worked as a CEO for a large corporation in Spokane, Washington, and Mrs. O'Brien came from a rich family and had inherited a great deal of money.

Darlene was also 13 years old and in the 8th grade, and her birthday was only one week before Hannah's. She had older twin sisters, named Rebecca and Rachel, who were seniors in high school and basically acted as if Darlene didn't exist. Because of Mrs. O'Brien's allergies, Darlene wasn't allowed to have any animals. This was unfortunate because Darlene absolutely loved animals; especially cats. Luckily, Hannah had two cats of her own named Lucky and Charms, and Darlene smothered them with affection whenever she came over.

Darlene actually spent the majority of her time at the Flannigan house for several reasons. The first and most obvious reason was that Hannah was her best friend in the whole world. Secondly, Darlene tended to get lonely at her house because her sisters were either pursuing their active social lives or ignoring her completely, and her parents were almost never home. Her father was a workaholic who seldom spent any quality time with his family. But he tried to make up for this by buying his daughters anything their hearts desired, and taking them on exotic vacations when his schedule would finally allow it.

Darlene's mother, on the other hand, had never had to have an actual job, but she was almost never at home either. This was because she spent most of her time serving on various committees for the Garden Club and the Country Club, or volunteering her time to numerous charities. Thus, Darlene spent most of her free time over at Hannah's house, and Tom and Molly were perfectly happy to have her over as often as she wanted.

Aside from their looks, the girls were almost carbon copies of each other. They both hated sports and math, but loved reading and writing. They were in the same clubs at school, and English Literature was also Darlene's favorite class. Unlike Hannah, Darlene was quite tall for her age and was so skinny that some of the more obnoxious kids at school called her "stork legs." She had bright red curly hair, sky blue eyes, and twice as many freckles as Hannah.

Darlene's house was directly across the street from Hannah's, and the girls' bedrooms were both on the upper floors facing the street, so they could look out their windows and see each other. To take further advantage of this arrangement, the girls had purchased walkie-talkies. This allowed them to carry on conversations well into the night, even when they were supposed to be in bed sleeping.

On one occasion they had promised themselves that they would stay up all night; talking to each other, telling jokes, and making up stories. The next morning, Hannah's mom had found her daughter sitting under her window fast asleep, with her head on the window sill and the walkie-talkie still clutched in her hand. Unfortunately, it was a school day, and both girls had to struggle to stay awake during their classes. The walkie-talkies were confiscated for an entire month after that little incident.

The girls were virtually inseparable; a fact which Mr. O'Brien was not exactly happy about. He was actually somewhat disapproving of the relationship because Hannah came from a middle-class working family, and he preferred that Darlene hang out with the kids at the country club. Mrs. O'Brien didn't disapprove of Hannah or her relationship with her daughter, although she also wished that her youngest would hang out with the more popular kids. Luckily, their main desire was that their daughters were happy, and so they accepted the friendship on that basis.

Hannah and Darlene's other best friend was a 13-year old boy named Ritchie Pearson, who lived three houses away on Darlene's side of the street. They had all been best friends since they were 6 years old, and Ritchie was in several of their classes at school. He was basically a "boy genius" when it came to computers and other electronic gadgetry, and his basement workshop was filled with half-finished projects. Ritchie felt he had already discovered several inventions that would make him rich and famous; if and when they were finally unveiled to an unsuspecting public. He shared most of these fabulous ideas with the girls, who agreed they definitely seemed promising.

However, Ritchie could never entirely finish one project, before his big brain was already thinking of another which could be even better. This explained why his basement was filled with so many half-finished projects, all of which Ritchie fully expected to complete at some future point in time. Unfortunately, Ritchie's genius IQ, combined with his love of science and computers, earned him the title of "nerd" at school. He was ignored by the jocks and cheerleaders, while being teased and ridiculed by the kids who hung out in the snobby, rich crowd. Ritchie breezed through life acting as if none of this bothered him, but Darlene and Hannah knew better. They were aware that the sarcastic, rude remarks from fellow classmates actually hurt his feelings a lot and contributed to his general feeling of loneliness.

His loneliness was further intensified by his home life, as he was the only child who still lived at home. His older brother lived in Oregon, where he was pursuing his postgraduate degree, and his sister was attending Whitman College in Walla Walla, Washington, on an academic scholarship. Ritchie knew that his parents had not intended to have more than two children, but they always reassured him that he was their "happy surprise."

Like his siblings, his parents were both brilliant and taught at Gonzaga University in Spokane, Washington. They were kind people who loved their son very much, but they were too absorbed in their teaching careers, as well as various academic pursuits, to pay much attention to their youngest child.

Thus, his friendship with Hannah and Darlene was quite likely the most important thing in his life. Ritchie had actually had a crush on Hannah for several years now, but Hannah had no clue whatsoever, and he planned on keeping it a secret forever...

Now that we have expanded our knowledge with a large amount of background information, we shall return to the meadow in the middle of the peaceful wooded glen. Hannah has just finished reading several chapters in her new book, and, as she inserts a bookmark to save her place, she lets a heartfelt sigh escape. The sigh sounds extremely loud in the soothing silence of the meadow, and for a brief moment Hannah looks around to make sure she hasn't been overheard. Once she is sure she is all alone, with the exception of birds, bugs, and a few squirrels; a feeling of relief washes over her.

The sigh was because she had to remove herself from the wondrous journey contained in the book's pages, and return back to the real world, which was nowhere near as exciting. In fact, Hannah thought, my life has got to be the most boring one in the entire world. She recognized that she was probably being a typical teenager and exaggerating her circumstances, yet it certainly felt like it was true.

Last year she had expected that 7th grade was going to be difficult, what with going to a brand new school, with new rules and new teachers, and a bunch of older kids. Also, the 7th grade class itself was made up of kids from several different elementary schools, which just compounded the number of unknown faces.

But Hannah had thought that 8th grade would be much different. She had expected that having her first year of junior high under her belt would result in her blossoming into a sophisticated and self-assured young lady, who would be invited into the popular clique with open arms. Unfortunately, the only thing which seemed to be blossoming this year was her acne, she thought gloomily; so much for an exciting life. Why couldn't some of the wonderful things that her books contained, happen to her? It just wasn't fair!

Hannah put down her novel and reluctantly picked up her journal, intending to start on this day's entry. She placed the end of the pencil in her mouth and gently nibbled on the eraser; yet another one of her habits which she was entirely unaware of. She abruptly decided on what she was going to write about, and removed the pencil from her mouth in preparation.

With the exception of having to deal with the cheerleaders and rich snobs, she was willing to admit that there were numerous aspects of 8th grade which she truly enjoyed. She was fond of her art class, and she loved her English

Literature class, which was taught by her favorite teacher, Mr. McKenzie. He was also the leader of the Debate Team, and was the one who had encouraged Hannah and her friends to join. Hannah was forever grateful for that because she loved participating on the team.

So although Hannah had to admit that she liked junior high for the most part, she still wanted to accomplish three major goals in what was left of the school year. She honestly didn't have the first clue about how she was going to achieve these goals, but being the disciplined child that she was, she dutifully recorded them in her daily journal. Her entry for the day looked like this:

I will let Sean know that I have a crush on him so he will decide to date me, instead of that snobby little cheerleader, Erika.

I will become part of the popular girls' group.

I will have my own adventure to make up for how boring my life has been up to this point.

Little did Hannah know how hectic and exciting her life was going to become; and all because of those three little wishes.

CHAPTER 3

HANNAH MEETS THE SPRITE

Hannah had barely finished writing down her goals, when she thought she heard a call for help floating by on the gentle breeze. She set her journal down with a surprised look on her face, and glanced around the meadow. She saw nothing out of the ordinary, and certainly nothing which suggested any presence besides her own. She listened carefully for a few more minutes before deciding that it must have been her imagination. She had just returned her journal to her lap and begun writing again, when she heard a slightly louder call for help. This time Hannah was quite positive she had actually heard a real voice, and was no longer willing to chalk it up to an overactive imagination.

She carefully put her writing stuff back into her backpack, and slowly stood up to look around. Once again, she saw absolutely nothing which would suggest another presence in the meadow. If this is Darlene or Ritchie playing a stupid joke on me, I'm going to be pretty upset with them, she thought to herself. While facing away from the rock, she heard several more calls for help, each one louder than the last, and she decided that the voice was coming from the other side of the rock. Hannah walked around the rock while her eyes roved around the meadow, scouring the grass and trees for the owner of the voice.

Thinking that the sounds were coming from beyond the meadow, in the woods themselves, she began to slowly walk in that direction. After walking ten or fifteen feet, and just as she lifted up her right foot and prepared to set it down; she distinctly heard a small, yet irate, voice call out and say, "If you don't mind, I'd rather not be squashed by your gigantic foot." Hannah stopped suddenly, with her foot frozen in the air, and angled her head down so that she could see the place she was about to walk through. To her surprise and amazement, there was a tiny girl about 4 inches tall, with tiny wings on her back, caught in a large spider web. She had golden blond hair tied back in a ponytail, bright blue eyes, and was clothed in a bright purple, sleeveless tunic which came down to just above her knees.

Hannah stood there frozen in place with an awestruck look on her face for what seemed like an eternity, but was actually only several seconds. Initially, her mind had gone entirely blank, but now the same thought kept running through it—this cannot really be happening to me! The tiny girl began to snap her impossibly tiny fingers together, while she glared up at Hannah impatiently.

"Hey, you big, dumb ox! Are you going to get me out of here before I become a spider's main course?" Hannah blinked her eyes in shock and looked more carefully around the web. Sure enough, a large, black spider had appeared at one corner of the web, attracted by the small girl's struggles.

Hannah quickly stooped down and began pulling strands of web off of the girl's wings, arms, and legs. When she felt she had removed enough of the webbing, she plucked the girl out and set her down on the grass; safe and in one piece. Without even a thank-you, the girl dove into the grass underneath the spider web and began frantically searching through it.

After watching her for several minutes, Hannah ventured to ask a question. "What are you looking for? "Maybe I can help you find it."

The girl pushed her head out of a clump of weeds and looked at Hannah appraisingly.

"I'm looking for my magic wand," she said. "That is, if you haven't already stepped on it and broken it into a bazillion tiny pieces."

Hannah crouched down and began to run her hands carefully through the grass, before she realized that she didn't even know what a magic wand looked like.

"Uh, could you kind of describe it to me?" Hannah asked. The girl poked her head up from the grass again, and looked at Hannah with a peeved expression on her face.

"Oh my goodness, you're almost as useless as a piece of dog poop!" she snapped, before crouching back down to resume her frantic search. Hannah's jaw dropped open in amazement, as she stared at the tiny girl's back. This was really getting to be too much. First, she had been forced to accept the presence of this small creature, and now she was being snapped at after she had just saved its life. Hannah blew a large puff of air up at her bangs, and placed her hands squarely on her hips.

"Now just a doggone minute," she started to say, when she was suddenly interrupted by a gleeful shout. The creature pounced on something hidden beneath a clump of grass, and then held the object aloft in triumph as she began skipping around merrily. The object she was holding was only about an inch in length, and was shiny gold in color with a silver star on top. All in all, Hannah didn't feel it was that impressive of a sight. Unfortunately, she ventured to repeat her opinion out loud, and the dancing stopped at once.

"For your information, this magic wand is called Twinkle and it is very powerful," the girl stated while glowering at Hannah. "Twinkle allows me to perform all of the magic that a sprite is capable of performing." Hannah permitted herself a moment to digest this bit of information.

"Then why weren't you able to free yourself from the spider web and how did you get stuck in there to begin with?" These questions caused the girl to scowl fiercely.

"One is only able to perform the magic, if the magic wand is being held in one's hand," she stated with frigid politeness. "And I was caught in the spider's web because I was trying to follow a group of fairies through the meadow on a little adventure last night. But I was trying too hard to keep up with them, rather than watching where I was going, and ran straight into this web. I was so surprised that I accidentally dropped my magic wand."

"But why didn't any of the fairies stop to set you free?" Hannah asked. At this question, the girl's face lost her scowl, and she stared sadly down at the pointed shoes on her tiny feet.

"Well," she started, and then hesitated. "They really didn't want me to come with them, I guess. It was just supposed to be a fairy night of adventure out in the Human World, and they wanted to keep it a secret. But I overheard one of my sisters talking to her friend about it, and threatened to tell our parents if she didn't let me come, too. My sister was pretty mad at first, but then she agreed to let me come along. She used her magic fairy dust to get me into your world, but then they ditched me when we got to this meadow. But I don't think they knew I got stuck in the web, or that I dropped my magic wand, because I'm sure my sister wouldn't just fly off and leave me alone like that."

A small tear slid down her tiny cheek and she sniffed quietly. "But now I've been away from home all night, and by the time I return my father is going to know everything that happened. Also, although only one day has passed in your world, close to a week has probably passed in mine, and my parents will be frantic. I'm going to get in big trouble and will probably have my wand taken away for at least a week!"

In spite of the girl's initially snappish behavior, Hannah found herself feeling sorry for her now. She looked around for something to use as a Kleenex and settled on a small blade of grass, which she plucked and then offered to the girl as a truce. The sprite gratefully accepted it and began wiping the tears off her tiny cheeks.

The sniffing slowly stopped and she finally looked up at Hannah with a shy grin. "I suppose we haven't been properly introduced yet. My name is Fatima, and I'm a sprite from Fairy Town," she told Hannah cheerfully, all thoughts of tears entirely forgotten.

"A sprite," Hannah repeated thoughtfully, "from Fairy Town." Hannah continued staring at the little sprite, while her brain struggled to process this impossible bit of information. "Oh my gosh," she said out loud, "I must be dreaming," and to test this theory she reached up and pinched herself on the arm. Realizing how rude this sounded, and remembering the sprite's previously prickly behavior, Hannah quickly rephrased her comment. "I mean, I can hardly believe this is happening to me. Not even in my wildest dreams would I ever have guessed that sprites and fairies actually existed."

The tiny sprite giggled and clapped her little hands together gleefully. "Oh, we exist all right," she replied. "It's just that we seldom let a human catch a glimpse of us, much less carry on a conversation with one."

Hannah mulled this information over in her head for a few moments before replying. "So why did you allow me to see you?" Fatima blushed and looked down at the toes of her shoes, obviously embarrassed.

"Well, I didn't actually have a choice for two important reasons. First of all, I couldn't free myself from the spider web without my magic wand, which I had already accidentally dropped. So, obviously, I needed to be visible in order for you to be able to help me. And second, sprites are only able to be invisible at night in the Human World, unless they have their magic wand available to cast an invisibility spell. Now that I have Twinkle back in my possession, I can give you a little demonstration."

Fatima pulled herself up to her full height and waved her magic wand over her head, while muttering a few words which were incomprehensible to Hannah. "Ta-da!" she proudly exclaimed when she was finished. Hannah stared at the place the sprite had been. All that remained were two tiny wings, hovering in the air all by themselves.

"Uh, I can still see your wings," Hannah replied hesitantly. Something that sounded like "Gosh, darn it" came floating out of the empty air, and then again she heard a few muttered words of magic. Suddenly, the tiny wings disappeared, and two tiny feet with pointy-toed shoes appeared to take their place. Hannah quickly put her hand up to her mouth to cover a smile, and then informed Fatima that she still wasn't completely invisible. Again the muttered words of magic, longer and more emphatic this time, and the tiny feet disappeared.

All that remained in the area where Fatima had been standing was the tiny magic wand, floating around in the air all by itself. Hannah clapped her hands together and exclaimed how amazing the trick was. Fatima suddenly reappeared with a big grin on her face, obviously pleased with herself.

"See," she said proudly, "if you hadn't already known it, you wouldn't have had a clue that I was standing there!" Hannah nodded her head vigorously in agreement. She had decided not to burst the little sprite's bubble by telling her she had failed to include her wand in the spell.

Instead, she decided to steer the conversation back to the whole issue of sprites and fairies even existing in the first place. Hannah described to Fatima the stories her father had told her since she was just a little girl. She especially focused on the ones involving leprechauns and fairies and such, living in the Old Country of Ireland. Fairly bursting with excitement, Hannah asked Fatima if any of these stories were indeed true. Fatima invited Hannah to sit down on the grass and make herself more comfortable. She then flew up and perched on a plant leaf, eye level with Hannah, and began to tell her all about the magical world of sprites and fairies.

Their conversation lasted for several hours, and the rest of that Saturday morning was gone in a flash. As Fatima started her long and detailed explanation, Hannah sat back comfortably and listened for the most part; although she did politely interrupt on several occasions to ask a question or two. Fatima was very patient with the questioning and was obviously enjoying the opportunity to teach her new friend all about her people and the world in which they lived.

In the interest of time, and the conservation of paper, I am not going to write out their entire conversation. However, I will describe to you the most important points of their discussion, and I assure you that the information which follows is entirely accurate.

Fatima began by explaining to Hannah that she is a junior sprite who comes from a place called Fairy Town, which exists in a world parallel to

Hannah's. Fairy Town is full of fairies and sprites. One must begin as a junior sprite and then, through education and the practice of magic, one becomes a senior sprite, and then ultimately becomes a fairy. Sprites' magical powers are much more limited than fairies' in several ways.

First of all, sprites have to possess their magic wands at all times in order to perform any magic. Fatima's magic wand is called Twinkle, and she has had it since the day she was born. The only powers she possesses without her wand are the ability to fly, and the ability to be invisible in the Human World. However, invisibility is only possible at nighttime unless an invisibility spell is cast, which is why Hannah was able to see her in the web.

As long as they have their magic wands, sprites are able to perform a variety of magic, but the most important are the three basic spells. Hannah later recorded these spells in her journal to help her remember them, and the entry looked like this:

Sprites can transfer themselves from one place to another instantly.

Sprites can freeze a human being in place for a certain amount of time and then unfreeze them, leaving the human with no memory of it.

Sprites can grant a human being simple wishes; senior sprites can grant more complex wishes.

A common punishment for sprites is to have their wands taken away for a certain period of time, depending on the offense. Fatima admits that she has been subjected to this form of punishment on more than a few occasions.

Fatima is the youngest of seven daughters, and all of her sisters are now fairies, except for the next youngest, Fatiana, who is a senior sprite. Both Fatima and Fatiana are required to attend Sprite School, which teaches them how to use the magic that they do possess correctly, as well as teaching them how to eventually become fairies. Fairies no longer require the use of a magic wand, but instead have magic fairy dust which gives them a much broader spectrum of magical powers.

On the day one graduates to fairy level, each fairy is given a chest which contains a self-perpetuating supply of magic fairy dust. The chest is always locked, and will only open with a secret command. This command is individual to each fairy, and is only supposed to be known by them. Every morning, the fairy removes some magic fairy dust and carries it in a small bag on his or her belt throughout the day. Whatever amount is left over at the end of the day is returned to the chest that night, before the fairy goes to bed. If he or she runs out of fairy dust before the day is finished, the fairy simply returns to the chest and replenishes their supply.

A fairy's magical powers are almost unlimited. They are immortal, at least in their world, and they can accomplish almost any feat of magic through the use of their magic fairy dust. They can conjure up anything, including gold and money, and can transform objects into other objects, as well as heal humans and animals. Unfortunately, although immortal in their world, they can be attacked and even killed in the Human World.

Entrance to the Human World from the World of Fairy can only be accomplished by the use of magic fairy dust. Sprites can only enter the Human World if they are accompanied by a fairy or fairies, or if they borrow (or steal) some fairy dust. However, the sprite's use of fairy dust is often erratic and unpredictable, so it can be dangerous to attempt. Also, if a sprite is caught using magic fairy dust without the fairy's permission, the punishment can be quite severe.

Besides becoming mortal in the Human World, the only other magical limitation that fairies have is the fact that if they perform acts of magic which are considered evil or malicious, they can be punished by the Fairy City Council. There's a wide range of punishments; like having to give up their fairy dust for a period of time, or even being banished to the realm between the worlds—a subject which Fatima refuses to say anything more about.

Hannah digested all of this information with equal parts of awe and amazement. She then asked Fatima to tell her more about the World of Fairy and the town in which she lived. Fatima promised she would indulge Hannah's curiosity further in just a few minutes. But, first she needed to carefully explain a very important topic. This topic needed to be discussed because Hannah had rescued Fatima from the spider's web, which had almost certainly saved her life. The topic was the Sprite Code of Honor.

CHAPTER 4

THE SPRITE CODE OF HONOR

Hannah had obviously never heard of the Sprite Code of Honor, and she couldn't even imagine what it was all about. Encouraged by Hannah's curiosity, Fatima began to explain the concept to her. According to the laws of Fairy Town, magical creatures must follow the rules of their own code if they are somehow either captured or rescued by a human being.

Leprechauns are required to take the human to their pot of gold which they have carefully hidden, usually aided by their special magic. Fairies are required to grant three wishes to their captor or rescuer, and sprites must grant them one special wish.

Hannah struggled to assimilate the mountain of information which Fatima had provided. Fatima had been talking for over three hours, and the sun was high overhead. Hannah was actually sweating freely, now that she was bathed directly in the sun's rays, but she noticed that the little sprite appeared as fresh as a daisy. The discomfort from the heat was further intensified by the way Fatima was staring at her, and by the fact that she was starting to squirm in an obviously impatient manner.

"Well," Hannah started, "I really don't know what to say exactly."

"Just tell me what you would like your wish to be, and Twinkle and I will get right on it," Fatima replied.

"But I didn't help you out of the web because I expected anything from you in return. It was just the right thing to do. Besides, it feels like enough of a reward to have met a sprite and to hear all about you and the fantastic world you live in." Hannah waited for the sprite's reply. However, Fatima didn't say a word, but instead hung her head, staring at the ground and letting her shoulders slump in obvious dejection. Hannah could swear she saw tiny tears begin to stream down the sprite's cheeks, and quickly grew alarmed. "I'm sorry," she blurted out. "I didn't mean to hurt your feelings, or make you sad. Please tell me what's wrong!"

The little sprite slowly raised her head and looked Hannah in the eye. "If you don't make a wish and allow me to grant it, then I will have failed the Sprite Code of Honor. It will automatically be recorded in the Sprite Code Book kept in the tallest tower at City Hall in Fairy Town. Everyone already thinks I'm a total screw-up as a sprite, and this will be the last straw. I'm going to be the laughingstock of the entire town for the rest of my life." After saying this, she threw herself facedown on the grass and began sobbing so hard that her wings shook violently.

Hannah stared at the tiny girl with her mouth hanging open, and felt a shameful blush turn her cheeks bright red. "I'm so sorry!" she stuttered, horrified that she had hurt the sprite's feelings. "I had no idea it was so important. In that case, I'll be more than happy to let you grant me a wish." Fatima's shoulders stopped heaving immediately, and she raised her tear-streaked face to look at Hannah.

"You would?" she asked hopefully.

"Of course I would," Hannah replied quickly. "Please don't cry anymore."

"You have no idea how much this means to me! Granting your wish would earn me lots of respect from the other sprites and fairies, and maybe they would finally have to admit that I'm better at magic than they think. Then all the other sprites at school would have to find someone else to pick on." After saying this, a self-satisfied smile appeared on Fatima's face.

Hannah was relieved that Fatima had stopped crying, but she still felt badly about hurting the tiny girl's feelings. "Why is everyone so hard on you? I thought sprites and fairies were supposed to be kind and compassionate."

"Well, we are for the most part," Fatima answered. "But I do tend to get myself into a bit of trouble at times, both at home and in school. You see, I enjoy playing harmless practical jokes and the jokes backfire on me sometimes. Also, I don't always pay attention to the teacher at school, and so I don't always follow directions exactly right. That means my magic spells don't turn out quite the way they're supposed to sometimes."

"Oh, I'm sure it's not that bad," Hannah replied in an attempt to comfort the sprite. "Everyone makes mistakes, and besides, I certainly have to deal with my share of teasing at school, too."

"Well, that's very nice of you to say, but I sincerely doubt that anyone makes as much of a mess out of things as I do."

"Well, give me some examples," Hannah answered, "because a lot of times things don't seem as bad when you share them with a friend." Fatima's brow furrowed while she thoughtfully considered Hannah's words.

"Okay," she replied after a few moments, "but you have to promise not to laugh." Hannah readily agreed, and Fatima began by telling Hannah about an incident which had happened at home several months ago. It had occurred at a time when the oldest of her six sisters, Faye, had still been living at home.

Faye was about to be married, and would soon be moving out to her own apartment with the young fairy who would be her husband. She was nervous about the upcoming wedding, and had been even more moody than usual. She was constantly yelling at her younger sisters, and they were all growing tired of her antics. Even Fawn, the next oldest sister, who was always kind and even-tempered, was beginning to show signs of being fed up with her older sister.

One day, Faye was unable to locate one of her favorite belts. She came stomping into Fatima's room, which she shared with Fatiana and Faith, and began throwing their stuff around the room looking for her belt. After ten minutes, she finally located it in Faith's closet. As Fatima was the only one in the room at the time, Faye began screaming at her. Fatima tried to dart out the door, but Faye used her fairy dust to freeze her in place.

Then she yelled at her for over an hour about how disrespectful her sisters were, and how they had better not take anymore of her stuff or she would turn them all into warthogs. She finally finished by saying how glad she would be to move out soon, so that she wouldn't have to see any of her sisters ever again if she didn't want to. She then huffed out of the room without even unfreezing Fatima; and she hadn't even done anything wrong for once!

Luckily, her favorite sister Fawn came home an hour later and used her fairy dust to unfreeze Fatima. By that time, Fatima was so frustrated with Faye's behavior that she began crying. While Fawn was hugging her little sister in an effort to comfort her, Fatima carefully reached into the bag on Fawn's belt and "borrowed" some of her fairy dust. She then flew off to the Fairy Town Library and looked up a particular spell, which she wanted to use to teach her oldest sister a lesson. She memorized the spell very carefully and headed back home, ready to carry out her plan.

As soon as she returned home, Fatima went straight to Faye's room, where she found her sister lounging on her bed reading the National Fairy Enquirer magazine. Without any explanation, Fatima flung the fairy dust at her and shouted the magic words of her chosen spell. Her intention had been to turn

Faye into a frog—just for the day to teach her an important lesson about how she should treat others.

But she must have mixed up some part of the spell, because all she succeeded in doing was turning Faye completely green. Everything was green: her hair, her skin, her clothes, and even her entire room. The rest of her sisters laughed uproariously at the spectacle. They laughed even harder when they discovered what Fatima's true intention had been. Unfortunately, her parents had not found it the least bit humorous. It took her mother all day to figure out how to reverse the screwed-up spell, and her father took away Twinkle and grounded her for an entire week. In spite of the loss of her wand, a small part of her had to admit that the expression on Faye's face when had she looked in the mirror was at least partly worth it.

As embarrassing as that whole thing had been, a recent incident at the sprite school had been even worse. Several days ago, Fatima and her classmates had been trying to learn several new spells at once. The directions were fairly complex, and all the sprites were supposed to be listening carefully. At one point, Fatima's attention had been captured for just the briefest of moments by a large, multicolored butterfly right outside the window. The next thing she knew, the teacher was asking them to practice the two spells she had just reviewed. The first spell required them to make themselves disappear completely, and then reappear on the other side of the room. The second spell involved transforming worms into big, fat slugs.

Everyone took turns practicing the spells, and eventually it was Fatima's turn. All of the other students had managed to duplicate the spells with only minor difficulties. Fatima managed to make herself disappear without any problem. However, she somehow managed to mix the two spells together, and reappeared as a large, fat slug with blond hair, stuck on the blackboard on the other side of the room. Her classmates had laughed hysterically, and just to teach her a lesson, the teacher had left her like that for the rest of the school day. Her classmates were still taunting her daily, and her current nickname was the Blond Slug. Now Fatima felt like an outcast at school, as well as at home.

After Fatima finished describing her recent misadventures to Hannah, she sat quietly, cupping her chin in her right hand. Her left hand clutched her magic wand, which hung dejectedly at her side. Hannah felt a wave of empathy wash over her, as she stared at the obviously depressed sprite. She searched for something to say which could help cheer up the tiny girl.

"Guess what?" Hannah began boldly. "I know exactly how you feel."

"You do?" Fatima asked, quickly raising her eyes to meet Hannah's, searching her face to gauge the truthfulness of her response.

"Oh yes! I really only have two good friends at school, and we are constantly being teased by the jocks and cheerleaders and all the other popular kids. They call us names and then either ignore us, or play mean jokes on us. Also, my older brother is always being a pain in the neck at home, and it seems like my parents always let him get away with stuff. So I really know almost exactly how you feel."

As soon as Hannah mentioned the word "home," the depressed look returned to Fatima's face. When Hannah asked her the reason for her sad face, Fatima reminded Hannah that she was going to be in a great deal of trouble when she returned home, for several reasons. First of all, she had skipped her classes at school yesterday afternoon so that she could accompany the other girls on their little adventure. Secondly, since the group had abandoned her when she became stuck in the spider web, she'd been gone for almost a week in Fairy time (missing even more class time), and she knew she was going to be in a great deal of trouble when she finally returned home.

The girls continued to share with each other their respective difficulties at home and school. Recognizing that, in spite of their obvious differences, they seemed to be kindred spirits, the girls decided then and there to be B.F.Fs (best friends forever), and then swore each other to total secrecy.

Fatima then explained to Hannah that when she returned to Fairy Town later that day, she would almost certainly be grounded for a significant amount of time. However, if Hannah could tell her what her wish was before she left, then she could use that time to think about how she would go about fulfilling it. Hannah took a deep breath, closed her eyes, and blurted out her wish—she wanted to be more popular at school, and she wanted Sean Adams to fall in love with her!

Fatima looked at Hannah dubiously for a minute. "Well actually, that's kind of two wishes, but I'll see what I can do."

"Oh, would you?" Hannah gushed excitedly. "That would be so wonderful!"

"There's not much that Twinkle and I can't accomplish when we work together," Fatima stated with confidence. Then the smug look on her face slowly dissolved, to be replaced by a puzzled frown.

"What's the matter?" Hannah asked anxiously.

"Well," Fatima said thoughtfully, "in order to grant your wish, I'm going to have to know a lot more about Sean Adams. And you're definitely going to have to tell me more about your school and the kids in it, so that I can figure out what I have to do to make you more popular."

"Okay," Hannah replied, "but explaining all of that is going to take awhile."

"Well, we might as well get it done and over with now, because I'm already going to be in enough trouble as it is. I'm sure another hour or two won't make much difference," Fatima said with a mischievous twinkle in her eye. So the little sprite made herself comfortable, and Hannah spent the rest of the afternoon giving her all of the details concerning the kids at Roseveldt Junior High—especially Sean Adams.

CHAPTER 5

ROSEVELDT JUNIOR HIGH

Roseveldt Junior High was the only public junior high school in Post Falls. It was located towards the center of town, and Lincoln High School was several blocks to the west of it. The junior high consisted of grades 7, 8, and 9; and the high school taught grades 10, 11, and 12. The only other school in town for those age groups was the private Catholic school Desales, which taught grades 8 through 12. This was the school that all of Hannah's cousins attended. As Post Falls was a fairly small town, the schools were fairly small, also. Roseveldt usually enrolled anywhere from 250 to 300 kids each year. The high school had a slightly higher enrollment of between 300 to 350 kids yearly.

Hannah's eighth grade class this year was composed of 89 kids. The benefit of having such a small class was that everyone pretty much knew everyone else. The bad part about having such a small class was ...well, that everyone pretty much knew everyone else.

Like most schools, Roseveldt Junior High had a variety of cliques which made up the general school population. The most popular kids were the athletes and the cheerleaders. The next most popular group was made up of kids from wealthy families, and the least popular group was the nerds. The kids that didn't fit into any of these groups made up the rest of the school population. They were neither popular nor rich, but weren't total losers either. These were kids who were the brains and got good grades, or whose parents didn't have a lot of money, or who didn't dress fashionably, or who weren't good at any type of sports. Hannah and her friends were part of this group. Hannah and Darlene referred to it as the grey zone, because there really wasn't a name for their group.

Even though it was better than being a nerd, being part of this group at Roseveldt Junior High was definitely no picnic. They were basically teased by all of the popular kids, and were especially tormented by a boy named Tony Parsons and his group of friends.

Tony was an eighth grader whose family was the richest in Post Falls. His father was the owner and director of a production company which filmed several movies each year. His dad was constantly flying back and forth between Post Falls and Hollywood, and Tony went with him whenever a business trip coincided with a school vacation. He had met several actors and actresses and was constantly bragging about it to anyone who would listen.

Tony surrounded himself with seven or eight other rich kids, although none of their parents made even close to as much money as Tony's father did. These kids idolized Tony Parsons and would do whatever he wanted them to do. Tony and his snobby friends felt it was their duty to make everyone else's life miserable. They earnestly disliked all of the nerds, and especially went out of their way to torture Ritchie Pearson at every opportunity.

No one knew exactly why Tony hated Ritchie so much. Even Hannah and Darlene couldn't remember any particular incident that started it all. For some reason, Tony always chose to pick on Ritchie, and because Ritchie was Ritchie, he never managed to shut his smart mouth in time to avoid a beating by Tony and his friends.

The only groups of people that Tony and his friends were ever nice to were the jocks and the cheerleaders. The leaders of the jocks, and probably the most popular boys in the 8th grade, were three boys who were best friends and were on the varsity football team together—Sean Adams, Shane Matthews, and Paul Andrews. The varsity football team was made up of 8th and 9th graders, and in spite of only being an 8th grader, Sean was the starting quarterback. He was a quiet, handsome boy with dark blond hair worn almost to his shoulders, bright blue eyes, and perfectly straight white teeth. He was almost 6 feet tall and had a lean, muscular build.

Sean was currently dating Erika Scott, who was the head of the cheerleading squad. He liked Erika because she was beautiful and popular; but he didn't like it when she acted snobby; and he definitely thought that she was spoiled. Sometimes he wasn't sure that her good qualities outweighed the bad. However, everyone seemed to expect the star quarterback to date the head cheerleader, so for now at least, he just went with the flow. Sean was a nice and likeable kid, although he did allow his friends and peers to dictate his actions at times. He was never actually mean to the less popular kids, but he often ignored them at school so his friends wouldn't consider him uncool.

Sean and Hannah knew each other fairly well, because their older brothers were best friends, and because Hannah often babysat his younger sisters. The girls were ages 6 and 8, and Sean and his older brother had to help out at home with them a lot. This was because their mother had died in a tragic automobile accident when Sean was 12 years old, and his father was busy working two jobs to support the family.

Besides his sports interests (Sean played football, baseball, and ran track), he also loved to read, but he didn't let any of his friends know this because it was considered uncool and nerdy. There were many people in town who felt that Sean had a good chance of becoming a professional athlete someday, but his dream was to become an author—although he had never shared that dream with anyone except for his mother before she died. Sean thought that Hannah was cute and very smart; something Hannah was totally in the dark about. However, he didn't talk to her much at school, because she wasn't considered to be one of the popular kids.

Sean's best friend was Shane Matthews, who played on the football team in one of the receiver positions. He was also quite popular at school, and was dating a cheerleader named Annika Iverson, who was the best friend of Sean's girlfriend, Erika Scott. Shane was very smart and didn't have to try very hard to get straight A's. However, he tried to keep his grades a secret so he wouldn't be considered uncool.

Shane was the middle child in a family of seven children. His parents didn't make a lot of money, so his only chance at affording college, where he wanted to study architecture, was to earn a football scholarship. Shane and Sean had been best friends since they were in day care together at the age of 4. Shane was instrumental in helping Sean get through his grief and depression following the death of his mother two years ago. He was about the only person besides his father that Sean felt he could talk to about that kind of that stuff.

The boys' other best friend was Paul Andrews, who was a tight end on the football team. Paul was very popular at school, in spite of the fact that his dad was the Vice Principal. He was a nice, but goofy kid, who frequently played the role of class clown. This tended to land him in hot water with his father, as he often ended up in the Principal's office because of one of his pranks. The three boys hung out together at school and at each others houses in the evenings and on the weekends. At school, they were usually surrounded by all the other jocks, as well as Hannah's favorite group of people—the cheerleaders.

Actually, the cheerleaders in general, and Erika Scott in particular, were easily Hannah and Darlene's *least* favorite group of kids at school; except for Tony Parsons and the kids he hung around with, of course. Erika Scott—the name alone could send shivers down Hannah's spine. Erika was the leader of the cheerleaders and was probably the most popular girl at school, even though she was only in the 8th grade. She was also Sean's girlfriend, but she mainly dated him because he was the quarterback of the football team and was one of the most popular boys at school.

Erika tended to make fun of the fact that Sean liked to read and got good grades. She was also quite snobbish about the fact that his family didn't have much money. But they continued dating, in part to fulfill the unspoken expectation that the star quarterback date the head cheerleader, and it was obvious to everyone that they would be the Prom Prince and Princess of the 8th graders this year.

In addition to having the star quarterback as her boyfriend, Erika Scott was one of those girls who had everything. She was tall and thin with long blond hair and beautiful blue eyes, and whether she was in her cheerleading outfit or her bikini, she looked like a model from a magazine. Her family had tons of money; because her mother had inherited a lot of money when Erika's grandparents died, and her father was a high-powered attorney who worked in medical malpractice.

She had two older brothers who were already in college, and she was very spoiled, because she was the youngest, as well as the only one who was still living at home. Her parents bought her almost anything she wanted, so she had all of the most expensive and fashionable clothes, and also had her own big-screen TV, computer, stereo system, and DVD player in her bedroom. She lived in a huge house with a live-in maid, and a huge swimming pool in the backyard that had both a slide and a diving board.

Erika and her best friend Annika were very mean to the unpopular kids at school, and Erika seemed to take a special delight in tormenting Hannah and Darlene. She had gone out of her way to make Hannah's 8th grade experience as miserable as she possibly could, even though Hannah had never done anything to warrant this unwanted attention.

Darlene had told Hannah on numerous occasions that she thought Erika was just jealous of her, but Hannah couldn't think of a single reason why that would be true. The only thing Hannah had that Erika didn't was good grades, and that was just because Erika didn't like reading or writing, and absolutely hated doing homework. Whenever Hannah and Darlene saw the trio of Erika, Annika, and Justine in a hallway at school, they quickly turned around and walked the other way.

Annika Iverson was Erika's best friend and was also on the cheerleading squad. She was also tall and thin, with strawberry blond hair and hazel eyes. She wasn't very smart and had trouble with her homework, so her boyfriend, Shane Matthews, had to help her with her schoolwork most of the time. Unlike Erika, Annika actually liked her boyfriend a lot, and the four of them went out together on double dates most weekends.

Her family was also very wealthy, and she was almost as spoiled as Erika. She and Erika and Justine hung out together at the mall a lot, and the rest of the time they hung out at Erika's house gossiping, practicing their cheer routines, and swimming in Erika's pool. Annika's family also had a swimming pool, but it didn't have a diving board or slide, so Erika thought hers was much better and they usually swam there. To be completely fair, Annika wasn't really as mean as Erika, but since she wanted to be popular and remain best friends with Erika, she ended up doing all of the mean things that Erika wanted her to do.

Justine Bates was also on the cheerleading squad, and spent most of her time hanging out with Erika and Annika. She really liked Paul Andrews, whom she had just started dating, and they went on group dates with the other two couples fairly often. She had beautiful, black curly hair and violet eyes and was naturally bronzed, especially in the summer. Her family was upper-middle class and pretty well-to-do, but they definitely weren't as wealthy as the other two girls' families were.

Justine was smart and did well in school. She also loved animals and volunteered her time at the local Humane Society. She was popular at school, both because of her looks and cheerleading position, as well as the fact that she was such good friends with Erika and Annika. She was also one of those rare teenagers who was quite comfortable in her own skin, and she was unwilling to be mean or snobbish to people just because her friends and peers expected it. Thus, she was never mean or spiteful to the less popular kids; unlike the other girls.

Both Hannah and Darlene would admit that Justine Bates was actually a pretty nice girl—in spite of being a cheerleader. Unfortunately, she was almost always found in the company of Erika, Annika, and all their snobby friends; and those were the girls that they spent a lot of their energy during the school day trying to avoid. But in spite of their attempts to avoid that group, it was almost impossible to get through an entire day at school without running into them somewhere.

This was especially true this semester, since they all had their Home Economics class together during first period. There was hardly a day that went by without Erika finding a way to make their lives miserable. One day in Home Economics, she had swapped Hannah and Darlene's sugar for salt when the girls weren't looking. Their teacher, Mrs. Oglivie, had given them an F for the day, after tasting that particular baking disaster.

Just talking about it caused Hannah to heave a great big sigh and grow silent; as she thought miserably about having to go back to school on Monday. While Hannah seemed lost in these depressing thoughts, Fatima cleared her throat loudly and tried to recapture Hannah's attention. When that didn't work, she began flying back and forth in front of Hannah's face.

"Earth to Hannah! Earth to Hannah! Are you there?" Hannah jumped in surprise as she tried to focus on the flying sprite.

"Oh, I'm so sorry," she exclaimed. "Telling you all about my school and Tony Parsons and Sean and his friends and those stupid cheerleaders . . . well, I just totally lost my train of thought for a moment. Now where was I?"

"Actually, I think I've heard about enough," Fatima replied angrily. "I just have to turn Tony Parsons into a toad, Erika Scott into a warthog, and then inject Sean Adams with some kind of love potion so that he falls in love with you. Then my work here will be done, and your wish will have come true. In fact, I think I'm going to enjoy teaching those little brats a lesson!" Fatima looked very satisfied with herself, as she hovered in midair with her hands on her hips.

"Oh, no!" Hannah exclaimed with a horrified look on her face. "That won't do at all! I don't want anyone hurt or anything like that. Even Erika Scott doesn't deserve to be turned into a warthog. Besides, as tempting as that is, it's not going to help make me more popular. And I want Sean Adams to fall in love with me because of me, not because he has to. We're going to have to come up with a much better plan than that. That's why I've been telling you all about school and Sean and his friends and the cheerleaders. I figured if I gave you enough information, you would be able to come up with a really good plan."

Fatima flew over to a large mushroom and plopped herself down on it. She crossed her legs, and then rested her chin in both hands with an elbow on each knee. Sighing deeply, she pondered their dilemma for a few minutes before replying. "Well, this is going to be a little harder than I thought."

"It's going to require quite a bit of planning. Fortunately, I'm going to have a lot of free time to be thinking about it, since I'll probably be grounded for the next 30 years," she said gloomily. Hannah's eyebrows arched up in surprise.

"Are you really going to be grounded for a whole 30 years?" she asked incredulously. Fatima couldn't suppress the amused giggle which slipped out of her mouth.

"Okay, maybe I was being a little melodramatic. But I'll probably be grounded for at least a month. Thankfully, time passes more quickly in the land of fairy, so a month there will only seem like a week or two to you. I'll be back before you know it, and by that time I'll have come up with a truly excellent plan!"

Fatima sprung to her feet and balanced on top of the mushroom, looking extremely proud of herself. Hannah couldn't help but share her infectious grin, and she felt a huge smile spread across her face. "Now in the meantime," Fatima cautioned her, "you can't tell anyone about our meeting. Not your parents, not your brother, not anyone. OK?" Hannah started to nod her head vigorously, but then a crestfallen look appeared on her face. "What's the matter?" Fatima asked anxiously.

"Well," Hannah replied, "I've just never kept a secret from my best friend Darlene before. It's going to be really hard because we've always told each other everything." Fatima thought about it carefully.

"Are you sure she'd keep it totally secret from everyone else?" she asked.

"Oh, I know she would," Hannah replied excitedly, "and she'd love to meet you!" Fatima grinned broadly.

"Of course she would," she said in a cocky tone, "I'm a sprite! Okay, this is what we're going to do. I'm going to get back to the World of Fairy and take my punishment like a true sprite. Then, while I'm serving out my sentence, I'll be busy coming up with a spectacularly fabulous plan. It will be so awesome that it will fulfill your wish beyond your wildest dreams, while at the same time making me famous in Fairy Town for my brilliant use of wit and magic in my attempt to fulfill the Sprite Code of Honor." Hannah laughed and clapped her hands together excitedly.

"That's marvelous!" she exclaimed. "And while you're gone, I'll explain all of this to Darlene, and we'll be thinking of ways we can help you out."

The girls talked enthusiastically about their plans, and then prepared to say their farewells. Fatima admitted that she wasn't sure when she would be able to come back. But, she assured Hannah that she would find her when she did return. Hannah pointed out her neighborhood across the meadow, and then described the location of the junior high school to Fatima. She explained to Fatima that she would probably either be at home or at school when Fatima returned. She then bent over and offered the little sprite her index finger, which Fatima shook solemnly between her tiny hands. "Until we meet again," she said cheerfully, and in a blinding flash of light, she disappeared.

CHAPTER 6

HANNAH TELLS DARLENE

Hannah blinked her eyes several times and looked wonderingly around the meadow. All traces of Fatima were gone, and for the briefest of moments, Hannah was afraid she had dreamed the entire thing. What if she had fallen asleep while reading her fantasy novel and just dreamed the little sprite into existence? That would be horrible!

Her eyes frantically searched the ground where Fatima had been, and she happened to glance over at the spider web which had imprisoned the struggling girl. There was a large hole in the very center of the web which was about 4 inches in size. Hannah bent over to look more closely, and noticed a tiny blond hair still stuck in the web, swinging in the breeze. She plucked it out, and felt the excitement growing within her. It had all been true! She had met an actual sprite, and even more amazing, the sprite was going to come back and grant her one special wish.

Hannah stood up and opened the golden locket which she always wore around her neck. It was in the shape of a heart and had been given to her by her parents on her 12th birthday. She placed the tiny hair carefully inside, and then refastened the clasp. She clenched the locket in her fist as she walked back to her backpack to collect her things. This hair was her proof that Fatima actually existed; proof for herself, and hopefully, proof for Darlene.

Having been best friends for so many years now, the girls had always shared all of their secrets and dreams with each other. However, trying to convince someone to believe in the existence of fairies and sprites was not your average, everyday event. Hannah couldn't imagine that Darlene would fail to believe her, as Hannah had never lied to her friend before; but this was going to be a little tricky.

Hannah reached the spot where she had left her stuff and grabbed her backpack. She slung it over her shoulder and began walking across the meadow. By the time she reached the trail through the woods, she was no longer able to contain her excitement, and she began skipping along, while humming a tune under her breath. As soon as she reached her neighborhood, she broke into a run and headed straight for Darlene's house.

She knew that Darlene had gone with her mom and twin sisters to shop for some new spring outfits, but that had been hours ago, and she had to be home by now. When Hannah neared the house, she slowed down to a walk, contemplating her strategy. Mrs. O'Brien's car was back in the driveway, which meant they had all returned from their shopping trip.

However, Hannah really didn't want to deal with either Mrs. O'Brien or the twins at this point, as she would prefer an atmosphere of complete privacy when she told her story to Darlene. She glanced across the street at her house, and noticed that both her father's truck and her mother's Subaru were missing from the driveway. She knew that Patrick was spending the day with Brian Adams at the water slides in Coeur d'Alene, so it looked like she had the house to herself.

Making her decision, she quickly raced across the street, entered through the side door into the kitchen, and ran up the stairs to her bedroom. Hannah grabbed her walkie-talkie off of the bedside table, and approached her front window. She looked out the window, across the street, and pressed the "talk" key on the walkie-talkie. "Red Racer to Blue Streak! Red Racer to Blue Streak! Come in Blue Streak!"

The girls had chosen their nicknames several years ago, when they had primarily used the walkie-talkies while riding their bikes around town. At that time, Hannah had a red racing bike, which she had gotten for her 10th birthday and Darlene had a blue mountain bike, which her father had bought her on a whim one Saturday afternoon. Since that time, the girls had both moved on to matching silver 10-speed bikes, but they had kept their nicknames in the spirit of nostalgia for their younger, more carefree days.

Hannah spied movement behind the curtains of Darlene's room, and suddenly her best friend's head popped into view. Darlene had a big smile on her face, as her voice came cheerfully out of Hannah's walkie-talkie. "Hey, Red Racer, this is Blue Streak. I'm back from shopping with the twin princesses, and my sanity is still intact." Hannah couldn't help but grin at Darlene's comment, which was obviously referring to her two older sisters, whom they both thought were a bit on the prissy side.

"Darlene, you need to come over to my house right away. I have the most amazing news to tell you!"

"Well, put an end to my suspense and just tell me now," Darlene replied excitedly.

"I can't," Hannah answered. "This is something that I need to tell you in person. I don't even know if you're going to believe it, because even though it happened to me, I can hardly believe it myself!"

"Oh my gosh!" Darlene exclaimed. "This sounds exciting. I'll be right over."

Hannah waited with barely contained excitement, as Darlene's front door opened and her friend dashed across the street. She heard footsteps pounding up the stairs, and then her bedroom door burst open. Darlene's freckled face was flushed with exertion and anticipation, as she plopped down on the floor in front of Hannah.

"Okay, I'm here," she announced. "Tell me what happened." Hannah rocked back and forth, sitting on the floor facing her friend, and tried to decide how she should begin. Unfortunately, Darlene wasn't going to tolerate any pauses or hesitations. "Tell me, tell me, tell me!" she cried. "The suspense is driving me crazy!"

"Okay, okay," Hannah began. "I'm going to tell you exactly how it happened from start to finish, but you have to promise not to interrupt until I'm completely done." Darlene quickly agreed, and Hannah began to tell her about her marvelous adventure.

She started by telling Darlene about her original plans for the morning. She had planned to go to her favorite spot in the meadow, and spend several hours enjoying the beautiful spring day, while reading her new book and writing in her journal. However, after reading several chapters in her book and barely starting the day's first journal entry, she had suddenly heard a cry for help. Hannah watched Darlene's face carefully, as she took a deep breath and began to share with her the discovery she had made in the spider's web. As she continued her story, Darlene's eyes got wider and wider, and her eyebrows arched higher and higher.

Hannah had just finished explaining the various rules that sprites and fairies must follow, when Darlene couldn't contain herself any longer. "Are you pulling my leg?" she blurted out suddenly, "because as much as I want to believe you, this all seems totally unbelievable. Are you sure you didn't fall asleep and dream the whole thing?" Darlene noticed the hurt look that crossed her friend's face, and immediately wished she could take back her words. "I'm sorry," she said quickly. "I didn't mean to hurt your feelings, but all this stuff about sprites and fairies and magic wands and fairy dust . . ."

Her words tapered off as she continued to watch Hannah's face anxiously. Her friend had never lied to her before, but all this stuff was just too much to take in all at once. Darlene had been present for Mr. Flannigan's stories of Irish folklore on many occasions, but she had never considered that there was even a grain of truth in them. Until now, she had always assumed that Hannah felt exactly the same way.

Hannah folded her hands in her lap and thought carefully about how to proceed. She had to get Darlene to believe her. She hadn't thought it would be this difficult, but as she herself had doubted the reality of the situation once Fatima had disappeared, she certainly understood her friend's disbelief. "Okay," Hannah started again, "let me think about how to convince you that this whole thing actually happened." She lay down on her bedroom floor, and blew her bangs up off of her forehead.

All of a sudden, she remembered the tiny golden hair she had carefully placed in her locket. She quickly sat up and took off the necklace. "All right, when Fatima disappeared to go back to Fairy Town, I was having a hard time convincing myself that it wasn't all a dream; just like I'm having a hard time convincing you now." Darlene looked slightly embarrassed when she heard these words, but continued to watch Hannah expectantly. "So, I looked around and noticed the big hole that was still in the spider web. It was exactly Fatima's size, and when I looked even more carefully, I found one of her tiny, golden hairs still stuck in the web."

Hannah unclasped the locket, gently removed the hair, and laid it on her palm. She then lifted it up towards Darlene's face so her friend could examine it more closely. Darlene stared at the hair for several minutes in silence. Her mind was racing, as she considered the implications of this evidence. She slowly raised her head and stared into Hannah's eyes. The look on her friend's face, so open and trusting, did almost as much to convince her as the evidence of that tiny hair. "It's true," she said quietly, to herself as much as to Hannah. "It's really true." Hannah's face broke into a broad grin.

"I told you it was amazing," she said breathlessly. "I had to pinch myself to make sure I wasn't dreaming. I can't believe anything like this could happen. Especially to me!" She placed the hair back in her locket, closed the clasp, and placed the chain back around her neck.

Both girls sat in silence for a few moments, and then broke into excited chatter at the same time. Once they realized they were both talking at once, they started giggling together. The giggling lasted until they both ran out of breath. Exhausted, they lay back on the floor with their arms crossed under their heads, as they thought about Hannah's experience. "So," Darlene finally stated, "this little sprite ..."

"Fatima," Hannah interjected.

"So this little sprite, Fatima, is going to grant you any wish you want for saving her life?" Hannah nodded her head in agreement. "Well, what are you going to wish for, and when's Fatima coming back, and when do I get to meet her?" Darlene's questions all jumbled together in her haste to get them out.

Hannah laughed gleefully, and began answering Darlene's questions one by one. "I told her that my wish would be for Sean Adams to fall in love with me," she stated firmly, although a blush of embarrassment appeared on her cheeks with this statement; even admitting this to her best friend in the whole wide world was kind of hard to do. "Also, I told her that I wanted to be more popular at school." Darlene looked a bit shocked at hearing this announcement from her best friend's lips.

"But," she started slowly, "don't you like hanging around Ritchie and me, and doing Debate Club and the Chess Club, and tinkering with Ritchie's experiments in his basement, and all the other stuff that we do together?"

"Of course I do, Darlene, but I just thought it might be easier for all of us if we were a little more popular at school. You know, so we wouldn't get teased so much by Tony Parsons and his friends, and so Erika Scott wouldn't be able to be so mean to us all the time."

Hannah watched Darlene's face carefully to see how she was going to react to this explanation. She was relieved to see the worry erase itself from Darlene's face almost at once. "So you don't want to change anything about our friendship together, or about Ritchie's friendship, or about the activities we love doing at school?"

"Oh, no," Hannah quickly assured her. "I just think that if Fatima could change some of the stuff we have to put up with at school, it could only make our lives easier. The thing is, we have to be thinking about how her magic can help us do that, before she returns to our world. She should be back in a week or two, and then you guys will get to meet each other, and we'll put our heads together and come up with some ideas about how to use her magic to grant my wish."

The girls happily spent the rest of the weekend coming up with various ideas for what they called "The Magic Plan." By Monday, they had thought of several ideas, and could hardly wait for Fatima to return from Fairy Town.

Fatima, on the other hand, was not having nearly as much fun as the girls were back in the Human World. In fact, for Fatima, life in the World of Fairy pretty much sucked right now.

CHAPTER 7

FATIMA RETURNS TO FAIRY TOWN

Immediately after saying goodbye to Hannah, Fatima had used her magic wand to instantly transport herself back to Fairy Town. Once she arrived, she quickly flew home and attempted to sneak up to her room. However, she had barely crossed the hallway leading to the stairs, when a stern voice stopped her in her tracks. Fatima turned around slowly, and faced what appeared to be a very angry father, as well as a concerned (and slightly angry) mother. The ensuing discussion was not at all pretty, and we'll spare Fatima the embarrassment of printing it word for word at this time. Instead, we'll content ourselves with a short summary of that rather one-sided conversation.

From what we can piece together from her father's lecture, Fatima has been in this kind of trouble on other occasions as well. In fact, during the course of her relatively short life, she has probably had her wand taken away for various transgressions more often than she can actually remember. With this information, we can assume that, while Fatima is both a bright and compassionate sprite, she also has a tendency to be impatient and impulsive, which often gets her into trouble.

After a time-consuming lecture, Fatima's father decides that she will lose possession of Twinkle for an entire month. She will still be allowed to use Twinkle at school, of course, but otherwise the wand will be confiscated by her parents. This not only leaves Fatima virtually powerless, but also leaves her unable to contact Hannah for at least a month. Thankfully, time passes much more quickly in the fairy realm, and so Hannah will only have to wait a week or two until Fatima returns. This also gives us plenty of time to learn more about Fatima's family, and the mysteries of Fairy Town.

Fatima's family consisted of her parents, Farthing and Fortunata, and six older sisters: Fatiana, Faith, Fransesca, Fountain, Fawn, and Faye. Fatima's father was quite strict in his discipline of his daughters, and was rather a stern fairy; although he loved his wife and daughters very much. However, he was often disappointed in his youngest daughter, because it seemed she was always getting into some kind of trouble or another. There were times when he was seriously concerned that Fatima was never going to make it to the level of senior sprite, much less ever become an actual fairy.

Farthing was a pretty important fairy, as he was a member of the City Council and so had quite a bit of power in Fairy Town. He also worked in the Liaison Office as the main supervisor of the fairy godmothers. The Liaison Office was a major establishment in Fairy Town, and its main function was to oversee the organization of its fairy godmothers. Part of Farthing's job was to make sure that the fairy godmothers helped the humans they were assigned to, without the human ever becoming aware of their presence. He also had to make sure that Fairy Town itself was never jeopardized by any of the fairy godmothers' interactions.

The institution of fairy godmothers was older than time itself, and had been around longer than even the oldest fairy could remember. In fact, the use of magic by various fairy godmothers had influenced some of the most important occurrences in human history. Thomas Jefferson's fairy godmother had helped inspire him to write the Declaration of Independence, a fact which the old biddy still bragged about to this day. Also, Ben Franklin's fairy godmother had helped him discover electricity; Henry Ford's fairy godmother had helped him develop the first automobile; and the fairy godmother team watching over those crazy Wright brothers, had helped them fly the first airplane. There were many similar episodes in our history, which are too numerous to list here. Suffice it to say that human beings would be no where near as prosperous as they are today without the help of fairy godmothers.

In spite of this, Farthing would definitely have been horrified to learn that his youngest daughter had interacted with an actual human being. He belonged to the old school of thought, which believed that fairies' interactions with humans should be limited solely to the invisible use of magic to assist humans at different times in their lives. Further, he believed that any other type of interaction could only spell disaster for fairies and Fairy Town. Although he neither hated humans, nor felt ill will towards them, he didn't trust humans in general and felt that fairies everywhere would be much safer if humans never became aware of their existence.

Fatima's mother, Fortunata, was both a beautiful and kind fairy, who absolutely doted on all her daughters. Unlike her husband, she had not been at all disappointed that they had never had a son. Although she was very careful to hide it, she was especially fond of her youngest daughter, and often felt that her husband was much too harsh when he disciplined Fatima. She also didn't share her husband's (and most of the rest of the City Council's) belief that visible interaction with humans would ultimately result in the destruction of all fairies, as well as the World of Fairy itself. However, in the interest of keeping peace in the household, she usually kept this point of view to herself.

Fortunata was very proficient in the use of her fairy magic. This was especially true when she used her magic as a source for her artistic expression, and several of her unique sculptures decorated the city. Besides her art work, she was very busy raising and caring for her seven daughters, and she had little time for anything else. Basically, she and Hannah's mother were kindred spirits, although obviously the two women had never met, and hadn't a clue the other even existed.

Unlike Farthing, she had no interest whatsoever in the politics of Fairy Town. She was not at all fond of the Grand Mayor of Fairy Town, Aristotle Fanconi, and she barely tolerated the other members of the City Council, with the obvious exception of her husband. On the other hand, she very much enjoyed the company of her sister-in-law, Fantastica, and the two spent a lot of time in each other's company.

Fantastica was Farthing's younger sister, and although their personalities and their beliefs (especially regarding humans) were very different, they were still quite fond of each other. Fantastica had never married and had no children of her own, so she made up for it by spoiling her nieces. Her favorites were undeniably Fatima and her older sister Fawn, and Fatima had often benefited from this, as her aunt had helped her out of numerous predicaments in the past. On most of those occasions, Fantastica had managed to keep Fatima's actions a secret from her brother, thus allowing Fatima to escape additional punishments.

She was an eccentric, but sweet creature, and Fatima and her sisters loved her dearly. In an incredible coincidence, she was actually Hannah's mother's fairy godmother, although of course, Molly had no idea that she existed. In fact, it was Fantastica's fairy magic that had saved Molly's life when she was in childbirth with Hannah. Boy, wouldn't Hannah have been surprised to find out that her mother's comment about "a little bit of magic" saving her life that day was actually right on the money!

Now we get to learn a little bit about Fatima's six older sisters. A note of caution here: all of the girls' names are remarkably alike, as they all begin with the letter F. The responsibility for this can all be laid at Fatima's mother's feet, and it had been a matter of confusion for both parents ever since the birth of their 3rd child. The reader should not dismay of ever keeping the sisters' names straight, because it is eventually possible to do so, as this writer has discovered. We will start with the next youngest sister after Fatima, and work our way up to the oldest from there.

Fatiana was the 2nd youngest of the seven sisters, and was the only one besides Fatima who was not yet a fairy. Instead, she was a senior sprite who was both well behaved and gifted in the use of magic, and she was expected to graduate to Fairy level before too much longer. Being the closest in age to Fatima, the two hung around together a lot, and were actually quite fond of each other – in spite of having to share a room.

Fatiana did wish, however, that Fatima would be more disciplined when using her magic, and that she would get into trouble less often. Because of that, she tended to be somewhat bossy with Fatima; which, of course, irritated Fatima to no end. On the other hand, Fatima couldn't help but be a little jealous of Fatiana at times, because she was so good at everything and never seemed to get into any trouble.

The 3rd youngest of the sisters was Faith, who was closer in age to Fatima and Fatiana than she was to the four older sisters. Thus, she had grown up playing with them, and studying in sprite school at the same time that they did. She had just completed her transition to Fairy level about three months ago, and because of this, she was full of herself lately and constantly taunted her younger sisters with her newly obtained magic. She made a big production of retrieving her magic fairy dust from her chest each morning, which Fatiana and Fatima had to watch, seething with envy. Similarly, each evening she replaced the extra fairy dust with a smug smile on her face directed at her sisters.

Because there was a limited number of rooms in the family's fairy town house, she still had to share a room with her younger sisters. She found this very annoying, as she now felt that sprites were very much beneath her. To make up for this, she thought of various plans for torturing Fatiana, and especially, Fatima. Currently, one of her favorite pastimes was getting Fatima into trouble by tattling on her as often as she could. In fact, Fatima's current punishment was largely Faith's fault, as she and her friends had been the ones responsible for ditching Fatima in the meadow during their adventure into the Human World.

To be fair to Faith, her youngest sister could definitely be a pest at times. As an example, Faith had a large collection of stuffed animals which she loved dearly. Fatima took great delight in using her magic wand to transform Faith's favorite ones into hideous creatures such as ogres, trolls, or hobgoblins. It wasn't very often that the two girls were actually speaking to each other, and Fatiana frequently had to be the referee during their fights.

Fransesca was the middle sister in the family, and had her own room in the town house; which she received when Faye, the oldest sister, moved out several months ago. She was almost always nice to her younger sisters, but wasn't around very often because she led such an active social life. She had been a fairy for a little over three years now, and was in her last year of fairy school, where she was studying to be a teacher for the sprites' school.

She had already completed several teaching assignments in Fatima's class, which her youngest sister always found quite embarrassing. Fransesca loved Fatima very much, but she felt like she had to treat her like all the other sprites when she was teaching them. Thus, when Fatima acted out in class or was obviously not paying attention, she was forced to send her to detention or to the office of the headmaster of the school, just like she would any other sprite. Fransesca was probably the smartest of all the sisters, and she and Fawn were the most advanced, magically speaking.

Fountain was the 3rd oldest sister, and like Fransesca, she also had her own room. She was quite a bit older than Fatima, and while she was certainly nice enough, she usually didn't spend much time with her youngest sister. She had already finished all of her required schooling, and was currently in her last year of training to be a fairy godmother.

She also had a busy social life, as she had a large group of friends who were in fairy godmother training with her. In addition, she was seriously dating a young fairy named Bartholomew. All of her sisters thought that she would most likely be the next one in the family to get married. At any rate, she was not home very often, and when she was home, she spent most of her time in her room reading or studying.

The 2nd oldest sister was named Fawn, and she was Fatima's favorite. Fawn was kind and loving towards all of her sisters, and spent most of her time doing charity work in both the fairy world and the human world. Unlike some of the older fairies, she felt no ill will towards humans, and actually found them to be fascinating creatures who were often very likeable. Fawn was very proficient in fairy magic, and enjoyed helping her younger sisters with their studies when needed.

Their oldest sister, Faye, was very jealous of Fawn's magical abilities, as well as her great beauty; but Fawn had never let this bother her, and had always treated Faye with love and respect. Fawn lived in a small apartment by herself, and although she went out on many dates, she was not serious about anyone yet. She still returned home often to visit her family, and Fatima loved to visit her at her apartment. She usually spent the night there once or twice a month, when she didn't have school the next day. Like Fatima, Fawn was also very close to their Aunt Fantastica.

Faye was the oldest of the seven sisters, and was the only one who was married. She and her husband were expecting a baby in several months, and all of the sisters were tremendously excited about being aunts for the first time. As mentioned, Faye had always felt inferior to Fawn, and because of this, she sometimes allowed her jealousy and selfishness to cause her to do things that she knew were wrong.

Thankfully though, once she realized this, she was usually able to redeem herself in some way. Faye worked in the Liaison Office, which dealt with all human-fairy interactions. Her official position involved minimizing or eliminating any unfavorable interactions between the parallel worlds, and her boss was Aristotle Fanconi – the fairy who was the Grand Mayor of Fairy Town, and whom we will learn a great deal about in the very near future.

CHAPTER 8

THE WORLD OF FAIRY

The World of Fairy was a fantastical and wondrous place. Having been there myself, I can assure you that no place on earth compares to it. Even the wildest imagination couldn't think up all of the amazing things which exist in the World of Fairy. Fatima had tried to explain it all to Hannah, but had eventually given up because she decided it would be much easier to just show it to her. She was certain that her Aunt Fantastica, or her older sister Fawn, would lend her some of their magic fairy dust so that she could secretly transport Hannah over to her world.

You do not have the luxury of being able to travel to the World of Fairy, so I will have to describe it to you as best as I can. I fear that mere words cannot adequately convey all the magical and fascinating qualities of this world – but rest assured that I will try my best to do just that.

The World of Fairy existed in a world that was parallel to the human world. This means that the two worlds existed in the same time period, but were separated by what could best be thought of as a thin membrane of magic. Human beings could neither see nor sense this membrane, and the vast majority of people had no idea that another world existed besides their own. Fairies could freely travel back and forth with the aid of their magic fairy dust. Although the two worlds existed in parallel to each other, there was a time difference between the two worlds, because time passed more quickly in the World of Fairy. This meant that when a week had passed in the fairy world, only a day or two may have passed in the human world.

The World of Fairy contained many different lands, all of which were populated by various magnificent creatures. Their world had many similarities to our world, as well as obvious differences. Like our world, it contained valleys, mountains, rivers, and seas, as well as the four seasons of spring, summer, winter, and fall. Most of the creatures in this world lived in their own land or region. For example, some lands were home to ogres and trolls, some to dwarves and elves, and some to leprechauns, sprites, and fairies.

As peace currently reigned throughout the lands, the different creatures traded goods and services with each other, and traveled to each others' lands for this purpose, among others. Some of the creatures even lived in the lands of others, either as a means of learning or teaching about each other, or just as a matter of choice. The World of Fairy had not always been a peaceful one, however.

Approximately twenty-three years ago, the infamous Century War, which had lasted for almost 100 years, finally ended. This war was started by a large band of ogres and trolls, who were led by the powerful ruler of their land, King Olag Leftfoot. Olag was an evil and crafty ogre, who desired to rule over the entire World of Fairy. But fairy magic proved to be too powerful for him to overthrow, so he set his sights on the Human World, instead.

First, he ordered one of his followers to befriend a young fairy named Sam. King Olag then promised Sam that his fairy powers would be greatly increased if he drank a magical potion that only ogres knew how to make. Sam foolishly drank the potion, and immediately fell into a deep sleep. In this state he was completely powerless, and he was then kidnapped by the evil group. King Olag and his army then used Sam's magic fairy dust to gain access to the Human World, their intention to achieve dominion over the entire world and its human inhabitants. Somehow, Sam was able to escape from their clutches and flew quickly back to Fairy Town, where he told the town leaders about the ogres' plot. The sprites and fairies, who because of their compassionate nature have always been protectors of the weaker, magic-less humans, banded together and used their powerful magic to banish the gruesome mob back to their own world. But despite the fairies' superior magic, the war lasted for an entire century, and many lives were lost; including that of fairies and sprites.

Some human lives were lost also, although not a single human being came even close to suspecting what the actual cause of death had been. They were simply forced to admit that the circumstances were very mysterious. If humans had actually realized that ogres and trolls were loose on earth, the entire world would have panicked, resulting in mass destruction and overwhelming fear. Thankfully, the fairies had used their magical powers to ensure that the humans never saw the hideous creatures, but they were unable to totally prevent the loss of human lives – although that number was minimal in comparison to the loss of fairies and sprites.

None of the fairies alive today had been spared from this loss. Everyone had at least one member of the family who had sacrificed his or her life during those terrible years. Both of Fatima's grandfathers had given their life for that cause, and one of her grandmothers had injured her wings so badly that she could no longer fly. The devastation had been great, and many of the older fairies had chosen to blame humans for at least part of that tragedy. This was in spite of the fact that human beings hadn't even an inkling of what was happening.

The full blame should have been laid at the feet of King Olag and his followers. Those that had survived the war (and King Olag wasn't one of them, as he had died a horrible death at the hands of the fairy general) were banished to the realm between the worlds, never to be heard from again. Still, the number of deaths had been great, and it would take many years of peace before Fairy Town would be fully populated again. This was especially true because fairy women had only a short period of time in their lives during which they could reproduce. It amounted to about ten human years and most fairy couples had only one or two children, if any. Fatima's parents were very unusual (and obviously quite lucky), as they had been blessed with seven children.

While the creatures of the World of Fairy lived unusually long lives, especially compared to a human being, only fairies, sprites, and leprechauns were immortal. Furthermore, remember that even they could be killed in the Human World, as they lost the ability to be immortal once they crossed that line of magic. If they were killed in the Human World, their bodies were immediately transported back to their world through the use of magic. That way there would be nothing left in the Human World to suggest their existence.

When a fairy was first born, it came into the world as a sprite. Sprites usually became fairies somewhere between 80-120 years of age. At that time, a large family celebration would occur, and the sprite would graduate to the level of fairy and start fairy school. As mentioned, fairies lived forever, but were most powerful until they were about 500-600 years of age. After that, they usually moved to large retirement communities, where they continued long friendships, pursued hobbies, and enjoyed visits from their younger family members. Once they reached a ripe old age, fairies tended to avoid traveling to the Human World. If the fairy had been a fairy godmother and her human assignment was still living, that assignment would be turned over to a younger fairy.

Technically, only fairies could enter the Human World, because it required the use of magic fairy dust. Sprites could only pass through to the Human World if they were accompanied by fairies, or if they were able to borrow (or steal) fairy dust. Scattered around Fairy Town were gateways or portals, which led to a large number of access points around the Human World. Since traveling there was dangerous enough for fairies, access was entirely denied to sprites, as their immature use of magic could prove deadly. Even if they were able to gain entrance by using fairy dust, the consequences could be undesirable, because a sprite's use of fairy dust could often be erratic and didn't always have the desired effect.

The vast majority of the sprites and fairies in the World of Fairy lived in a place called Fairy Town. No one knew exactly how old Fairy Town was, but it had been there for as long as anyone could remember. Even the oldest fairy in town, whose name was Methuselah and was rumored to be 2,048 years old, couldn't remember a time when there hadn't been a Fairy Town. Fairy Town itself was a large and sprawling place with thousands of houses and buildings, all of which were multileveled. The newest businesses and homes were on the topmost levels, as fairy builders would just add new levels to the existing structure. Many of the buildings had 90 or 100 levels. Everything was beautifully decorated and painted in the brightest of colors, and all of it was perfectly maintained. The town had numerous schools, parks, businesses, and government buildings; and was a humdrum of activity throughout the day and well into the night.

Fairies were busy little creatures by nature, and they seldom wasted any of the time that they didn't spend sleeping. Each individual fairy had his or her own talent or area of expertise, and this was what their magic fairy dust was based upon. For example, some fairies were skilled at building or engineering. When they finally graduated from fairy school, their magic chest contained fairy dust which helped them excel in that area. Thus, the fairies' magic chests were individual to each, and helped them become experts in their chosen occupation. Of course, every fairy was also able to use the fairy dust to perform all of the spells which were considered basic to being a fairy. So all of them could fly, become invisible, transform objects into other objects, produce an object from thin air, etc., etc.

The most common occupation for female fairies was that of fairy god-mother, while the male fairies were much more diverse in their occupations.

They held jobs which were very similar to those in the Human World; such as firemen, lawyers, doctors, judges, government workers, and many more. Female fairies could work at these jobs also, but the majority of them became fairy godmothers. This was a thriving business, because there were always more humans being born, and most of them could really use a fairy godmother.

To be a fairy godmother, the female fairies had to continue on to fairy godmother school, after they were finished with sprite and fairy school. There they learned the skill of protecting their assigned human, while providing them with special and wonderful things in life, as well as the art of keeping the human unaware of their presence. When the fairy godmothers graduated, they would draw a human name randomly from a huge bin. They would then pay an invisible visit to their human being, and attempt to learn as much about them as possible. Then they would be able to assist them to the best of their abilities, while at the same time discovering how they could most enrich their lives.

Periodically, depending on each fairy's schedule, they would check up on their human, so they could continue to provide for their wants and needs. They would also have a special magical bond with their human, so that they would be instantly aware when trouble arose, and could usually arrive in time to prevent death or serious injury. Unfortunately, not even fairy magic could change the fact that all humans must die eventually. When that happened, the fairy would receive some vacation time to recover and mourn during this time of sadness. They would then be reassigned to another human, who was usually a member of that same family. As humans vastly outnumbered fairies, only a small number of individuals actually had a fairy godmother. Ultimately, after hundreds of years, the fairy would retire, and a younger fairy would assume the duty.

Law enforcement was not really a requirement for Fairy Town because fairies, in general, were peaceful, law-abiding folk. Occasionally, rogue fairies did exist, but they were the exception, rather than the rule. If it did become evident that a sprite or fairy was either misusing its magic or participating in an activity which could result in harm to another, then that fairy was brought before the City Council to answer for its crime. The City Council would then determine a punishment appropriate for that crime. Punishments ranged from community service, to loss of magic for a period of time, to banishment from Fairy Town. The absolute worst punishment which an individual could receive was to be banished to the realm between the worlds.

Everyone in the World of Fairy was aware of the horrible entity called the realm between the worlds, but no one ever wanted to talk about it. It had existed for as long as the two worlds had existed next to each other, but no one actually knew how long that was. Individuals could only be banished there by an unanimous vote of the City Council, because it required using the magic fairy dust of all the council members together to accomplish it. There was no known escape from the realm, and certainly no one had ever escaped from there before. It was a barren and desolate place, very much unlike the fairy world. No other living things existed there, and most horrible of all, there was no magic in the realm. A meager amount of food and water was somehow provided for each banished individual, but nothing more than that. Banishment there was a truly awful punishment, reserved for only the most heinous of crimes.

Although no law enforcement was required in Fairy Town, there was an army led by a fairy named General Mazzarati. The purpose of this army was to protect the city in the event that Fairy Town was attacked or threatened by another group of the land's inhabitants, such as ogres or trolls. It was the General who was the military commander during the majority of the Century War, and most of Fairy Town credited him with their eventual victory. General Mazzarati was an older fairy who had been in power for over 100 years now. He was the most important fairy in the land, next to the Grand Mayor, Aristotle Fanconi.

Aristotle was a middle-aged fairy, which meant he was several hundred years old. He had been the Grand Mayor of Fairy Town for the last 57 years. He was supposed to allow the City Council to assist him in passing laws and forming rules and regulations concerning fairy behavior, as well as the duty of deciding punishment for misbehavior or breaking the law. However, he was both a cruel and unethical fairy, and he and the General frequently took care of a lot of the Town's business in private, while attempting to keep it a secret from the City Council. Unfortunately, no one in town realized this at the time, and it would be awhile yet before this discovery was made. Aristotle hated humans with a passion, and his secret goal was to destroy the Liaison Office specifically, and the whole tradition of fairy godmothers in general.

This deep-seated hatred stemmed from the fact that his beloved and only daughter Tinkerbell had run away with a human named Peter Pan. Unknown to her father at the time, Tinkerbell had traveled to the Human World to check on another human, whose name has been long forgotten and is unimportant to this story. Her grandmother had been the fairy godmother for this human, but had come down with the sniffles, and was spending a few days in bed to rest and recuperate from her illness. Worried about her human assignment, she had asked her granddaughter, Tinkerbell, to check up on the human, which Tinkerbell had cheerfully agreed to do.

Tinkerbell was on her way to the human's house, when she spied a young boy, all alone and crying in his backyard. His tears had pierced her kind heart, and she appeared before him to see if there was any comfort she could provide. The boy, whose name was Peter Pan, had confided to the young fairy that he was afraid of growing up, and wished to remain a boy forever. Tinkerbell had listened compassionately at the time, and then had continued to visit the boy over the next several months. They developed a close friendship, which grew over time and eventually became mutual admiration and affection. When her father became suspicious of her frequent trips to the Human World, he followed her one day and caught her with Peter Pan. Her father threatened to destroy the boy, and to protect him Tinkerbell used her magical powers to bestow upon him the ultimate gift of immortality.

Unfortunately, that act itself broke the main rule that the entire Fairy Code is based on, and Tinkerbell was banished from Fairy Town forever. For this reason, Aristotle had declared a personal war on all humans, and he and the General were continually scheming together to concoct a plan that would bring their goal to fruition, and destroy all human-fairy interaction. Whether they would eventually be successful remains to be seen, and it is altogether possible that the budding new friendship between Hannah and Fatima would ultimately have some effect on the mens' evil goal.

CHAPTER 9

BACK TO SCHOOL

Monday finally came around – just like all Mondays have to eventually. Spring break had been filled with beautiful, sunny days, so it seemed only fitting that the first day back at school was overcast and threatening to rain. In spite of the weather, Hannah and Darlene had decided to ride their bikes to school. They had stopped at Ritchie's house and rang the doorbell, but no one answered, so they figured that Ritchie must have gotten a ride from one of his parents. Now they were making their way slowly towards the junior high school, walking their bikes side by side so they could talk more easily.

The obvious topic of conversation was Fatima and the wish she was going to grant Hannah. As they chattered excitedly together, a familiar voice shouted at them from down the street. They turned around quickly, and spotted Ritchie coasting towards them on a rather interesting contraption. He pulled up along side the girls, grinning broadly from underneath an oversized motorcycle helmet. Because of its sensitive nature, the girls' conversation had stopped abruptly when Ritchie had come into view.

"What are you guys talking about?" Ritchie gasped, as he tried to catch his breath. "Whatever it is, it must be exciting, because I could hear you chattering and laughing two blocks away." The girls stared at Ritchie and then at each other, struggling to think of something to say. Noticing the stricken looks on their faces, Ritchie suddenly blushed and looked down at the ground. "OK," he muttered, "it must be some girl thing, so let's just forget that I even asked." The girls looked at each other guiltily, although they were relieved they'd been spared from trying to come up with an explanation. They didn't feel good about keeping a secret from Ritchie, but since Fatima had made Hannah promise not to tell anyone but Darlene, they really didn't have much choice. Hannah racked her brain for something to say.

"What in the heck is that wacky thing you're riding?" she asked.

Ritchie's face brightened instantly, as he looked up at the girls with a gleam in his eyes. "It's my Ritchiemobile," he answered proudly.

"Uh, what's a Ritchiemobile?" Darlene asked uncertainly.

"It's this," Ritchie said, spreading his hands out with the palms turned up. "It's like a super, spectacular tricycle, except it's even better!"

Hannah and Darlene walked slowly around the bike, trying to figure out exactly how it worked. The entire thing was about four feet long and three feet high, and it looked like a cross between a go-cart and a tricycle. There were two large spoked wheels in back, a much smaller wheel at the very front, and the entire frame sat evenly on those three wheels. The frame was made from some kind of light-weight metal, and was painted a bright blue. The seat was positioned in the middle of the frame, and consisted of a flat part for the rider to sit on and a reclined back. Ritchie had built it so that the rider's legs stretched straight out from the seat, and the feet were then positioned on two small pedals towards the front. There was a steering wheel hooked to the frame in front of the seat, while a large box sat behind the seat and was also attached to the frame.

"Well, what do you guys think?" Ritchie asked with a pleased grin on his face.

"It's awesome!" Hannah and Darlene both said at once.

"How does it work?" Darlene asked.

"It should be obvious, but since you're just girls, I'll go ahead and explain it to you." Ritchie grinned at them good-naturedly, but both girls glared at him following that comment. "Oh, come on guys! I'm just kidding, and besides, there actually are a few hidden surprises that need to be explained before either of you can try it out." That statement caused the girls to look at each other worriedly. Ritchie was too excited about his invention to notice, though.

"OK, here's how it works," he began. "The back wheels provide all the power, while the front wheel is primarily used for steering. The steering wheel connects directly to the axle of the front wheel and the handbrake, down here by the seat, connects to the axle of the back wheels. That way both of the back wheels brake at the same time, so you don't skid when you try to stop. Now, the bike can either be driven manually, in which case your speed is determined by how hard you pedal, or it can be powered by this baby behind the wheel." As he said this, he proudly patted the box behind him. "In here, I've hooked up a 60 horsepower, internal combustion engine with a nitrous oxide bleed in." The girls just stared at him.

"Ritchie, would you mind telling us that last part again. And this time use words that are actually part of the English language."

Ritchie glared at Hannah for a moment, and then sighed in surrender. "It's a small motor that let's you reach a speed of 10mph, and if you push this red button on the steering wheel, you can go up to 25mph for short periods of time. It uses very little gas and runs clean, so you don't have to worry about polluting the environment with a bunch of exhaust. It's going to revolutionize the whole travel industry. People can use this to commute to work or school. They can use the pedals for exercise, or the motor for longer trips, or to get up steep hills, or if they just want to get somewhere faster. As soon as I get this baby into mass production, it's going to sell like mad, and I'll be rich in no time at all." Ritchie crossed his arms with a smug smile on his face, and waited for his friends' response.

Hannah and Darlene looked at the bike warily. There was no question that Ritchie came up with truly excellent ideas on a regular basis. He was also able to build things in an incredibly short amount of time, as anyone who had seen his basement workshop could attest to. But sometimes he got so excited about a project that he worked too fast, and too long without sleeping, and forgot some important part. This had led to a few glitches with previous demonstrations, and was often punctuated with, say, a minor explosion or two. Ritchie noticed the expression on the girls' faces, and immediately knew what they were thinking.

"OK, maybe a few of my other projects had some problems," he admitted grudgingly.

"A few!" Darlene started to say.

"But," Ritchie interrupted firmly, "I've thought this through carefully and completely, and it's ready for extensive test driving. I can say with complete confidence that this sweet little machine is entirely safe."

The girls exchanged nervous glances, before Hannah spoke up. "Uh, Ritchie, it's not that we don't believe you or anything, but I'm sure we can both recall other times when you said the same thing. I'll tell you what, why don't you go ahead and give us a little demonstration. That way we can see for ourselves how safe it is."

"I would be more than happy to," Ritchie replied in a cocky tone. "I rode this far just using the pedals, because I wanted to find you guys before I gave the motor a try." After saying this, he reached behind the seat and lifted the lid off of the box. The girls leaned in closer and peered inside. Sure enough, a small motor sat inside surrounded by a jumble of cables and wires, some of which were attached to a long, thin canister, which was hooked onto one side of the engine.

"That canister contains the nitrous oxide," Ritchie said proudly. "That's what gives it a little extra power. I control the bike's speed with this lever on the steering wheel, and then when I really want to cruise, I push this red button beside it. Now you guys ride up ahead on your bikes, and when you get to the end of the street, turn around and prepare to be dazzled." Ritchie reached into the box and flipped the switch to the motor. The engine immediately began running smoothly, and Ritchie placed the lid back on the box and latched it firmly in place. He refastened the chin strap on his helmet, placed his hands on the steering wheel, and gave the girls a thumbs up sign.

Hannah and Darlene got on their bikes, and quickly pedaled to the end of the street. They were both starting to get excited, in spite of their initial misgivings. The girls parked their bikes at the end of the street and stepped up on the sidewalk, where they stood together waiting for Ritchie's demonstration. Suddenly, the Ritchiemobile began moving, picking up speed as it neared the spot where the girls were standing. Just before he reached them, Ritchie pushed the red button on the steering wheel. In a burst of speed, he zoomed by the girls, who were left standing on the sidewalk in slack-jawed amazement.

Ritchie had turned around with a big grin on his face, when the girls suddenly spied a black cat starting to cross the street in front of him. They began waving their arms and yelling at Ritchie to turn around. A look of puzzlement crossed Ritchie's face, as he turned his head to look up the street. Noting the cat standing frozen in his path, he reached for the brake lever beside his seat. His speed immediately decreased, but the bike was obviously not going to stop in time to miss the cat. He swerved towards the sidewalk, bounced over the curb, and crashed into a large mailbox that sat on the corner of the sidewalk. The cat, entirely unscathed, ambled slowly across the street, as the girls broke into a run.

When they reached Ritchie, they were relieved to see that he appeared to be uninjured. He slowly shook his head back and forth in a daze, and then glanced around. The Ritchiemobile was definitely not in as good as shape as its rider. In fact, pieces of it were strewn all over the sidewalk and the adjacent street. Ritchie looked around and groaned. "My invention is demolished!" he said in a dejected tone. "It's going to take who knows how many days for me to put it back together. Plus, it's obvious that the current braking system isn't powerful enough to stop the bike, after I push the button for the nitrous oxide. Man, this completely sucks." Ritchie looked so depressed that it almost broke Hannah's heart. She attempted to lighten the mood with a little bit of humor.

"Well, I guess that's why they say it's bad luck for a black cat to cross your path."

Ritchie glared at Hannah for a few moments, until he couldn't help it anymore, and started to chuckle in spite of the circumstances. In no time at all, the three friends were laughing so hard they thought their sides would split. As their laughter tapered off, they wiped the tears it had caused off their faces, and began picking up the scattered pieces of the Ritchiemobile. They placed the loose parts in a pile on the bike's seat. The two back tires were still in pretty good shape, so Ritchie decided to lift up the front end, and push the bike home backwards. The girls offered to help, but Ritchie declined, saying that it would be better if they at least got to school on time. "I'll catch up to you guys in 2nd period," he said, and started back towards his house. The girls waved goodbye and got on their bikes, riding quickly towards the junior high school.

As soon as they got to school, they locked their bikes up in the bike rack, and hurried to the locker they shared. Surrounded by the other students, they opted to continue their conversation about Fatima at a later time. Instead, they began talking about the Home Economics project that was due next week. The project required each team to come up with its own special cake recipe. They were to do the baking themselves, and then they were supposed to come up with a unique and creative frosting design. The girls had thought of several ideas, but none of them seemed to be quite good enough. It had to be a super special cake to make up for the F they'd gotten several weeks ago when that snot, Erika, had swapped their ingredients when they weren't looking.

"This is going to be impossible," Darlene moaned to Hannah. "How are we going to come up with something good enough to make Mrs. Oglivie forget about our last disaster?"

"That wasn't our fault, Darlene. If that little brat hadn't switched our sugar for salt, our cookies would have turned out just fine," Hannah said in an uncharacteristically bitter tone.

"Okay, I know that, and you know that, but Mrs. Oglivie doesn't know that. She already treats the cheerleaders like little princesses, while she acts like we hardly even exist. And since that cookie fiasco, she glares at us every time we walk in the room." Darlene finished this last statement at the same moment they walked through the door of their Home Economics class.

Sure enough, Mrs. Oglivie had a big smile on her face as she stood near the desks where the cheerleaders sat, listening to Erika Scott babble on about something. She glanced up when Hannah and Darlene entered the room, and the smile immediately vanished and was replaced by a scowl. Darlene heaved a sigh and gave Hannah an I-told-you-so look, as she walked over to her desk and sat down. Hannah shrugged helplessly and slid into the seat next to her. They both turned and stared at Mrs. Oglivie, who had approached the blackboard, as she waited for the school bell to ring, announcing the beginning of class.

Sonja Oglivie was in her late 50's, and had taught at Roseveldt Junior High for almost 20 years. She was totally dedicated to her job, and she expected all of her students to treat Home Economics as seriously as she did. She was quite overweight and had a hideous sense of fashion – a combination which was unattractive, to say the least. She was married to a mousy little man named Herbert, who worked at a bank downtown, and she was obviously the dominant one at home. She tore through the house like a tornado on the loose whenever something upset her which was, unfortunately for Herbert, fairly often. The couple had two daughters who had grown up and moved away several years ago. The girls did not come home to visit very much, and most people in town felt it was because their mother was such a bossy pain in the butt.

As soon as the bell rang, Mrs. Oglivie clapped her hands together impatiently, waiting for the students to settle down so she could start class. When everyone was quiet, she started writing a list of requirements for next week's project on the blackboard. She then reminded the students that this special cake project would represent 25% of their final grade for the class. In other words, they had all better do a really good job. Hannah and Darlene looked at each other glumly. The class then divided into teams of two, and worked on making pie crust for the rest of the class period. By the time the bell rang signaling the end of class, Hannah and Darlene had finished making a pretty impressive looking pie crust. However, as Mrs. Oglivie walked around the room evaluating each team's effort, their crust barely registered a grunt, while she stopped in front of Erika and Annika's desks and praised them effusively.

Truthfully, Hannah didn't notice any difference between the cheerleaders' crust and hers and Darlene's, but apparently Mrs. Oglivie did.

As soon as the bell rang, she and Darlene gathered up their stuff and hurried towards the door. They had barely made it out of the room when they heard Erika's voice right behind them. "Apparently, some people are just natural cooks, while others just can't seem to do anything right," Erika said to Annika, before they pushed their way past Hannah and Darlene. Erika turned her head as they passed and gave Hannah a sickly sweet smile. Hannah quickly looked down at her shoes and gritted her teeth together, so she wouldn't be tempted to make a snotty comment while Erika was still in earshot. Once the girls reached their locker, the cheerleaders were completely out of sight, and Hannah decided it was safe to let off a little steam.

"Can you believe her?" she asked Darlene. "I mean the only reason we got a bad grade on the last assignment was because she cheated. Otherwise our cookies would have been perfect. I really can't stand her."

"No argument here," Darlene responded. "Thank goodness English Literature is next, and you know what that means."

"No cheerleaders!" both girls said at the same time. This caused the girls to start laughing loudly, and their giggles were just tapering off as they walked into their English Literature classroom. Their teacher, Mr. McKenzie, was standing at the front of the room writing the next reading assignment on the blackboard. Hearing their laughter, he turned around with raised eyebrows, and asked the girls a question. "Hey, you guys aren't laughing at my new vest are you? I had to wear it since my mother got it for me for my birthday." This caused the girls to laugh even harder, but Hannah finally managed to get out a few words.

"Don't worry, it's not your vest we're laughing at," she reassured him. "Just something that happened last period."

Mr. McKenzie grinned, and turned back around to finish writing. Mr. McKenzie had been teaching English Literature at the junior high school for almost 10 years now. He was in his late 30's and already balding, and often wore somewhat old-fashioned clothing, such as sweater vests and bowties. He had never married or had children, and currently lived with his elderly mother, who was in poor health. He loved his work, and often got very excited about introducing his students to all of the fascinating worlds they could visit in books.

The cheerleaders and the rich, snobby kids thought he was a nerd because of his passion for teaching; but he was definitely Hannah's favorite teacher, especially since he had provided her with so much encouragement regarding her reading and writing abilities. Sean Adams also enjoyed his class immensely, as he secretly desired to be an author someday. Mr. McKenzie recognized the fact that Sean had a lot of talent when it came to writing, and he tried to encourage him as often as he could. Mr. McKenzie was also the leader of the Debate Club, and it was his opinion that Hannah, Darlene, and Ritchie were the best and brightest of his students.

The girls sat down at their desks, and Ritchie raced in just as the class bell rang, sliding into his seat by Hannah. "Whew, just made it," he whispered to the girls. Class began, and the three friends enjoyed a delightful hour listening to Mr. McKenzie highlight the important points of Mark Twain's "A Connecticut Yankee in King Arthur's Court." The rest of the school day passed by quickly. An hour before the end of school, everyone gathered in the cafeteria for the spring assembly. The main purpose of this meeting was to discuss the Science Fair, which would be held in about three weeks.

The initial announcements were made by the Principal of the school, Ms. Peterson. She had been the Principal at Roseveldt Junior High for the last eight years. Ms. Peterson was in her late 40's, and had also never been married or had any children of her own. She loved working with the kids at school, and was very dedicated to her job. She was a fair-minded person who was well-liked by most of the students, in spite of the fact that she expected them to follow all of the school rules.

She was very fond of Hannah, Darlene, and Ritchie because they were such nice kids, as well as excellent students. She was a little less fond of Erika and her friends, because they were often snobby and petty, but she worked on trying to change their behavior using positive feedback. She was not at all fond of Tony Parsons and his group of friends, and she and the Assistant Principal were always on the lookout to put a stop to their bullying behavior. After Ms. Peterson had finished the general announcements, she turned the microphone over to Mr. Andrews, so that he could talk about the Science Fair.

Mr. Andrews was the Assistant Principal at the junior high, and had been there even longer than Ms. Peterson; as he had been there for almost 15 years now. His son, Paul, was an eighth grader at the school, and he ended up in the Principal's office quite regularly, much to his father's embarrassment. Like Ms. Peterson, he was kind and fair-minded, but also made sure the kids followed the school rules. He was the leader of the Chess Club, as well as a big fan of the football team, and he usually helped Coach Harris with football practices and various team functions. His favorite part of the school year was during the spring when they held the annual science fair competition, and that was what he wanted to talk to the kids about today.

Apparently, this year's competition was going to be a little bit different than previous years' had been. Students would be designing and building their own projects, and could work individually or in groups of two or three people. The competition would be unveiled on Wednesday night, April 20th, and several of the teachers, as well as he and Ms. Peterson, would be the judges. The entry that won the grand prize would be getting something very special this year. After saying this, Mr. Andrews waited a few seconds for all the whispering and speculation to die down. Then he announced the grand prize.

The kid or kids who had the winning entry would receive an all-expense paid trip to the Seattle Science Center, where they would get to put their very own project on display. It was the chance of a lifetime, and after hearing the news, a collective gasp was heard throughout the auditorium, followed by loud applause. Clapping furiously, Ritchie turned around and winked at the girls with a confident smile on his face. He was certain their project would be the winner!

After the assembly was finished, the three friends walked home together, excitedly discussing what they needed to do to finish their project. They just had to win that prize. The rest of the school week passed by uneventfully, and the kids worked on their project in Ritchie's basement every evening. Each night before she fell asleep, Hannah wondered if the next day would be the day when Fatima returned – and, soon enough, it was.

CHAPTER 10

SHE'S BACK!

A month had slowly passed in the World of Fairy. Today was the day Fatima would finally get her wand back – and it was Fatima's opinion that it was about time. It felt like the last month had lasted for about 348 years. As each day had plodded by, Fatima found herself growing more and more excited about returning to the Human World. Part of her excitement was because she was about to set off on an adventure that was all her own. But, most of her excitement was due to the fact that she would soon be seeing her new best friend again.

She had never had a best friend before; especially one that was human! She couldn't wait to see Hannah again, and she was going to get to meet Darlene, too. Plus, she would finally have a chance to grant Hannah's wish. That would practically guarantee that she was going to be the most famous sprite ever. They would probably let her skip being a senior sprite, and allow her to automatically graduate to fairy level. The town might even erect a statue in her honor in the town square!

While Fatima had been daydreaming about how famous she would become, she had been walking down the long hallway that led to her father's study. Suddenly, she found herself outside the door, and her daydreams immediately vanished, to be replaced by a great deal of nervousness regarding the upcoming conversation. Getting back her magic wand was never an easy process. Fatima steeled herself for the lecture that was sure to follow, and bravely knocked on the large oak door.

"Come in," answered the stern voice of her father. Fatima opened the door and stepped inside. Her father was seated behind his enormous oak desk, which was positioned at the far side of the room, beneath the large windows that looked down on the town square.

"Please close the door and have a seat," her father stated firmly. Fatima swallowed a lump in her throat, as she closed the door behind her and took a seat in one of the uncomfortable wooden chairs that faced the desk. As her father watched her silently, Fatima began to squirm on the chair's hard surface. All at once, her father cleared his throat loudly, causing Fatima to freeze in her seat.

"Well, Fatima," her father started, "it seems that a month has passed, and miraculously, you have managed to stay out of further trouble during that time. I suppose it is time for me to return Twinkle to you, but first a note of caution. If you do not change your ways, you will never reach the level of fairy. I have had more trouble with you, than your six sisters combined. I would like you to promise me that your future behavior will be more appropriate for a sprite in training, and that you will concentrate on making your mother and me proud, rather than continuing to disappoint us."

Fatima swallowed hard before she replied. Her answer came out in a quavering voice. "I promise, father."

Farthing's face softened immediately, and he reached into one of the desk's many drawers and took out Twinkle. He smiled at his daughter as he held the wand out to her.

"Thank you, father," Fatima said, grasping the familiar handle of her wand.

"Make me proud, Fatima."

"I will, father."

"You may go, daughter," Farthing said, and bent his head back over the paperwork spread out on the desk before him. Fatima stared at her father for a moment. She then walked to the door, opened it, and closed it behind her as she stepped out into the hallway. Her expression changed to one of fierce determination, as she thought to herself; I will make you proud father, just you wait and see.

Fatima flew through the rooms of the townhouse, until she found her mother, busy at work in her art studio. Fatima hesitated in the doorway, watching her mother work on a clay sculpture. Every sprinkle of her mother's fairy dust caused a precise change in the clay, and as she watched Fatima felt her chest swell with love and admiration for her mother. Fortunata suddenly looked up from her work and noticed her youngest daughter hovering in the doorway. Her beautiful face broke into a big smile and she waved Fatima over.

"Come here, little one. I would like your opinion."

Fatima grinned and flew around the sculpture, taking in every bit of her mother's creation. "It's beautiful, mother," Fatima exclaimed.

"Thank you, Fatima, but it still needs a lot of work. Now what can I do for you? You look about ready to burst with excitement. Is it because this long month is finally over, and you now have Twinkle back?"

"Oh yes, mother. That's definitely part of it. Also, Aunt Fantastica has asked me to spend my four day weekend with her, and it will just be the two of us. I'm sure we'll have all kinds of fun, because Aunt Fantastica always manages to come up with the most enjoyable activities. Can I go, mother? Can I?" Fatima hopped up and down with impatience, waiting for her mother's answer.

"Why, of course you can, Fatima. I hope you two have lots of fun. Just remember to be good and stay out of trouble."

"Oh, I will, mother. Thank you!" Fatima flew up to place a kiss on her mother's cheek, and then raced out of the townhouse.

As she flew over to her Aunt Fantastica's apartment, Fatima thought carefully about how she would approach this rather delicate situation. She had originally considered attempting to steal magic fairy dust from one of her sisters in order to get back to the Human World. However, if she was caught in the act, she would be in even more trouble than she had been. Besides, even Fatima realized how dangerous it would be for a sprite to use fairy dust to cross over to the Human World without any fairy supervision. Attempting it herself would only be used as a last resort. No, she thought, I definitely need help with this, and there's no one better to depend on than Aunt Fantastica. Also, she can cover for me if it takes a few days to achieve my goal for Hannah. This way my parents won't even miss me, because they'll think I'm at Aunt Fantastica's.

Satisfied with her plan, Fatima quickly covered the distance to her aunt's house in seven short minutes, and rang the doorbell out front.

"Who is it?" Fantastica's voice came crooning out of the speaker box mounted by the front door.

"It's me, auntie," Fatima spoke into the receiver. "It's your niece Fatima."

"Well, of course it is. I'd know that sweet little voice anywhere. Come on up, darling, the door is open."

Fatima heard the latch click, and the door swung open. She ducked inside, and flew up the stairs to her aunt's apartment. Fantastica was waiting in the doorway, and she enveloped Fatima in a huge hug.

"To what do I owe the pleasure of this visit?" she asked.

Fatima bit her bottom lip, trying to figure out the best way to start. Watching her niece carefully, Fantastica realized that Fatima needed to discuss something serious. Without another word, Fantastica led Fatima over to a comfortable, overstuffed couch, and sat down beside her.

"Tell me everything, dearie; and start at the beginning."

Fatima began by telling her aunt about the secret fairy adventure into the Human World, which had quickly become a disaster for Fatima. Her voice was halting at first, but as she gained confidence from her aunt's neutral expression, the words began to spill out; faster and faster. On several occasions, Fantastica had to ask her to slow down, or to repeat an important point. When Fatima had finished, they both sat silently for a few minutes. Fatima watched her aunt's face anxiously, trying to gauge her reaction. Finally, her aunt heaved a great sigh, and then stared thoughtfully at Fatima.

"Well, you got yourself into a bit of a pickle, didn't you?"

Fatima said nothing, as she bowed her head and stared at her hands, clenched tightly in her lap. If her aunt wouldn't help her, it was going to make things a lot more complicated. Also, if her aunt told her father, she'd be grounded until she was 200 years old, and she'd never see Hannah again. A single tear trickled down one cheek. Fantastica placed her hand under Fatima's chin and gently lifted her head, until she could look into Fatima's eyes.

"Don't fret, sweetie. Between the two of us, we'll get this all figured out. And, most importantly, I see no reason why your father needs to know about this."

Fatima let out an earsplitting shriek of happiness, and threw her arms around her aunt, squeezing her so hard she had trouble catching her breath.

Fatima finally released her aunt and began flitting about the room, turning somersaults in midair and yelling at the top of her lungs. After a few minutes of this frenzied activity, she finally returned to the couch and plopped down, panting for air. The look of complete happiness on her niece's face made Fantastica feel that she had definitely made the right decision.

"All right now; when do we leave?"

Fatima stared at her aunt in complete bewilderment, before a look of understanding washed over her face. "Uh, what do you mean we?" she asked.

"Well, of course, I need to go with you to keep you safe, and to help you out with your little plan. Your parents would never forgive me if something happened to you in the Human World. You've already found out for yourself how dangerous that world can be. Besides, it seems to me that you're going to need some magic fairy dust to accomplish your mission. I don't think that Twinkle is going to be quite enough."

Fatima hung her head again, before quietly replying. "So you don't think I can do this on my own. I thought that if anybody would have faith in me, it would be you. Obviously, you think I'm a screw-up too; just like everyone else in Fairy Town." Fatima's shoulders began to shake gently, and she sniffed repeatedly. Her tiny hands reached up to wipe the tears off of her cheeks. Watching this, Fantastica felt as if her heart would break into a million pieces. She had a very important decision to make. A look of resolve crossed her face, and she cleared her throat to recapture Fatima's attention.

"I see your point, and I happen to agree with you. I'll use my magic fairy dust to get you across, but then I'll let you go ahead on your own. If your parents ask, I'll say we're having a great time together. In the meantime, I'll just wait for your return. But you have to do one thing for me, so that I won't be worrying about you the whole time."

"Oh, I'll do anything, Aunt Fantastica!" Fatima said breathlessly.

"You have to carry a small magic button with you in your belt pouch. If you get into any trouble, or you run into a problem which requires my assistance, you only have to push the button and I'll be by your side in no time at all. The button has another purpose as well. Since time passes more quickly in the World of Fairy, you will only have a day or two at most in the Human World, before your four day weekend here is over. But, since time here doesn't pass at a constant rate, you will have no idea when you need to come home. So, when it reaches that point in time, I will use my fairy magic to cause the button to light up and vibrate. Then you will know it's time to come home immediately."

Fatima eagerly agreed to her aunt's condition. Secretly, she was amazed that Fantastica had agreed to let her go on this adventure by herself. She was tremendously excited, but she had to admit that she was a little frightened, too. This was a big responsibility for a little sprite. But with Hannah's help, she was sure she would accomplish her goal. While her aunt went upstairs to retrieve the magic button, Fatima bounced up and down on the couch with excitement.

When Fantastica returned with the button, Fatima examined it curiously. It was smaller than her hand, and the button was bright red and sat on top of a sparkling rock. In spite of this, it weighed next to nothing. Fatima carefully placed the magic button into the small pouch that hung on her belt. She gave her aunt a big grin, and announced that she was ready to go. They then flew to the nearest gateway, which was just around the corner from Fantastica's apartment, in a little side alley off of the busy Main Street. Fantastica gave her niece a big hug and kissed her on the cheek.

"You be very careful," she said seriously. "Push the button to call me at the slightest bit of trouble." Fatima promised her aunt she would do just that. She then drew herself up proudly, and waited for Fantastica to transport her over to the Human World. In a sprinkle of fairy dust, and a few muttered words of magic, Fatima vanished from sight.

Aunt Fantastica stood at the portal for a moment, deep in thought. She sincerely hoped she was doing the right thing. Unknown to Fatima, the magic button she carried at her belt was also a small transmitter, which Fantastica had created herself. It emitted a signal which Fantastica could use to follow her niece anywhere. The signal could only be tracked using a small, hand-held computer unit, which would not be leaving her hand until her niece returned. Best of all, Fatima would have no idea that she was being monitored.

You see, Fantastica had no intention of remaining behind; especially when Fatima could find herself in a heap of trouble at any moment. She would be keeping an eye on her niece at all times. The best part was that Fatima would never even suspect her presence, because she would be using her fairy dust to stay completely hidden. With that thought in mind, she sprinkled another dose of magic fairy dust over the portal, and in an instant, she too was gone.

In the Human World, a blinding flash of light signaled Fatima's entrance. She had emerged from the gateway in Hannah's world at the edge of the wooded glen by the meadow. She had already used her invisibility spell while in transit, so she wasn't at all worried that someone would notice her entrance. She hovered at the edge of the meadow for a moment, and tried to get her bearings. Once she was certain that she knew the direction she needed to go to find Hannah's house, she set off towards Hannah's neighborhood. Hannah had told her which street she lived on, and Fatima found Sycamore Street in no time at all. She located the brick house set in the middle of the block, and from Hannah's previous description, she immediately knew this was the Flannigan home. Hannah was going to be so excited to see her again, she thought to herself.

Fatima flew around the outside of the house, until she found an open window on the 2nd floor. Sliding through a rip in the screen, she emerged into a room which she guessed must be Patrick's. Dirty clothes littered the floor, and posters of rock groups and sports cars decorated the walls. Fatima's nose wrinkled in disgust. Boys were such gross creatures. It didn't matter if they were fairies or humans – they were all just gross!

Fatima flew out into the hallway, where she spotted a door with a pink sign just around the corner. The sign read 'Hannah's Room – Please Knock Before Entering.' Fatima obediently reached out and rapped her tiny knuckles against the door. Unfortunately, the door was so thick compared to the size of her tiny hand, that her knock hadn't made any sound at all. Well, I tried, Fatima thought, as she wiggled through the crack under the door.

Her first thought when she saw the room was that Hannah wasn't even there. Her second thought was that Hannah's room was awesome. The room was mainly decorated in pinks and yellows, with a large canopied bed occupying the center. The bed was pink, and so were the night table and lamp beside it. Spread around the room were a desk, a dresser, and a book case, which were all painted a light yellow. The carpet was light pink with yellow flowers, and hanging from the ceiling were numerous Indian dream-catchers in various colors. There was also a yellow hope chest at the bottom of the bed, and light pink curtains framed both of the windows.

Fatima sincerely wished that she had a room like this; especially since Hannah had her room all to herself. While Fatima hovered in the air admiring the room, she suddenly remembered her mission. She needed to quit wasting time and find Hannah. She flew over to the window facing the street, and looked out at the neighborhood. Remembering Hannah telling her that her best friend lived directly across the street, she decided that the large white house directly across from her must be Darlene's. That had to be where Hannah was, she thought to herself, because it was still too early in the morning for her to be at school.

Fatima retraced her way back to Patrick's room, and exited through the hole in the screen. She flew over to Darlene's house, and slipped under the front door. She searched the entire house, but found it to be completely empty. Where could those girls be? She hoped that nothing had happened to Hannah while she was gone. She wasn't entirely certain how many earth days had passed since their good-bye, but it couldn't have been more than a week or two. Fatima exited Darlene's house, and hovered uncertainly outside. She remembered Hannah talking about her other friend, Ritchie Pearson, and while she knew he also lived on this street, she didn't know exactly which house was his.

Fatima flew up and down the street slowly, checking out each house she passed. Three houses down from Darlene's, she noticed the sun glinting off some metal on the house's front porch. Zooming down for a closer look, she saw a bunch of pieces from some kind of riding contraption lying in a pile. Fatima obviously knew nothing about the infamous Ritchiemobile, but she did remember Hannah talking about how her friend Ritchie was always building one thing or another.

This must be Ritchie's house, Fatima thought to herself. I'll bet Hannah and Darlene are both here. Remembering that Ritchie's workshop was in the basement, she flew down to one of the basement windows. Wiping the grime from a small area of the glass, she pressed her tiny nose against the window and peered inside. Bingo! Fatima thought excitedly to herself. Standing around a table in the workshop were Hannah, Darlene, and Ritchie. Now I just have to find a way to get Hannah's attention, without Darlene and Ritchie noticing.

The little sprite thought hard for a moment, and if she hadn't been invisible, one would have been able to see the tiny creases in her forehead. Suddenly, she had an idea. She flew around the perimeter of the basement until she discovered a window which was cracked and missing a pane of glass. She squeezed through the hole without any problem, and flew over to where the kids were working.

Fatima zoomed down and perched on Hannah's right shoulder, intending to whisper into Hannah's ear to announce her return. But when she leaned in and started to whisper, her hair accidentally tickled Hannah's ear. Before Fatima knew what was happening, Hannah yanked her hand up to scratch her ear, and knocked Fatima right off her shoulder. Fatima was so surprised, that she lost her grip on Twinkle and forgot to flap her wings, all at the same time. She fell through the air, and landed in an undignified heap on the worktable.

Since her invisibility spell had been broken when she dropped her wand, she was completely visible for everyone to see. Ritchie was the first one to react to this unexpected intrusion. He stared at the tiny girl, completely flabbergasted. Unable to comprehend what he was seeing, he removed his glasses, rubbed his eyes furiously, and then replaced his glasses. Fatima, meanwhile, was feeling a wee bit grumpy about the whole situation.

"What are you looking at?" she snapped at Ritchie.

"Uh, I'm not exactly sure," Ritchie replied slowly. He hesitantly reached out a finger and stroked one of the sprite's wings.

"Hey! No touching!" Fatima shouted. "What are you, some kind of pervert?"

"No, of course not," Ritchie said, with a shocked look on his face. "I just wanted to see if your wings were real."

"Of course they're real. I thought you were supposed to be some kind of boy genius or something. Why don't you quit acting like an idiot."

Darlene had watched this whole exchange with her hands pressed to her cheeks, a look of awe and amazement on her face. "Oh my gosh!" she squealed. "You're the little sprite Hannah was telling me about. You're Fatima. Hannah's told me so much about you. We've been waiting like forever for you to come back. I'm Darlene, and it's such a pleasure to meet you." Darlene's words practically tumbled over each other in her excitement. Fatima sniffed archly, as she stood up and brushed off her clothes in an effort to look more presentable.

"Thank you," she replied. "It's nice to meet you, too, which is more than I can say for your friend," and she jerked a tiny thumb in Ritchie's direction. Hannah was so thrilled to see her little friend again, that she could barely stand it.

"I'm so sorry that I knocked you off my shoulder. I just thought a bug or something had flown into my ear. I had no idea it was you." Fatima gave a humph and bent over to retrieve her wand. Ritchie still looked like he was about to faint.

"Why does Darlene know all about this little person, when I wasn't told a thing?" he said in a wounded tone.

"Oh, Ritchie, I'm so sorry," Hannah gushed. "Fatima made me promise to only tell Darlene, and besides, you're always so scientific and rational about everything, that I didn't think you would believe me."

"Well, I guess I can see your point. I'm having a hard time believing it right now, even though she's standing right in front of me."

Hannah took that remark as a sign of forgiveness. She and Darlene sat Ritchie down on a nearby workbench, and began to explain the whole story to him. They told him everything that had happened, from start to finish, with Fatima occasionally interrupting to clarify certain points. When they were finished, Ritchie still looked like he was in a daze. But, at least he finally understood and accepted the little sprite's presence.

"Well, what do we do now?" he asked the group.

"That's easy," Fatima replied. "Take me to school with you this morning, so that I can get started on fulfilling Hannah's wish," she said with a twinkle in her eye. The three friends agreed enthusiastically and they all set off for school – with Fatima perched on Hannah's shoulder, invisible once again.

CHAPTER 11

A DISASTER IN HOME ECONOMICS

On their way to school, the three friends could hardly contain their excitement. All of them still found it hard to believe that something like this could actually be happening to them. Hannah was reassured by the feeling of pressure on her right shoulder, but Ritchie and Darlene kept staring at the spot the invisible Fatima occupied; as if they were worried that the whole thing had just been a figment of their imagination. While there was still time, and before they got too close to school, Hannah explained her class schedule to Fatima. She went into the most detail about first period, which was Home Economics with Mrs. Oglivie. Fatima asked questions periodically, and all three of the kids found it kind of spooky to hear a voice coming out of thin air.

Nearing the school, Hannah reminded Fatima how important it was for her to stay still and quiet, and most importantly, invisible. Fatima promised her that she would be as quiet as a mouse, but Hannah still had a somewhat doubtful look on her face. She sincerely hoped that Fatima would keep her promise. When they entered the school building, Ritchie said a quick good-bye and then headed off towards his locker on the other side of the building. Hannah and Darlene's locker was just down the hall, and they hurried towards it, after glancing up at the clock on the wall. Mrs. Oglivies's class was definitely not a class you wanted to be late to.

As soon as they reached it, the girls opened their locker and placed their backpacks inside. Warning Fatima with a whisper that she had to remove her jacket, Hannah felt the sprite move off of her shoulder. After placing their jackets in the locker too, they trudged off to their least favorite class of the day. Feeling the sprite's comforting weight back on her shoulder, Hannah thought, at least Fatima will be there with us. So maybe it won't be as horrible as it usually is, or at least I hope that's the case.

The girls entered the classroom and scurried to their desks, just as the 1st period bell rang. Mrs. Oglivie immediately stood up and waddled towards the blackboard. "All right, class," she said in her shrill voice, "let's not be wasting anymore time. I want you all to get started on your special cake recipes, right this moment." Hannah suddenly heard a tiny whisper in her right ear.

"Oh, I don't like her at all," Fatima said.

"Shh!" Hannah said, horrified that the little sprite was already breaking her promise. Darlene glanced over at Hannah with a questioning look on her face. Hannah shook her head firmly, and resumed paying attention to Mrs. Oglivie.

"Each team is responsible for preparing and baking its own original cake recipe. You are also required to frost your cake, and part of your grade will depend on your frosting design. You have one hour to finish your cake. When the bell rings, I want you to bring your cake up to this table beside my desk, and leave it here with a slip of paper that has your names on it. I will judge the cakes by lunchtime, and the winning team will get to do a special project with me for tomorrow's class. You may now begin!" she said, and clapped her hands sharply together.

Hannah and Darlene looked at each other and rolled their eyes. They had discussed their project in great detail last night; and had decided to make a raisin-carrot cake with orange-peel, sour cream frosting, and a design of orange and white flowers on top. The final touch would be walnut halves, positioned in a circle, around the edge of the cake. Even if they didn't win, the girls were certain they would at least get an A for their efforts. As they started to mix the initial ingredients together, Hannah heard a soft whisper in her ear. "Are you sure you don't want me to help out? Because, Twinkle and I could whip something up in no time at all."

"No!" Hannah whispered fiercely. "You promised to sit still, and stay quiet."

"All right, all right," the grumpy voice replied. "I'll just sit here with my mouth shut, even if I'm so bored that I fall asleep. Just don't blame me if I start snoring." Hannah pressed the back of her hand against her mouth, and suppressed a giggle.

After the ingredients were all mixed together, Hannah and Darlene placed the cake in the oven to bake, and got started on their frosting. Hannah glanced around the room, and was relieved to see that everyone else was pretty much at the same stage they were. The girls finished mixing the frosting, and then concentrated on breaking all of the walnuts into halves. By this time, the cake was almost finished baking, and as soon as the timer went off, Darlene removed it from the oven. She set it down carefully at their table, and they both admired their work so far. The cake looked beautiful, and more importantly, it had turned out exactly as they had planned.

While Darlene set to work frosting the cooled cake, Hannah filled the squeeze tubes with orange and white frosting. The tubes would be used to make the flowers on top of the cake. When they had each finished their frosting jobs, both of them set to work placing the walnut halves around the edge of the cake. The finished project looked awesome, and promised to be delicious.

Sitting on Hannah's shoulder, the invisible sprite had quickly grown bored with the whole cake baking process, and had begun watching the other students instead. She had no trouble figuring out which of the girls were the despised cheerleaders. Just as Hannah was about to carry the finished cake up to the table by Mrs. Oglivie's desk, Fatima noticed Erika and Annika whispering together and glancing over in Hannah's direction. Her suspicion aroused, she flew over by the cheerleaders to see if she could eavesdrop on their conversation. Landing on their desk, she listened intently to the two girls.

"I'm telling you that their cake looks better than ours," Erika was saying to Annika. "I'm not going to let those two win the chance to do the special project with Mrs. Oglivie. It should obviously be the two of us up there tomorrow," she said haughtily.

"But I won't even be here. I have a dentist appointment tomorrow morning," Annika answered.

"Well, I don't care," Erika said angrily. "I will be here tomorrow, and I'm the one that should get to do that project. I always win everything, and besides, I refuse to lose to those two morons. Now, here's what we're going to do. When she walks down the aisle with that cake, you're going to stick out your foot and trip her."

"Wait a minute," Annika said, "why do I have to be the one to trip her?"

"Because you're the one next to the aisle and because I told you to!" Erika hissed, glaring at her friend.

As soon as Fatima heard this last exchange, she was determined to fly back to Hannah and warn her of the cheerleaders' plan. However, before she even had a chance to flap her wings, things began to happen way too fast. Fatima turned around, and saw that Hannah was already starting down the aisle with the cake in her hands and a big smile on her face. As she approached the cheerleaders' desks, Annika's foot shot out like greased lightning, and hooked around Hannah's left ankle. Hannah's face registered a quick look of shock and surprise, and then she began falling. Fatima knew exactly what was going to happen next, but she couldn't turn away or even close her eyes; she was frozen in horror.

While Hannah continued to fall, she did her best to try and save the cake. Alas, Hannah's athletic skills left much to be desired. The cake landed with a plop on the floor, and Hannah immediately followed, her face landing smack dab in the middle of the cake. The cake was completely ruined, and when Hannah lifted her face (which was, of course, covered with orange and white frosting), the entire class began to laugh uproariously. Hannah's look of dismay and embarrassment was still visible, even through the layers of frosting.

Her glasses had remained stuck in the cake when she lifted her head, so her eyes were the only part of her face that wasn't covered with frosting. Looking behind her, she noticed that Annika's foot was still sticking out in the middle of the aisle. Quick as a wink, Annika whipped her foot back underneath her desk, and then sat there with an innocent expression on her face. Over the classes' laughter, Hannah could hear Mrs. Oglivie screeching at the top of her lungs.

"What is going on here?" Struggling to move her bulk down the aisle, she continued to yell. "I want all of you to quiet down, and someone needs to tell me what's going on here!" Erika raised her hand and smiled sweetly at her teacher.

"Mrs. Oglivie! I saw it all and would be happy to explain it to you," she simpered.

"Please go ahead, Erika; I'm all ears."

"Well, Hannah was carrying her cake down the aisle, when she suddenly lost her balance and fell, landing right on top of her cake."

By this time, Mrs. Oglivie had managed to squeeze her way down the aisle, and was looming over Hannah's prostrate form. She was wearing a hideous red and white striped dress, which most closely resembled a circus tent. "Well, Hannah, what do you have to say for yourself?"

Hannah tried to wipe some of the frosting off of her face, and then slowly blinked her eyes. She was obviously still dazed from the fall itself.

"Hannah Flannigan, you answer me this instant or you'll be going straight to the Principal's office!"

"But Mrs. Oglivie, I didn't lose my balance. I was tripped. You have to believe me," she begged.

"Oh, so now you want to place the blame on someone else. Why don't you just admit that it was your own clumsiness that caused this? In fact, maybe it wasn't even an accident at all."

"What do you mean?" Hannah asked in a wounded tone.

"Maybe you were worried about your grade, because your cake didn't turn out the way you planned. So, in an effort to hide that fact from me, you deliberately sabotaged your own cake."

Hannah stared at Mrs. Oglivie with a horrified expression on her face. "But I wouldn't do that," she protested, "and besides, our cake was perfect."

"Well, I guess we'll never know, now will we, because your cake is entirely ruined. There's no way I can even judge your finished project now."

"But, that's not fair! I'm telling you the truth. I know that Annika tripped me, whether it was accidental or not," Hannah stated firmly.

"Annika," Mrs. Oglivie replied, "did you trip Hannah while she was carrying her cake?"

"Oh, my gosh!" Annika said, with a shocked expression on her face and one hand pressed to her chest in disbelief. "I would never do something like that, would I Erika?"

"Of course not," Erika said in support of her friend. "I was sitting right here and saw the whole thing. It happened exactly like I said, and anyone who says differently is a liar."

Following this last statement, she glanced around the room with her icy blue eyes, wordlessly challenging anyone else to argue with her. Hannah also looked around the room with a pleading expression on her face. Hadn't anybody seen what had really happened? Sean Adams immediately turned his gaze away from Hannah, unable to meet her eyes. He had happened to look up from his project, just as Annika's foot had snaked out into the aisle and tripped Hannah. But, in spite of how badly he felt for Hannah, he didn't feel brave enough to lock horns with Erika or Mrs. Oglivie. Instead, he kept his eyes glued to the desk in front of him, as a feeling of shame crept over him. Fatima looked at him with disgust written all over her face, but being invisible, it obviously had no effect. Darlene had unfortunately been cleaning up their baking area, and hadn't noticed a thing, so even she was unable to come to her friend's defense.

Hannah sighed in defeat, and looked down at the mess which had once been a beautiful cake. She pulled her glasses out of the middle of the cake, and tried to wipe most of the frosting off of the lenses. Then she slowly stood up and waited for Mrs. Oglivie's verdict.

"Hannah, I have no choice, but to give you and Darlene an F for today's assignment. I will also expect you to spend your lunch hour here, cleaning up the mess you've made. Luckily, I have already rescheduled my other morning classes, so that I'll have ample time to judge everyone else's cakes. I'll leave this mess exactly as it is, and I expect you here at noon sharp. Now go get cleaned up as best you can before your next class."

Finished with Hannah, she addressed the rest of the class. "Students, you have five minutes until the bell rings. By that time, I expect you all to have cleaned up your work areas, and to have your cakes placed on the judging table. Then, you're all excused." Giving Hannah one more look of disgust, she waddled back to her desk and placed her large butt on her chair, which creaked and groaned under the massive weight.

Hannah began walking back to her desk, trying to brush the frosting and cake crumbs off of her hands. Realizing it was useless without soap and water, she gave up, and settled for using a Kleenex in her pocket to wipe the frosting away from her eyes. Darlene gave her a look of sympathy and a whispered "I'm sorry," as she stopped to collect her things. Hannah gave her a wan smile and started to walk out the door.

Over the noise of continued snickering from the rest of the class, Hannah heard Darlene ask her to wait in the girls' restroom, until she got there. Hannah gave a quick wave over her shoulder to acknowledge Darlene's request, and continued trudging towards the door. It felt like the door was a mile away, and she was being forced to walk through a gauntlet, while everyone stared at her and continued laughing; everyone except Sean Adams, who watched her sympathetically and shrugged his shoulders helplessly when she passed his desk.

Once Hannah reached the hallway, she quickly made her way to the girls' restroom, which was thankfully just around the corner. By lunchtime, everyone at school would know about the whole embarrassing incident, because word was sure to spread like wildfire. But until then, the fewer people who saw her with frosting all over her face and hair, the better. As it was, she was sure to be teased until high school graduation – or maybe even for the rest of my life, she thought gloomily. Hannah checked the bathroom stalls to make sure she was alone, and then looked in the mirror over the sinks.

Well, no wonder everyone had laughed so hard, she looked like an idiot! There was orange and white frosting all over her face and hair, and some of it had even gotten into her nostrils.

She gave a heartfelt sigh and turned on the water at the sink. Grabbing a large handful of paper towels, she set to work scrubbing. She had barely started cleaning up, when Fatima suddenly appeared on the edge of the sink. The little sprite was obviously furious. Her face was bright red and she was stomping back and forth along the sink's edge, waving her magic wand around, as she ranted and raved. Hannah thought that if she looked hard enough, she would probably see smoke coming out of the sprite's tiny ears.

"I have never been so angry in my entire life!" she seethed, and sparks seemed to shoot from her eyes. "I can't believe those girls would do something like that, and then lie about it. And you're teacher is such a fat nincompoop that she believed them. Twinkle and I are going to get busy right this very minute. We're going to turn your teacher into a warthog, those two cheerleaders into a couple of slimy toads, and everyone who laughed at you into little, fat slugs!"

At this point, Fatima finally stopped to take a breath, so Hannah took immediate advantage of the opportunity and attempted to calm the girl down.

"As mad as I am right now, I can't let you turn my teacher and classmates into toads and slugs." Fatima started to open her mouth, and Hannah quickly continued. "I just want to get cleaned up as much as I can, and then try to forget this ever happened."

"Well, how about turning your teacher into a warthog? You didn't say anything about warthogs," Fatima said, with a pleading tone in her voice.

"Absolutely not," Hannah stated firmly. "I'll take care of this myself. I'm going to have a talk with Erika and Annika, and I'm going to ask them to tell Mrs. Oglivie the truth."

Fatima sneered as she replied. "Those girls are just going to laugh in your face. They'll never agree to do that. You have to let me help you; that's what I'm here for."

At that moment the class bell rang, and not thirty seconds later, Darlene rushed into the bathroom. Fatima quickly repeated the conversation that had taken place, and then asked Darlene for her opinion.

"Well," Darlene said, biting her lower lip and thinking for a moment. "I have to say that I agree with Fatima, Hannah. I mean not about turning them into toads and slugs, but about the part where she could use her magic to help you out somehow."

"Ha!" Fatima said, crossing her arms across her chest in victory. "Darlene agrees with doing it my way."

Hannah closed her eyes for a moment, and then blew a puff of air up at her bangs. "Okay," she said finally, "but it has to be something relatively harmless and temporary. That means you can't turn them into anything."

Fatima immediately agreed, before Hannah had a chance to change her mind. Hannah finished cleaning herself up, just as the bell rang for 2nd period. The girls hurried out of the restroom, and jogged down the hall to their English Literature class. Fatima had returned to her spot on Hannah's shoulder, her invisibility spell back in place. Hannah somehow managed to get through the rest of her morning classes without rolling herself into a ball and crying. It was difficult though, because word had already spread throughout the school, and kids were constantly pointing and laughing when she walked by. She couldn't wait for the day to finally be over.

When the noon bell rang, Hannah hastily ate a banana on her way back to Mrs. Oglivie's room. Entering the room, she noticed that Mrs. Oglivie had done exactly what she promised and left the entire mess for Hannah to clean up by herself. "Boy, one of your spells would come in handy about now," she muttered over her shoulder. "Just kidding," she added quickly, afraid that Fatima would take her seriously. Mrs. Oglivie looked up, as Hannah walked towards her desk.

"You're just in time," she said with a thin, unpleasant smile on her face that didn't reach her eyes. "I was just going to announce the winners of this morning's assignment." Hannah watched her teacher expectantly. "The winners are Erika Scott and Annika Iverson. Annika will be absent tomorrow, so Erika will be my special assistant for tomorrow's project. I just need to finish getting our ingredients ready for tomorrow, and then I'm going down to the office to make the announcement over the loudspeaker."

Hannah nodded her head in resignation, feeling not the slightest bit surprised that Mrs. Oglivie had selected Erika as the winner. Truthfully, the outcome was exactly what she had expected it to be. Mrs. Oglivie grunted as she stood up and walked over to the table where she would be arranging the ingredients for tomorrow. Hannah heard a few muttered words, and suddenly, Mrs. Oglivie froze in place. Hannah looked at her teacher in shock. "Mrs. Oglivie?" she asked hesitantly. "Are you okay?" Her teacher didn't say a word. In fact, she didn't make even the tiniest movement; not even a blink of her eyelids.

"Of course, she's okay," Fatima said, as she suddenly reappeared, hovering in the air in front of Hannah. "She's just feeling a bit frozen at the moment." Fatima giggled at her own joke.

"Well, it's not hurting her or anything, is it?"

"Nope, she'll be fit as a fiddle with no memory of this at all, as soon as I cancel the spell. But I'm not going to do that until I mess around a bit with her ingredients for tomorrow's special, little project," she said in a sarcastic tone.

"Fatima, you promised not to hurt anyone, or do anything that would be permanent," Hannah reminded her anxiously.

"I know, and I'll keep my promise to you. I'm just going to cook up a little surprise for everyone; pun definitely intended," she said with a huge grin.

"What are you going to do?" Hannah asked.

"That's for me to know, and everyone else to find out!"

Fatima flew over to the table and began waving her wand around the ingredients, casting her spell with unintelligible words of magic. Hannah bent down and resumed cleaning up, keeping one eye on the door to make sure no one came in and found Mrs. Oglivie frozen, with a sprite flying around the room.

As soon as Fatima announced she was finished, Hannah breathed a sigh of relief. The sprite flew back to her perch on Hannah's shoulder, and became invisible once again. At almost the same moment, Mrs. Oglivie began moving again, adjusting various containers on the table as if nothing out of the ordinary had taken place. She looked only mildly surprised when Hannah informed her several minutes later that she was already done cleaning up.

Mrs. Oglivie excused her, and then followed Hannah out of the room on her way to the office. Several minutes later, her booming voice came over the school PA system, announcing the winner of that morning's baking contest. Hannah had just entered the cafeteria, intending to find Darlene and Ritchie and finish her lunch. She heard a shriek of joy, and turned around to see Erika clapping her hands ecstatically, while the other cheerleaders gathered around to congratulate her. Hannah grunted in disgust, and walked over to the table where Ritchie and Darlene were sitting.

"Wow, that was fast," Ritchie said cheerfully.

"Did Fatima take care of things?" Darlene asked.

"She sure did," Hannah replied, "but she won't tell me exactly what she did. I have no idea what to expect, so tomorrow's class should be very interesting."

Just then the bell rang, and the kids hurried off to their afternoon classes. The rest of the day passed slowly for Hannah, who had to endure the nearly constant teasing from the other students. As the three friends walked home after school, Hannah professed her relief that the awful day was finally over. When they came to Ritchie's house, he told the girls good-bye and went inside to continue working on the demolished Ritchiemobile. Darlene had piano lessons that afternoon, so she and Hannah said their good-byes, too.

"Are you sure you don't have any idea what Fatima has planned for tomorrow?"

"Not a clue," Hannah answered. "Fatima, no one's around; can't you just tell us what's going to happen?"

A small voice came out of the air by Hannah's shoulder.

"Sorry girls, but you're just going to have to wait until tomorrow," Fatima said gleefully. "I will tell you one thing, though."

"What's that?" the girls asked in unison.

"Don't eat the cake that Erika and Mrs. Oglivie are going to make." – and, in spite of the girls' continued pleading, Fatima would say no more.

CHAPTER 12

BACK AT THE FLANNIGAN HOME

After saying good-bye to Darlene, Hannah crossed the street, and went inside her house. She had to use her own key for the front door, because no one else was home yet. She stopped in the kitchen for a quick snack and a glass of milk, and then climbed the stairs to her bedroom. Once inside, she closed her door, and threw her backpack on the bed.

"Fatima! Come out, come out, wherever you are!" she said in a singsong voice, giggling at her own silliness.

The sprite appeared suddenly, perched on a stack of books on Hannah's desk. She tried to keep a straight face, but soon gave up, and joined Hannah in her giggling fit. When the girls had finished, Fatima straightened up and tried to look more serious, as she asked Hannah a couple of questions.

"Where's the rest of your family?"

"My parents are still at work, and Patrick's at football practice."

"Well, when will they be home, because I don't want to take any chances and accidentally have someone see me?"

"Don't worry," Hannah replied, "no one will be home until at least 5:30, which means we have the next two hours to ourselves."

Feeling a sense of freedom, the girls relaxed and began to talk about the horrible day. Fatima started out by telling Hannah about the conversation which had taken place between Annika and Erika, word for word. The girls then discussed all of the events which happened after that. When they finished their spirited dialogue, both of them agreed that today belonged in the Top Ten of crappy days. But, tomorrow was sure to be much better, or at least that's what Fatima promised. As soon as Hannah resumed trying to get Fatima to tell her what was going to happen the next day, Fatima declared the conversation over. Feeling slightly frustrated, but determined not to bug the little sprite anymore, Hannah decided to get started on her homework. Fatima used the opportunity to take a quick nap, as the events of the day (especially the magic spell at lunchtime) had proven to be quite exhausting.

Around 5:45, Hannah heard the front door slam shut, followed by heavy footsteps racing up the stairs. Without warning, Hannah yelled at Fatima to hide, causing the sprite to practically jump out of her skin in surprise. She darted into Hannah's open backpack, quickly chanting the invisibility spell once again. Several loud knocks hammered on Hannah's door, and when the door swung open, Patrick stood framed in the doorway.

"Hey Hans, what's up?"

"My name is Hannah, and nothing's up. Why don't you go take a shower? You're filthy, and you stink, and I'm not sitting at the same dinner table with you until you do."

Patrick appeared to be totally unimpressed by her little speech.

"Yeah, whatever. Catch up to you later," he said, as he headed towards his room.

"Please, close my door!" Hannah shouted. The only answer was the sound of Patrick's own door slamming. "Honestly," Hannah fumed, "big brothers are a huge pain in the butt." Then, she slammed her own door.

"Hey!" a voice downstairs yelled, "what's with all the door slamming?"

"Oops, that's my dad," Hannah said in Fatima's direction. She opened her door again, and stepped out into the hall. "Sorry, dad," she called downstairs, "the big ape was just bugging me again."

"Well let's keep it down; it sounds like a herd of elephants got loose up there. Finish up your homework, and I'll call you when dinner's ready."

"Okay, dad!" Hannah yelled; and softly closed her door.

Hannah walked back to her bed and flopped down on it. A voice near the end of the bed quickly piped up, and said, "Hey, watch what you're doing! You almost sat on me!"

"Oh, my gosh! I'm so sorry. Where are you?" Hannah asked worriedly, her eyes darting right and left in an attempt to locate the sprite.

Hannah heard giggling by her ear, and the sprite reappeared, hovering in the air beside her head.

"Fatima, you little stinker! You weren't even on my bed." Fatima laughed even harder, as she plopped down on the bed beside Hannah.

"Sorry," she said in a tone which suggested otherwise, "I just couldn't resist."

Hannah gave an exasperated sigh, which was immediately followed by a few giggles of her own.

"Fatima, what are you going to do while I'm eating dinner with my family?"

"Well, I'm going to be with you, silly."

"Like that?" Hannah asked quickly, a worried expression on her face.

"Of course not, you big dummy. I'll be invisible and perched on your shoulder, just like I was for most of the school day."

"Oh," Hannah said in a tone of relief, "I get it."

"But," Fatima added, "I would definitely appreciate it if you could save me a little bit of your dinner for later, because I am famished."

Just then, Hannah's mom called up the stairs, informing her kids that dinner was ready. Fatima suddenly vanished into thin air, and within seconds Hannah felt the now familiar presence on her right shoulder. Hannah walked to her door and reached her hand out towards the knob, but then hesitated for a moment. "Now, Fatima, remember," she started to say.

"I know, I know," Fatima said in a huffy tone, "be quiet and stay invisible."

"Thanks," Hannah said gratefully, and opened her bedroom door.

"Talking to yourself again, retard?" Patrick asked cheerfully, pushing past his sister, and bounding down the stairs without waiting for her reply. Hannah barely resisted the urge to strangle him, as she walked downstairs and took her place at the dining room table. She settled for sticking her tongue out at him when her parents weren't looking.

"So, kids," Tom said, after he'd finishing saying grace, "how was school today?"

Hannah mumbled something under her breath.

"What was that, sweetheart?" Molly asked brightly. "I couldn't hear you over the noise of your brother inhaling his food."

Patrick shot her a grin, his mouth full of mashed potatoes.

"I said it was fine," Hannah said quietly, before she resumed picking at her dinner. She barely finished her sentence, before Patrick broke in and began telling his dad about that afternoon's football practice. From that point on, the majority of the dinner conversation involved Tom and Patrick discussing this year's team, and how it matched up against the other high school teams. Hannah pushed her food around her plate, while she stared off into space, neither listening nor participating in the conversation. Molly was the only one who seemed to notice her daughter's unusual silence. When Tom and

Patrick had finally exhausted the whole subject of football, Molly tried to draw Hannah into the dinner table banter.

"So, honey, what did you do at school today?"

"Nothing exciting," Hannah answered. Molly waited for a moment, but when it became obvious that Hannah wasn't going to continue, Molly tried again.

"Well, what about that special baking project that you and Darlene spent all weekend thinking about?"

Hannah sat there silently, trying to think of a way to downplay the whole incident. Thank goodness her brother was in high school now or he would have already heard about it, and would be teasing her mercilessly by now. As if he had read her mind, Patrick leaned in closer and carefully studied Hannah's face.

"Is that frosting in your bangs and eyebrows?" Patrick asked suddenly. "Oh my gosh, it is! And you have it in the sides of your hair, and even in your ear. What did you do, fall into a frosting bowl?"

Hannah glared at her brother, tears threatening to well up in her eyes. Sensing a delicate subject, Molly cut off her son. "That's enough, Patrick. Hannah, why don't you tell us what happened."

Hannah set down her fork, and folded her hands in her lap. Staring down at the table, and speaking in a monotone, she quickly told them about the incident in Home Economics. However, she omitted the part about Annika tripping her on Erika's orders, because she didn't see any reason why she should share that part with her family. But, she did share the fact that Mrs. Oglivie had decided to give her and Darlene an F for the project, because either way, she still felt like that was totally unfair. Before Tom or Molly could say a word in response, Patrick, sensing a unique opportunity, jumped right in and resumed teasing his sister.

"You have got to be the biggest klutz in the universe!" he crowed. "How in the world did you manage to trip while walking across the room? Did your huge rabbit feet get tangled up together, or did you trip on a speck of dust?" Patrick paused just long enough to catch his breath, before starting in again. "And how in the heck did you happen to plant your freckled face in the middle of your cake? Oh, man, I can see it now," he said, as he started laughing. "You must have looked hilarious. I'm almost glad I wasn't there to see it, because I'm sure I would have laughed hard enough to pee my pants!" As if to prove his point, Patrick paused again to wipe tears from the corners of his eyes, and then continued laughing with his hands pressed against his stomach.

Tom's face had grown angrier and angrier as Patrick continued, and he had just opened his mouth to apparently reprimand his son, when Hannah completely lost her temper. She began yelling at her brother at the top of her lungs, while holding her dinner fork in an obviously threatening manner. Her parents had a look of total shock on their faces, and both of them were momentarily at a loss for words. Tom regained his composure first, and placing his hand on Hannah's shoulder (thankfully, it was her left shoulder, or Fatima might have ended up an inch or two shorter) in a calming gesture, he spoke to each of his children in turn.

"Hannah, I understand that you're upset about the incident at school, and angry at your brother's stupid remarks, but I need you to sit back down and quit yelling." Hannah, looking surprised that she had gotten out of her seat to loom over Patrick, sat down quickly with a mumbled apology. She continued to glare across the table at her brother, however. "Patrick, I am very surprised at you. This was obviously a very upsetting incident for your sister, and frankly I'm appalled at your lack of compassion. I want you to apologize to your sister right this minute, and then you may spend the rest of the evening in your room – that means no TV, no video games, and no telephone." Patrick started to open his mouth to protest, but after one look from his father, he quickly shut it again.

"I'm sorry, Hannah," he said, before beating a hasty retreat to his room.

Hannah waited until her brother had left the room, and then quietly apologized to her parents for her behavior. Both Tom and Molly reassured her that they understood why she was so upset. They then invited her to tell them more about the whole incident. Hannah explained in great detail about the mess she had made in the classroom, and then described to her parents how she had looked when she finally got a chance to glance in the mirror. By the time she had finished telling them about how everyone had laughed at her for the rest of the day, her parents were sitting quietly with expressions of genuine sympathy on their faces. Molly was the first one to speak.

"Oh, honey, what a horrible day! I'm so sorry you had to go through all of that. It seems especially unfair that Mrs. Oglivie gave you and Darlene an F for your project. I know how hard you girls worked to try and come up with the perfect recipe. If you'd like me to have a talk with her, I'd be more than happy to."

Hannah was just about to tell her mom that it would definitely not be necessary for her to do that, when they suddenly heard a lot of crashing and banging coming from upstairs. They all looked at each other in surprise, and then raised their eyes to the ceiling in total confusion. The ruckus continued, getting louder and louder and now accompanied by Patrick yelling and screaming like a banshee. Tom was the first to get up from his chair, and as he started climbing the stairs, Molly and Hannah were right behind him. As Tom strode down the hall, the noise began to die down; and by the time he reached Patrick's door, it was completely quiet again. Tom opened the door, stepped inside the room, and abruptly came to a complete stop. He slowly looked around the room in amazement. Hannah walked up behind him and craned her neck around the door, in an effort to get a better view of the room.

What she saw stopped her in her tracks, and she only dimly heard her father ask what the heck had happened. Patrick was standing in the middle of his room, wild-eyed, and with his hair practically standing on end. All of the books from his bookshelf were scattered around the room, with the majority of them piled up around him. Patrick looked a little banged up, with a slight bloody nose, and areas on his face and arms which looked like they were already starting to bruise. Posters had been ripped off of the walls, and the whole room seemed to be in more disarray than usual. Tom went from flabbergasted to extremely angry in about 4.5 seconds.

"What in heaven's name is going on here? This place is a pig sty. Just because you're angry about being sent to your room, does not give you the right to come up here, and start throwing stuff around. You have about five seconds to give me an explanation for this, or you're going to be grounded for the rest of the week."

Patrick stared at his dad with a pleading expression on his face. "Dad," he started, "you have to believe me. I didn't do any of this. I came up here and was just about to start on my homework, when books started flying off my bookcase, hitting me in the head and face and stuff. I put my arms up to protect myself, but they just kept flying at me, and so all I could do was yell to you guys for help. It's like there was a ghost in here or something."

Tom listened to his son with an expression of disbelief on his face. Realizing that his dad wasn't buying his explanation, Patrick let his shoulders slump and looked around miserably at his trashed room. Tom shook his head in disgust, and turned around to exit the room. He herded Molly and Hannah out in front of him, then turned back around and gave Patrick his final verdict before pulling the door shut. "Grounded for the rest of the week," he said in a firm, no-nonsense tone, and then he slammed the door behind him. As the three of them walked down the hall, Hannah paused in front of her bedroom door.

"I'm going to go ahead and finish my homework," she informed her parents.

"Okay, sweetheart," Molly replied. "I'm going to clean up the kitchen, and then I'll make some brownies to help cheer you up."

"Thanks, mom," Hannah said, as she stepped into her room and closed the door behind her. Hannah leaned back against her door, and puffed her bangs up off of her forehead. In a tentative voice, she quietly called out Fatima's name. Not getting an immediate response, she tried again in a slightly louder voice. All of a sudden Fatima appeared, sitting calmly with her legs crossed on top of Hannah's desk.

"You called?" she said, with an innocent expression on her face.

"Fatima," Hannah started, "you weren't in Patrick's room a few minutes ago, were you?"

Fatima's only reply was, "Who me?" while she continued to try and maintain a look of innocence. Hannah stared at Fatima with her forehead wrinkled, deep in thought. Fatima began to study her fingernails, obviously trying to avoid Hannah's gaze. Eventually, Fatima glanced up and found that Hannah was still staring at her.

"Okay," she finally admitted. "Maybe I was in there for a few minutes. But I didn't mean to cause any trouble; I was just looking for a good book to read, while you finished your homework."

Hannah slapped both hands over her mouth in an effort to muffle her laughter. Fatima's tinkling laugh filled the room, and Hannah dove for her bed and buried her face in her pillow. Her shoulders were shaking violently, and even through the stuffing of the pillow, her laughter could still be faintly heard. Fatima flew over to the bed and collapsed beside her, continuing to laugh until her stomach muscles ached. Just as the girls' laughter finally tapered off, Darlene's voice crackled out of the walkie-talkie.

"Blue Streak to Red Racer; Blue Streak to Red Racer! Are you there, Red Racer?"

Hannah grabbed her walkie-talkie off the bedside table and answered Darlene, giggles still slipping out between her words.

"Hey, Darlene, I'm here. How was your piano lesson?"

"Extremely boring as usual, but it doesn't sound like your evening's been boring. What's going on over there?"

Hannah described the events at the dinner table, followed by the noisy little mishap which Patrick had suffered at the mercy of Fatima's magic. By the time she had finished her story, Darlene was laughing just as hard as the two girls had been earlier. When Darlene finally caught her breath, she asked Hannah if she'd been able to get any further information out of Fatima regarding her plan for tomorrow. Hannah admitted that Fatima hadn't given her any more clues, and that she was still just as much in the dark as Darlene was. Her friend let out a disappointed sigh and signed off for the night. After putting down her walkie-talkie, Hannah turned around and stared at the little sprite thoughtfully.

"No way," Fatima said, noting the look on Hannah's face. "I'm not saying another word about my plan for tomorrow, and if you bug me anymore about it, I'm not going to speak to you for the rest of the night." Hannah held up her hands in defeat.

"Okay, okay, I won't say another word about it. But I'm probably going to die of suspense tonight.

"Oh, I'm sure you'll be fine," Fatima said, with an impish grin on her face.

Just then Hannah's mom called up the stairs, telling Hannah that the brownies were ready. As Hannah stepped out of her room, Patrick's door opened a crack.

"Can I have a brownie?" he called down the stairs.

"No!" his father yelled. "Get back in your room, and keep that door closed."

Hannah stuck out her tongue at her brother, and then sauntered down to the kitchen. She grabbed two brownies, and called out a "good night" to her parents. Then she headed back upstairs, intending to finish her homework and go to bed. She certainly wouldn't be sad to put this awful day behind her. After she had stepped inside her room and closed the door, she walked over to her dresser, where Fatima was waiting patiently. Hannah broke off a chunk from one of the brownies, and tore it into smaller pieces. Then she reached into her pocket, and pulled out a napkin spotted with small drops of grease. She opened it up on top of the dresser, and presented it to Fatima. The sprite's little nose wrinkled up, as she gazed at the food in front of her.

"Uh, what's that?" she asked Hannah warily.

"Well, we had beef stew for dinner, so I brought you some pieces of meat, and a few carrots and peas. My mom's a wonderful cook. You're going to love it," Hannah assured her.

"So that's what those disgusting brown chunks are. Hannah, I apparently forgot to mention this, but all fairies and sprites are vegetarians. We don't eat meat, because we would never harm another living creature."

"I'm so sorry," Hannah exclaimed, quickly wrapping up the pieces of meat and throwing them into the garbage can.

"That's okay," Fatima insisted, "I'll just eat the brownie." In two seconds flat, she had settled herself down on top of the dresser, and started stuffing bits of brownie into her mouth. Something that sounded vaguely like "mmm, this is good," came out of her mouth in between bites.

"Shouldn't you have something a little healthier?" Hannah suggested.

The little sprite stopped chewing for a brief moment, and shot Hannah a peeved look. "Hey, come on," she said around a mouthful of brownie, "I'm on vacation here, with no parents or older sisters to tell me what to do. I'm taking full advantage of that."

Hannah smiled in agreement, but then a worried expression passed over her face, as she suddenly thought of something. "Fatima, if time passes more quickly in the World of Fairy, then how do you know you'll get back in time? I mean your parents are expecting you home after the weekend, and you also have to be back in school by the beginning of the week.

Fatima stopped chewing for a moment, while she thought about how to explain the whole time concept to Hannah. "Well, you see, time passes more quickly in our world, but it doesn't pass at the same speed all of the time." Hannah appeared very confused by this answer. "Okay, I'll give you an example. I was grounded in my world for an entire month, but when I returned to your world, only a week or so had gone by. But now I could be in your world for one or two days, and only have three or four days pass in my world. Time goes more quickly for awhile, and then it slows down for awhile. Hopefully, this is one of the times when it goes more slowly. Besides, we're on a mini-break from school, which means we have a four day weekend. If time is passing more quickly than that, my Aunt Fantastica will be able to warn me, and I'll simply head home."

Hannah seemed a little less confused than she'd been before this detailed explanation.

"But how will your aunt be able to warn you?"

"That's easy; with this," Fatima proclaimed, and she reached into the pouch on her belt and pulled out the magic button. "This is a magic button, and it has two purposes. If I get into trouble over here, then I just push this button, and my aunt will come to my rescue. Also, if I run out of time before I've finished my duty here, then this button starts to vibrate and light up, and I know to come home right away." Seeing the expression on Hannah's face,

Fatima was quick to reassure her. "Don't worry, if I have to go home before I'm done here, I'll be back as soon as I can."

"Okay," Hannah said in a relieved tone, "just as long as I know that I can count on you."

"I give you my word on that. Now, go finish your homework so we can get some sleep."

Hannah went over to her desk, and sat down to finish studying. In less than an hour, she had finished everything, and the girls got ready for bed. Hannah pulled out one of her dresser drawers, and Fatima settled down among the socks. Hannah retired to her bed, and was asleep as soon as her head hit the pillow. Fatima, on the other hand, tossed and turned for quite awhile. She couldn't fall asleep, because she kept worrying about how her spell was going to turn out the next day. She was pretty sure that she had performed the spell correctly, but she wouldn't know for sure until tomorrow. After an hour or two, she finally fell asleep, but her dreams that night were anything but comforting. Every dream involved the spell she had cast in Mrs. Oglivie's room – and in every one of them, the spell definitely didn't turn out the way she had intended.

CHAPTER 13

FATIMA'S REVENGE

The next morning ushered in the arrival of a beautiful spring day. Sun rays peeked through the half-drawn blinds of Hannah's window, and spread their dappled light across the walls. Fatima felt the sun's warmth on her face, and snuggled deeper into the downy softness of the socks. Suddenly, her eyelids sprang open and she sat bolt upright in the drawer. Today was the day she would get to see the results of her first magic spell cast in the Human World.

Her stomach bunched up with excitement, as she bounced out of the drawer, and skipped across the top of the dresser. Glancing over at Hannah's bed, she spied a lump beneath the covers, with tangled brown hair sticking out of the top of the blankets. A grin crossed her face, and she was just about to fly over and rouse the sleepy head, when there was a loud knock on Hannah's door. Wasting no time, Fatima dove back into the open drawer, and burrowed beneath the socks.

She barely made it, before the door creaked open and footsteps crossed the room. Fatima's pointy, little ears twitched, as she heard Molly's voice trying to wake Hannah so she wouldn't be late for school. Her mother had barely started speaking, when Hannah shot out from under the covers, scaring Molly half to death. Startled, she took a step backwards with one hand pressed to her chest and exclaimed, "My goodness, you've never woken up that quickly before!"

Hannah rubbed the sleep from her eyes and bounded out of bed, dancing around the room with the hem of her nightgown in her hands and singing "Today is the day; today is the day."

"Today is the day for what?" Molly asked, confusion written all over her face.

Hannah stopped abruptly and stared at her mom, her brain racing like a chugging locomotive, as she struggled to come up with a reasonable explanation. "Uh..." she said uncertainly. Suddenly her expression brightened. "Why, today is the day that Ritchie, Darlene, and I put the finishing touches on our science project. It's going to be totally awesome, and we're definitely going to win the grand prize."

"Well, that sounds great," Molly said, walking back towards the door. "But for right now, why don't you just concentrate on getting to school on time."

"Yes, mother," Hannah said with exaggerated politeness. She strode over to her dresser, and started digging out the clothes she'd need to put on, after a quick shower. Rummaging through her socks, she spied two bright blue eyes peering out at her. Momentarily startled, she let out a little squeal. Already out in the hallway, Molly stuck her head back in the room, and stared at her daughter with raised eyebrows. Slamming the drawer shut, Hannah gave her mom an innocent smile, and then shrugged her shoulders. Molly stared at her for a moment, and then slowly shook her head back and forth, before heading down the hallway to wake up Patrick.

Hannah waited until she heard her mother enter Patrick's room, and then carefully slid the drawer back open. Two little legs with pointed shoes at the end stuck straight up in the air between the rows of socks. While Hannah watched with great interest, the legs began kicking around, until a blond head finally broke free and stuck itself out. The same bright blue eyes that had peered at her from between the socks a moment ago, were now glaring at her from beneath arched eyebrows.

"What in the heck do you think you're doing?" Fatima whispered fiercely. "I've probably got bruises all over now, thanks to your careless handling of my delicate, little body."

Hannah stared at her solemnly, trying not to let out the grin that was threatening to break through to the surface. In spite of her mighty effort, Fatima was not fooled in the least.

"You obviously find this to be quite funny," Fatima began, "but I can assure you that I fail to find the humor in this situation." The sprite's tone was very serious, but the twitching at the corners of her mouth suggested otherwise.

Hannah finally succeeded in burying her grin and keeping a straight face. She quickly offered Fatima a sincere apology for slamming the drawer. "I just didn't want to risk having my mother see you in there," she explained.

"Humph," Fatima answered. "Well, I accept your apology then. Now can you hurry up and get ready. I can't wait to get to school."

"You got it," Hannah replied over her shoulder, grabbing her clothes and racing down the hall to the bathroom. Fatima heard the sound of the shower turning on, and flew over to settle herself on top of Hannah's backpack. In less time than it takes to toast a piece of bread, Hannah was all ready, and the girls headed downstairs. Fatima had already completed her invisibility spell and taken her customary position on Hannah's right shoulder.

Hannah grabbed a pop tart from a kitchen cupboard, scooped the lunch her mom had made for her off the counter, and stuffed it in her backpack. Yelling good-bye to her mom, she ran out the front door. Ritchie and Darlene were already waiting on the curb in front of the Flannigan house. Spying Hannah, they both stood up and brushed off the back of their pants. As she walked up to join them, Hannah noticed Ritchie staring intently at the pop tart in her hand.

"Hey Ritchie, do you want me to grab you one before we go?"

"No," Ritchie replied slowly, "but you might want to grab one for someone else."

Hannah, totally confused by his answer, was just about to ask whom he was talking about, when she happened to glance down at her pop tart. While she stared at it in disbelief, tiny little bites appeared in it, one by one. Quickly solving the mystery at the same time, all three of them began laughing.

"Guess Fatima's hungry this morning," Ritchie snorted between guffaws.

"I guess so," Hannah said with a grin.

The three friends then headed off down the street towards the junior high school. The closer and closer they got to the school, the more nervous the little group became. It was a safe bet that each of them felt as if butterflies were doing somersaults in their stomachs. Approaching Hannah and Darlene's locker, Ritchie started shuffling his feet, moving more and more slowly, until finally he was going so slow that a turtle would have been able to pass him. Hannah turned around to face her lagging friend. "What is up with you?" she snapped. "The bell's going to ring any minute, and we're all going to be late to class. That would be a wonderful way to start the day," she said sarcastically.

"I know," Ritchie mumbled, "but it's just not fair. I'm gonna miss all of the excitement. Man, I never thought there would come a day when I would rather be in a Home Economics class, than Advanced Science. This totally sucks," he muttered, and slowly walked away towards his locker.

Poor Ritchie, Hannah thought to herself. Out loud she called to him, "Don't worry, we'll fill you in on everything later!" Ritchie's only reply was a half-hearted wave over his shoulder.

Hannah and Darlene placed their jackets and backpacks in their locker, and then stood there for a moment staring at each other, wondering what surprises the first class of the day would hold. A whispered voice spoke from the vicinity of Hannah's right ear. "Get going you two. We don't want to miss out on any of the fun and excitement."

Hannah swallowed hard, past a lump in her throat that felt the size of a small elephant, and started walking towards the Home Economics classroom. Darlene followed close behind her, and they both entered the room just as the first period bell rang. Sliding quickly into their seats, they glanced up to the front of the classroom, and noticed that Erika and Mrs. Oglivie were already cheerfully at work on their project. When the rest of the students had settled into their seats, Mrs. Oglivie called for everyone's attention.

"Today, class, my lovely assistant and I," she started, pausing to beam at Erika, "will be making a special recipe together. The recipe is for a large cinnamon-raisin bundt cake with white powdered sugar frosting. You'll notice that the recipe has already been written out on the blackboard, so I expect everyone to follow along." She paused, once again, and cast a rather pointed look in Hannah and Darlene's direction. "In addition, Miss Scott will be describing each step as we go along, so please listen to her very carefully. All right, Erika, now that we have everything arranged to our satisfaction, we can begin."

The two of them began mixing the initial ingredients together, and Erika described each step in the recipe using her best cheerleader voice, which seemed a little too loud and peppy for the occasion. Hannah watched the performance, trying to ignore the sensation of nausea building in the pit of her stomach. Erika was obviously enjoying her chance to be in the spotlight, yet again. Hannah was dead certain that she had even bought new clothes for the occasion, because the outfit she was wearing was one that Hannah had never seen before. Although, Hannah thought sighing to herself, how could anyone keep track of all the clothes Erika had.

Today's wardrobe consisted of beige Capri pants and a short-sleeved pink blouse, with tails that were pulled forward and tied in a bow, just above her belly button. It was Hannah's firm opinion that the outfit was somewhat brief for a spring morning in April; not to mention the fact that it also seemed a bit brief to wear at school. The Capri pants had large, pink sequins all over them, which spelled out various words and phrases; such as "I'm cute," "drama queen," "spoiled," and "#1," to name just a few.

Erika's hair was done up in a formal looking bun, with curled strands hanging down in ringlets on either side of her face. She wore five or six thin gold bracelets on each arm, which jangled almost continuously (and annoyingly) while she mixed the cake's ingredients. The sound alone was enough to set Hannah's teeth on edge, kind of like the feeling one gets after hearing the sound of fingernails on a blackboard. Hannah's grim observation was interrupted by Darlene's whispered comment that Erika looked like "Mrs. Oglivie's trained poodle."

As the girls giggled quietly together, Sean Adams, who sat several desks away and had somehow managed to overhear Darlene's comment, added a few snickers of his own. Carefully keeping an eye on the front of the room to make sure Mrs. Oglivie hadn't noticed the brief disruption, Hannah risked a glance back in Sean's direction. It was obvious that Sean had already grown bored with the whole baking production, because his attention was now focused on the window near the back of the classroom. Rather than watch the gruesome twosome mix their stupid recipe, Hannah decided to take advantage of Sean's current distraction, and stare at him safely without him noticing. This was really the only class where she had that opportunity, because the only other class they shared was English Literature, and that class was so interesting that Mr. McKenzie always had her full and undivided attention.

Hannah planted an elbow on her desk and rested her cheek on that hand. She slowly tilted her head to the left, until she had a completely unobstructed view of Sean. This way, she would be able to quickly tilt her head down towards her desk if Sean turned his attention away from the window. If he ever caught her staring at him, she'd be so embarrassed that she'd probably melt into the seat of her chair. Watching him out of the corner of her eye, she had to admit that he was a very handsome young man.

Unlike his fancy girlfriend, Sean tended to dress like a normal junior high school boy. He was wearing faded Levis jeans, obviously well worn, but without any holes or frayed edges, illustrating his tendency towards neatness. On top, he wore a long-sleeved shirt which resembled a baseball T-shirt with a dark green front and back, and white sleeves. His favorite baseball cap sat backwards on his head; the entire thing white, except for a large purple W over the bill, which represented his favorite college football team, the Washington Huskies.

Sean's bright blue eyes were fixed on a couple of squirrels, frolicking around outside on the school lawn. His dark blond hair reached down to his shoulders in back, and a small thatch of bangs poked through the little semicircle in the back of his hat. Still focused on the squirrels, Sean reached up to remove his hat and used his fingers to brush his bangs back in place, before placing the hat on backwards again. Hannah smiled to herself, as she dreamily imagined using her fingers to comb through that tousled blond hair. He was just so gorgeous, she thought to herself.

Suddenly, Sean's attention was yanked back into the classroom by Mrs. Oglivie's shrill voice announcing the baking instructions for the cake. Before Hannah had time to pull her gaze away, he turned around and caught her staring right at him. Sean started to give her a hesitant smile, as she felt a red blush creep up her neck and spread across her face.

Hannah jerked her eyes away to stare at the top of her desk, conflicting emotions rolling around inside her, like her own personal tornado. Part of her wanted to raise her head back up and smile boldly back at him, but another (and bigger) part of her was way too embarrassed to acknowledge her feelings for Sean that openly. Instead, Hannah glanced over at her best friend to see if Darlene had noticed any part of the exchange. She breathed a silent sigh of relief, once she had verified that Darlene's attention remained fixed on the whole baking production. Apparently someone had noticed though, because a tiny whisper said in her right ear, "I think he might like you." Hannah gave a firm little shake of her head, as the blush on her face intensified to a color brighter than fire engine red.

Focusing her attention once again on the gruesome twosome, she noticed that the mixing of the ingredients was finally finished, and the cake had been placed in a large oven. While the cake was baking, Erika and Mrs. Oglivie started on the frosting, and the rest of the students dutifully copied down the recipe in their notebooks. Hannah and Darlene had just finished writing down the entire recipe, when the timer went off, signaling that the cake was done baking. Mrs. Oglivie waddled over to the oven and pulled the cake out, setting it down on a large plate to cool.

While the cake finished cooling, she and Erika completed preparing the frosting. As soon as the cake had cooled, Mrs. Oglivie pulled the metal bundt mold off of it, and showed the class their work of art. Even Hannah had to admit that the cake looked spectacular, and the smell was already making her mouth water. The rest of the class seemed to agree, because everyone was already clamoring for a piece of the cake. But first, Erika grabbed the frosting bowl and tipped it upside down, dribbling the powdered sugar frosting over the top and sides of the cake. Now the finished product looked even more delicious than before. Maybe Fatima's spell hadn't worked, because nothing seemed to be wrong with the cake.

As if she had sensed Hannah's doubt, Fatima whispered in Hannah's ear, "Remember: do not eat a single bite of that cake. I know it looks and smells wonderful, but I promise you that eating it will definitely not be a wonderful experience." Hannah nodded her head slightly, and refocused her determination. She tapped Darlene on the leg to get her friend's attention. Darlene looked over at her with a questioning look on her face. Without saying a word, Hannah glanced at the cake, then back at her friend, and gave her head a firm shake back and forth. Darlene nodded immediately, indicating that she understood Hannah's unspoken warning. There was no way she was taking even the tiniest of bites from that cake.

Meanwhile, once the frosted cake had been properly "oohed" and "aahed" over, Mrs. Oglivie proceeded to cut it into enough pieces for everyone in the class to have some. First, though, she had one of the students in the front row take a picture of her and Erika, standing proudly by their lovely cake. While Mrs. Oglivie placed each slice on a paper plate, Erika began passing out the pieces to the students. Still playing the role of prima donna, she ordered some of the kids in the front row to help her pass out the slices of cake. When it was Sean's turn for a piece of cake, she personally delivered it to him, adding a little curtsey and a big smile, as she placed the plate in front of him. Surprisingly, she also personally delivered plates to Hannah and Darlene. The motive became clear, however, when she placed the cake slices on their desks, and then bent over to whisper to Hannah.

"Sorry you didn't win, cake-face," she said, with a sickly, sweet smile on her face. She then flounced back to the front of the room, and supervised the other students while they finished passing out the slices. Sean Adams, who had overheard Darlene's comment about the trained poodle, also managed to catch Erika's snotty comment to Hannah. With an expression of disgust on his face, he pushed his slice of cake to the corner of his desk, and then sat back with his arms crossed across his chest. He obviously had no intention of eating the cake, and for this stroke of good luck, Hannah was sincerely grateful.

The other students, however, were poised over their plates with forks in hand, waiting for Mrs. Oglivie to give the signal that would allow them to begin eating. Before giving the okay, Erika and Mrs. Oglivie picked up the large slices of cake which they had reserved for themselves, and took a huge bite at the same time. With an expression of pure bliss on her face, Mrs. Oglivie raised her flabby arm, signaling that the rest of the class could now join them in their culinary delight.

Hannah and Darlene watched anxiously as the other students began shoving bites of cake into their mouths. After a minute or two, Hannah realized that she was clenching the edge of her desk so tightly, that the knuckles of her fingers had turned white. Forcing herself to relax, she continued scanning the room, her eyes darting back and forth in an effort to detect any signs of magic. Five long minutes passed without any evidence of trouble or disorder, and Hannah had just about given up hope, when she happened to direct her gaze towards the front of the room.

Both Erika and Mrs. Oglivie had almost finished their super-sized slices of cake, when Hannah thought she noticed small purple spots beginning to form on their faces. Hannah removed her glasses and rubbed her eyes furiously with her fists. Putting her glasses back on, she resumed staring at Erika's face. Her eyes hadn't been playing tricks on her! Sure enough, the purple spots on Erika's face were multiplying right before her eyes. She nudged Darlene in the ribs with her elbow, and pointed towards the front of the classroom. Darlene's jaw immediately dropped open in amazement, indicating that she saw the purple spots, too. Fortunately, the other kids were fully concentrating on eating, so no one else had noticed yet.

While Darlene and Hannah watched in horror, the spots began swelling until they resembled large purple blisters. The very tops of the blisters were turning bright red, and the largest ones had burst, causing a mixture of purple goo and bright yellow specks that looked like popcorn kernels to ooze out. Glancing around the room, Hannah noticed the appearance of small purple spots on other student's faces, too. But none had advanced as far in size and frequency, as Erika's and Mrs. Oglivie's had.

Turning around in her seat, Hannah saw that Sean was also staring in disbelief, his gaze fixed on his girlfriend's face. Almost as if she had sensed his attention, Erika looked up and gave him her prettiest smile. She frowned uncertainly, though, when Sean continued to stare at her with wide open eyes without even the suggestion of a returning smile on his face. Continuing to frown, Erika reached up to scratch her nose, her fingernails raking across the spot where a particularly large blister was forming. At her touch, the blister burst, and Erika pulled her hand away to stare at the mixture of purple goo and yellow specks on her fingers.

She lifted her face to her teacher, a question forming on her lips, but one glance at Mrs. Oglivie's face and her unasked question was immediately answered. Noticing Erika's stare, Mrs. Oglivie turned towards her star pupil. For what seemed like an eternity, but was actually only several seconds, the two stared at each other in terror. Then they both opened their mouths at the same time, and emitted ear-splitting shrieks. The rest of the class froze immediately, and every pair of eyes focused on Erika and Mrs. Oglivie.

At first, everyone seemed unsure about exactly what was happening; but realization began to dawn on their faces, as they looked down at the cake they were eating and then at each other. Every student who had eaten a piece of the cake was beginning to break out in the horrid purple blisters. The more cake they had eaten, the more blisters they had. As Erika and Mrs. Oglivie had consumed the most cake, they definitely suffered the worst.

The blisters had spread from their faces, down their necks, and now covered their hands and arms, also. They were obviously extremely itchy, because both Erika and Mrs. Oglivie had already scratched the bright red tops off of numerous blisters, and they were now covered in the purple goo with yellow specks. It was equally obvious that the blisters had also spread down to their legs, as evidenced by the interesting dance the two were doing.

Out of the entire class, only Hannah, Darlene, and Sean were unaffected. Soon the screaming and jostling around had reached such a high level, that chaos and pandemonium reigned in the classroom. Just when it seemed that it couldn't get any worse, several things began happening all at once. Hannah first noticed the change in Mrs. Oglivie. While staring helplessly at her teacher, she saw her stomach begin to swell visibly beneath her dress. Within a minute or two at the very most, Mrs. Oglivie's stomach (which was already quite large) had begun to resemble a hot air balloon; especially since it was encased in one of her bright, colorful, tent dresses.

Hannah was still trying to figure out what surprises this new development would hold, when she suddenly got her answer. Without any warning, Mrs. Oglivie opened her mouth and let out one of the largest and loudest burps that Hannah had ever heard in her entire life. Even Patrick with a bellyful of pop couldn't have come close to the sheer volume and length of that burp. What was even more amazing was that one of the largest farts in the history of the world, followed immediately on the heels of the belch. Before Hannah could recover from this shock, the entire classroom began to fill with the sounds and fragrance of multiple farts and burps. Hannah had never even had a dream that was this bizarre before. She and Darlene stared at each other in amazement.

"Do you think we should go get someone?" Darlene asked Hannah.

"I don't know," Hannah replied, "what do you think?"

"I think we better get out of here before we need gas masks. I hope no one strikes a match around here. It could blow up the whole school!"

In spite of the overwhelming situation, Hannah couldn't help but giggle at Darlene's comment. "Let's go get Ms. Peterson and Mr. Andrews," Hannah said, getting up from her chair. Racing down the hall, Hannah made one last comment. "I know one thing," she told Darlene. "Fatima is going to have an awful lot of explaining to do."

CHAPTER 14

BETTER THAN WARTHOGS

Hannah and Darlene raced down the main hallway, skidding around the corner to the right, at the end of the hall. They both burst through the door of the office at the same time, panting and red-faced from their run. The secretary, who had been typing at her desk, jumped in her seat at their noisy arrival and hit several keys all at once causing the typewriter to jam. Looking flustered, she started to reprimand the girls for their behavior, but after glancing at their faces, she instead asked them what was wrong.

"We need to talk to Ms. Peterson or Mr. Andrews right away!" Hannah said, between gasps for air.

"Something's happened in Mrs. Oglivie's class!" Darlene stated, picking up where Hannah had left off.

Hearing panicked voices outside their doors, both Ms. Peterson and Mr. Andrews stepped out of their respective offices.

"What's wrong, girls?" Ms. Peterson asked immediately.

"Something awful is happening in Mrs. Oglivie's classroom," Darlene repeated, "and we need your help."

Mr. Andrews herded the girls out of the office and into the hallway. Ms. Peterson was right behind them, and the little group hurried back down the hallway. Hannah and Darlene's noisy race down the hall moments before had already attracted some attention. A few students were standing in the doorways of some of the classrooms trying to find out what was happening. Several of the kids called out questions to Hannah and Darlene as they passed by, but Mr. Andrews kept a firm hand on their backs, gently pushing them ahead of him so that they were unable to share any information. He did not want any rumors or gossip floating around until he had a chance to assess the situation. Half-way down the long hall, screams and shouts from Mrs.

Oglivie's room could already be heard. Mr. Andrews and Ms. Peterson picked up their pace, and began jogging down the last part of the hallway. They reached the door to the classroom at the same time, and then froze in place.

Only their eyes moved as they looked around the room, struggling to figure out exactly what was going on, and even more importantly, trying to decide how they could gain control of the situation. Mrs. Oglivie was rolled up in a very large ball on top of her desk with her head on her arms, sobbing uncontrollably. Erika was standing behind her, screaming at her to look at what her stupid cake had done to her face. The rest of the students were either screaming or crying or both, and all of them were milling around the room blindly, like mice caught in a maze. Mr. Andrews blinked his eyes in amazement, and then purposely strode to the front of the room, while Ms. Peterson zeroed in on Erika and Mrs. Oglivie.

Mr. Andrews had to shout three times at the top of his lungs, before he was able to get the entire class's attention. Once the students had quieted down, he asked them all to please take their seats. Directing Hannah to close the classroom door, he asked Darlene to explain what had happened. Darlene took a deep breath, and then told Mr. Andrews exactly what had occurred after everyone ate the cake. She further explained that Sean, Hannah, and herself were the only ones spared, and that they had also been the only ones who hadn't eaten any of the cake. Meanwhile, Ms. Peterson had finally gotten Erika to quit screaming and sit down; but she refused to speak, choosing instead to bury her face in her hands and cry. She was even less successful in calming Mrs. Oglivie, but finally with Mr. Andrew's help, they were able to get her off of her desk and into her chair; although the sobbing still continued.

Still entirely confused about the whole incident, Mr. Andrews examined what was left of the cake, and then checked out the skin lesions on a couple of the calmer students. Although he had no medical training, he figured it was a pretty good guess that this had to be one of the weirdest ailments that anyone had ever seen. Thankfully, besides the blisters and excess intestinal gas, the kids didn't seem to otherwise be sick or in distress. All he could think of was that it must have been some kind of unique allergic reaction to an ingredient in the cake. Boy, was this whole thing going to be a mess to sort out, he thought to himself. He would probably be dealing with parents' complaints and phone calls for quite a few weeks after this. Glancing over at Ms. Peterson, he could tell by her expression that she was most likely thinking the same thing.

With everyone except Erika and Mrs. Oglivie relatively calm at this point, Ms. Peterson instructed the students to go ahead and return home for the rest of the day. If they lived close by, they could walk or ride their bikes, and if they lived farther away they could use the phone in the office to call their parents for a ride. As Sean, Darlene, and Hannah had escaped entirely unscathed, they were excused to go to their 2nd period class.

The students began rushing around, as they gathered their things and headed for the door. They were all feeling better at this point, and the majority of the students were actually pleased to get a day off from school. Before they left, Mr. Andrews informed them that this was most likely an allergic reaction which should resolve in the next day or two, so no one was too worried any longer. The two principals were then stuck with Erika and Mrs. Oglivie, both of whom were still complete basket cases.

Dividing up the duty, Mr. Andrews called Mr. Oglivie down at the bank and explained the situation as best he could, while Ms. Peterson called Erika's mother and did the same. Herbert arrived first, and immediately attempted to soothe his distraught wife. Her initial response was to yell at him for taking so long to come rescue her from such an utterly terrifying experience. As he bundled her up in a blanket he had brought in from the car, she continued to nag him all the way out the door. As soon as the couple disappeared through the doorway, Mr. Andrews and Ms. Peterson breathed a collective sigh of relief.

Not five minutes later, Mrs. Scott arrived to take her precious baby home. One look at Erika's face was enough to send the poor woman into complete hysterics, and eventually Mr. Andrews had to call Mr. Scott to come pick up both of them. Finally, Mr. Scott arrived and hustled his wife and daughter out the door. However, before he left he informed the Principal and Vice Principal that they had better hope his daughter recovered quickly without any permanent marks, or he would be suing the school district for every dollar he could wring out of them.

Compared to 1st period, the rest of Hannah's morning was as relaxing and tranquil as floating on an ocean wave. However, when lunchtime finally came around, Hannah was so sick of all the other students asking her questions about what had happened in Mrs. Oglivies's class, that she was going to have a meltdown if one more person approached her about it. Luckily, she was able to locate Darlene and Ritchie as soon as she walked into the cafeteria, and they all headed for a small table in the back corner, hoping for a little peace and quiet. Hannah was perfectly content to eat her lunch, while Darlene filled Ritchie in on all of the details concerning the incident in Home Economics. Just as she finished, and before Ritchie was done chuckling about the whole thing, Hannah noticed a group of cheerleaders led by Annika Iverson approaching their table. Uh oh, she thought to herself, here comes trouble.

Annika walked over until she was about five feet away from their table, and then came to a complete stop. Her cheeks were flushed and her eyes were flashing with anger, as she put her hands on her hips and started to speak. Hannah had a split second to notice the new flash of metal on her teeth, before her attention was captured by Annika's shrill voice, raised just loud enough to allow the students surrounding them to hear everything she was saying.

"Hannah Flannigan, you should be ashamed of yourself! Erika called me on her cell phone when I was leaving the dentist's office, and told me the whole story, although I have to admit it was difficult to understand her since she was crying the entire time. You and Darlene obviously put something in that cake, because you two were the only ones that didn't have that stupid allergic reaction, or whatever it was. So, what do you have to say for yourself?"

Hannah just stared at her, completely flabbergasted by the unfair accusation. Before she could gather her wits about her and think of a way to answer Annika, Sean Adams came over; pushing through the crowd of people that had started to gather, attracted by the sounds of a commotion. His face was cloudy with anger, as he walked up to Annika and placed himself between her and Hannah.

"What's your problem, Annika?"

"This is none of your business, Sean. I just want Hannah and Darlene to admit that they did something to that cake, and caused all those horrible things to happen."

"Why would they do something like that?"

"Well, because they're jealous of Erika, of course."

"Oh, I see," he said sarcastically, "so to teach Erika a lesson, they did something that affected Mrs. Oglivie and the rest of the students, too. Now I get it."

"Honestly, Sean, I would think that you would want to help me get to the bottom of this. I mean, Erika is your girlfriend, after all."

"Well, Annika, if you're looking for someone to blame this on, then why don't you give me the 3rd degree, too. I didn't eat the cake either, so maybe I'm the one that put something in it. Besides, what do you think someone could do to a cake to make it cause an allergic reaction?"

Annika was appearing more and more flustered as the conversation continued. In spite of the fact that she was a cheerleader, and Erika's best friend, Hannah was actually starting to feel a little bit sorry for her. Suddenly, Justine stepped out from the crowd, and walked over to stand by her friend. Annika gave her a grateful smile, and Justine returned it, before she began speaking.

"Annika, I think what Sean is trying to point out, is that Hannah and Darlene weren't the only ones who didn't eat any of the cake, so that fact alone doesn't prove anything. Plus, no one even knows exactly what happened to the kids who ate the cake, so how could anyone have planned for all of that horrible stuff to happen?"

Annika's smile had become smaller and smaller as Justine had continued. Now, she had a look of disbelief on her face, as if she couldn't believe that her friend hadn't taken her side of the argument. She stomped her foot on the ground, and crossed her arms over her chest.

"Well, I don't care if you guys are on my side or not. I still think that those two girls (she paused and pointed at Hannah and Darlene with a sneer on her face) did something to that cake, and I'm standing right here until they admit it."

Hannah was about to open her mouth and stick up for herself, when she heard someone mumbling in her right ear. Distracted for a moment, she paused and tried to regain her train of thought. Before she could say a word, Annika flounced over until she was right in Hannah's face.

"Well," she said threateningly, "what do you have to say . . ."

All of a sudden her words cut off, and she just stood there with her mouth closed, and her jaw muscles clenching and unclenching. Hannah sat there waiting for her to continue. But only grunts and muffled sounds came out of Annika's mouth. As her lips spread apart in an effort to speak, Hannah noticed that the metal glint she had spied earlier was from new braces. Figuring that she must have gotten them at her dentist appointment that morning, Hannah leaned forward to examine them more closely.

It appeared that Annika's braces had become stuck together. Annika was becoming red in the face from the effort of trying to open her mouth and continue talking. Tears of frustration began to run down her cheeks as she turned towards Justine, and began pointing wildly at her mouth. Confused, but wanting to help, Justine leaned in closer and peered into her friend's mouth. A look of surprise, and then understanding, crossed her face, and she grasped Annika's arm in an attempt to both calm and comfort her.

"Oh, my gosh! Your braces are stuck together. Oh, you poor little thing. Let's get you down to the nurse's office right this instant. I'm sure the nurse will be able to figure out what to do, or at least she can call your dentist for help. Come on, Annika."

Justine took her friend's hand, and led her out of the cafeteria. Most of the kids who had gathered around were either snickering behind their hands, or laughing openly. Annika felt completely humiliated, and the tears began running faster and faster. Just before they left the lunchroom, Justine turned around and gave Hannah a reassuring smile, and Sean a conspiratorial wink. Once the two girls had left, Sean stuffed both hands in the front pockets of his jeans, and glanced down at the floor shyly. Hannah turned towards him, slightly embarrassed, but determined to let him know how much she appreciated his help.

"Uh, Sean, thanks a lot for sticking up for us. It was really nice of you, and I totally appreciate it."

Sean scuffed the toe of his sneaker on the ground, peering at her through his bangs. "Don't worry about it," he replied. "I'm just sorry she attacked you like that. It was totally uncool. Well, I'll catch you later, bye."

"Bye," Hannah said, and Sean walked back over to his table to finish his lunch. "Wow," Hannah said after a moment, looking at Ritchie and Darlene in amazement. "That was such a cool thing for Sean to do. I'll bet you nobody else will have the guts to bug us about the whole cake thing. Not after the way Sean stood up for us."

"Yeah," Ritchie replied in agreement, "especially anyone who has braces."

Hannah and Darlene couldn't help but bust into a fit of giggles after that comment. However, after a few minutes, when their laughter had finally tapered off, Hannah became a little more serious. "You know," she told Ritchie and Darlene thoughtfully, "I think there's been just a bit too much unauthorized magic going on around here. I think it's about time that I had a little talk with you-know-who. If you'll excuse me for a few minutes, I'm going to take that someone with me to the bathroom for a brief discussion."

Ritchie and Darlene exchanged a knowing glance, and then gave Hannah a nod of agreement. Hannah got up from the table and walked out of the cafeteria. She knew of a girls' restroom on the 2nd floor that was clear down at the end of the hallway by a janitor's closet. It was hardly ever used by any of the students, and should definitely be empty at lunchtime. Just to be on the safe side though, she carefully checked under both of the stall doors, before entering the 2nd stall and locking the door. This was the best place she could think of to have a little talk with Fatima in relative privacy.

As soon as Hannah had locked the door to the stall, Fatima appeared and took a seat on the toilet paper dispenser. Hannah remained standing, leaning against the wall opposite Fatima. She stared thoughtfully at the little sprite, waiting for her to start explaining exactly what had gone wrong with her magic spell. Fatima refused to meet Hannah's gaze though, and instead stared down at the ground, looking as if she was wishing for a large hole to suddenly open up and suck her into it. It was Hannah who finally broke the silence.

"Fatima, what in the world happened this morning? I sincerely hope that things didn't turn out the way you had planned, because what happened to those kids was awful. Even Erika and Mrs. Oglivie didn't deserve that horrible of a punishment. I don't even know if they're going to be all right. Please tell me that those awful blisters will go away soon. I mean they're not going to keep growing and multiplying are they?"

"Oh, no!" Fatima blurted out, "in fact, they should all be gone by tomorrow, or the next day at the latest. They'll just shrink and disappear, and no one will even be able to tell they were ever there at all. There won't be any permanent changes whatsoever. I promise you that you can trust me regarding that," Fatima implored.

"Well, that's a relief at least," Hannah answered. "But you didn't answer my first question – is that what you were trying to do, or did something get screwed up?"

Fatima didn't answer Hannah right away. She just sat there, staring down at Twinkle lying across her lap. Hannah, who was beginning to get quite frustrated with the tiny sprite, blew a puff of air up at her bangs and tried again.

"Fatima, you need to tell me the truth, because best friends don't hide things from each other, and they definitely don't lie to each other." Fatima's head whipped up, and she stared intently at Hannah's face, searching for any sign that Hannah was teasing her or just joking around. The serious look on her friend's face proved that certainly wasn't the case. She screwed up her courage, and looked Hannah directly in the eye.

"Do you promise not to be mad at me?" she asked in a quavering voice.

"No," Hannah replied instantly. "I can't promise that I won't be angry with you, especially if you broke your promise to me. But, I do promise you that I'll still be your best friend."

"Even if what I did was wrong?" Fatima asked hopefully. She held her breath as she waited for Hannah's answer.

"Yes, Fatima, even if what you did was wrong. I just need you to tell me the truth, and then I need you to tell me that you won't break your promises to me anymore. It's hard to build a friendship when that friendship is based on lies and broken promises."

Fatima thought hard for a few moments, wrinkles forming in her tiny forehead. "I understand, and I promise to be a better friend in the future." She offered Hannah a tentative smile, which grew even bigger once she noticed that her friend was smiling in return. Fatima took a deep breath, and was about to confess the true intention of her magic spell, when she suddenly gave a startled jump and stared down at her waist.

"What's wrong?" Hannah asked with a touch of concern in her tone.

"My button just went off," she exclaimed, and then reached into the pouch on her belt and pulled it out as proof. Sure enough, the magic button was glowing bright red and vibrating at the same time. "I have to go right this minute! Aunt Fantastica is calling me which means my time over here has just run out. If I don't get home immediately, I'm going to be in a lot of trouble!"

"But when will you be back? It seems like you barely got here, and now you already have to go home."

"I know," Fatima replied, "but I promise to return as soon as I can. My spring vacation is only a month away, so I'm sure I'll be back in time for your Science Fair."

"Okay," Hannah sighed, "but I'm sure going to miss you."

"I'll miss you, too, but don't worry I'll be back before you know it."

Fatima gave her friend a big smile, then placed the magic button back in her pouch and stood up. "Well, I'm off! I need to get back to the gateway, pronto."

"Wait!" Hannah yelled, as Fatima flew into the air preparing to leave. "You still haven't told me the truth about the spell." Hannah unlocked the stall door, and followed Fatima as she flew over to the door and beckoned for Hannah to open it. Hannah pulled open the door, and the sprite flew out into the hallway and hovered there for a moment, waiting for Hannah to catch up.

"I've really got to go," she said, while Hannah approached her.

"But Fatima, you promised; remember what I said about best friends?"

"Okay, okay, you were right," she said quickly. "The spell didn't turn out the way it was supposed to, but those kids really are going to be perfectly fine in a day or two." She began flying down the hallway, and Hannah had to jog to keep up with her.

"So what was the spell supposed to do?"

"It was supposed to turn them into warthogs for a few days, but I guess I screwed it up somehow. See ya soon!" and she zipped off down the hall and out of sight, before Hannah could say another word.

Hannah slowed down to a walk, and then stopped moving altogether. That little brat! she thought to herself. I can't believe she was going to turn them into warthogs. That would have been a total disaster. Shaking her head in total disbelief, Hannah walked towards the stairs and started down, intending to return to the cafeteria to finish her lunch. What a day this had been; and it was only halfway over.

At least with Fatima gone, there shouldn't be any more nasty surprises. The adventure this morning would certainly be enough to last her for a very long time, or at least until Fatima returned. Boy, Hannah thought, I don't know why I wanted to have a more adventurous life. After this, I need a boring week or two. There's been just a little too much excitement lately. I guess that's where the old saying comes from- you better be careful what you wish for, because you just might get it!

Hannah had just finished this train of thought when she found herself back at the table where she had left Darlene and Ritchie sitting. They looked up questioningly, as she sat down and began eating her lunch. After a few minutes of silence, Darlene couldn't stand it any longer. "Well, what happened? Did Fatima tell you whether her magic spell turned out the way she intended?" Darlene's voice dropped down to a whisper with her next question. "Is she still sitting on your shoulder?"

Hannah gave her a weary smile, before she answered. "No, her magic button went off during our conversation, so she had to go back home. But, she said she'd be back as soon as she could, and that she would definitely return before the Science Fair." Hannah paused long enough to take a few deep breaths, before she continued. "As for her magic spell, it didn't turn out the way she planned, thank goodness. We can thank our lucky stars for that at least."

"Why?" Ritchie blurted out. "What was supposed to happen?"

"You guys are probably going to find this hard to believe, but the spell was supposed to turn everyone into a warthog. But only for a few days," she added sarcastically.

"Oh my goodness!" Darlene exclaimed. "That would have been a huge disaster. I mean how do you explain the fact that eating a piece of cake could turn someone into a warthog? There would have been reporters and TV crews all over the place. People would have been freaking out right and left. How did she think she'd be able to get away with that?"

Hannah closed her eyes, took another deep breath, and let it out in a big sigh. "I have no idea," she answered slowly. "Let's just be glad it only turned out to be some blisters and gas. More importantly, Fatima promised to never do anything like that again. Hopefully, that's a promise she intends to keep."

The three friends sat silently for awhile as they each contemplated the panic and chaos which would have occurred if Fatima's magic had actually worked the way it was supposed to. After several minutes, Ritchie got a twinkle in his eyes and let out a few chuckles. Hannah glanced over at him in amazement, and then looked over at Darlene. Her best friend was trying to keep a straight face, but Hannah could tell that she was struggling to keep a serious case of the giggles at bay.

You can only imagine Hannah's surprise when she discovered that she was about to burst out laughing herself. In a matter of seconds, all three of them were laughing so hard they thought their sides would split. More than a few of the other students were beginning to stare at them, wondering what could possibly be that funny. Finally, their laughter tapered off, and they resumed eating their lunches.

"Well," Ritchie said, as the last few chuckles escaped, "at least we have something to occupy our time until Fatima comes back. The Science Fair is only two weeks away, and we need to spend a lot more time on our project if we want to win the grand prize."

The girls nodded their heads in agreement. When the last bell before 5th period rang, they picked up their lunch stuff and headed off to class. Before they split up, they all agreed to meet at Ritchie's house after dinner. Then they rushed off to their respective classes.

Back in Fairy Town, Fatima popped out of the portal by her aunt's apartment, where Fantastica was already waiting. Fatima flew over to her aunt and gave her a giant hug. Aunt Fantastica returned her niece's warm embrace, before informing her that she only had an hour to spare before she was due at school. The two decided to walk there together, giving them a chance to discuss Fatima's recent adventure. Fatima quickly filled her aunt in on the events over the last two days. She omitted nothing, even confessing how she managed to screw up the magic spell, and about breaking her promise to Hannah. When Fatima finally finished, her aunt looked at her thoughtfully for a minute or two before replying.

"Well, Fatima, it appears that you learned a valuable lesson."

"Oh, I did auntie," Fatima replied. "I learned that I need to be more careful with my magic, because I'm never going to be able to fulfill Hannah's wish, unless I'm more disciplined with my magic spells. Twinkle and I have to get everything exactly right, or it won't turn out the way it's supposed to. I'm going to do much better next time," Fatima promised, her eyes shining with renewed energy and purpose.

"Fatima," Fantastica said quietly, "that's not the lesson I was referring to." Fatima looked confused by this statement, so her aunt continued. "I meant that I hoped you had learned a lesson about friendship. Being someone's best friend isn't about granting a wish. It's about keeping your promises, and always telling the truth. If you can't do that, then the bond of trust will be broken – and once that happens, the friendship is over. Instead of practicing your magic skills, you need to practice being a good friend, because I can promise you that will be the most important thing to Hannah. Now off you go," and she gently pushed her niece in the direction of the sprite's school.

Fatima slowly flew the rest of the way to school with her aunt's words replaying in her mind. She bit her bottom lip, as she thought about the true meaning of friendship. She had never had a best friend before, and she didn't want to ruin her friendship with Hannah. Determination etched itself on her face as she made a decision. I'm going to be the bestest best friend ever, she thought to herself. With that in mind, she continued on her way, whistling happily and looking forward to her next visit to the Human World.

CHAPTER 15

THE SCIENCE FAIR

The next two weeks passed quickly for Hannah and her friends – just like it always seems to when you're trying to get something done in a certain period of time. The kids worked hard on their Science Fair project, which still wasn't finished, although they had been spending most of their free time on it for the last month. But with the deadline right around the corner, they had spent every evening and weekend day on it since Fatima's abrupt departure. Now, with the Science Fair only two days away, they were finally putting the finishing touches on their marvelous creation.

School had been boring and humdrum ever since Fatima left, but Hannah and her friends were definitely not complaining. Erika had finally come back to school, after hiding in her room for almost a week. During that time, she had not so much as stuck her nose out of her house. By the time she returned to school, there wasn't a single blemish remaining on her skin, and her intestinal tract had returned to normal, or at least Hannah assumed it had.

Mrs. Oglivie had returned just yesterday, and even Hannah and Darlene had to admit that they were glad to see her, although that feeling only lasted for about half of the class period. Annika had returned the very next day, but it was quite obvious that she had been forced to get a new pair of braces. These braces were a light blue, which was one of the school colors, so it matched her cheerleading outfit. The rumor was that her old pair had to be cut off because even the dentist couldn't get them unstuck.

So basically things were pretty much back to normal, with the minor exception that both Erika and Annika entirely ignored Hannah and Darlene now; which was a major improvement over their previous snotty behavior. However, poor Ritchie still had to endure the annoying taunts and mean-spirited teasing from his arch enemy, Tony Parsons. In fact, over the last couple of weeks Tony's annoying behavior had reached a new high. Now he was bugging Ritchie about the Science Fair every day. Ritchie wanted to win the grand prize so badly, he could almost taste it. Mr. Andrews had announced what the grand prize would be at their last assembly, and it was definitely spectacular.

The winning team would win an all-expense paid trip to the Pacific Science Center in Seattle, Washington. They would spend three days and three nights at a luxurious hotel with an indoor swimming pool, and all of their meals would be paid for, too. They would also receive a three-day pass to the Science Center, which included all of the rides at the Seattle Center, like the giant rollercoaster and the monorail. Most importantly, the winners would get to demonstrate their science project at the Science Center for an entire day. This was unquestionably the best prize the school had ever offered, and Ritchie wanted to win it so badly he could hardly stand it.

Unfortunately, Tony Parsons was bound and determined to win the grand prize too, although Ritchie couldn't figure out why it was so important to him. For one thing, Tony hated science and probably couldn't care less if he ever set foot in the Pacific Science Center. Secondly, if Tony really wanted to go to the Science Center, his father could easily fly him there in his movie company's private jet without batting an eyelash. As everyone knew, he had already flown Tony to Hollywood and New York (as well as numerous other cities) more times than anyone could possibly keep track of. With those facts in mind, the only thing Ritchie could think of was that Tony wanted to win, just so Ritchie couldn't. As far as Ritchie was concerned, there was no way a complete idiot like Tony Parsons was going to beat him in a science contest; Ritchie just wasn't going to let that happen. Not in this lifetime, or any other, for that matter.

Meanwhile, back in Fairy Town, time was not passing at all quickly for Fatima. She could hardly wait for the start of spring vacation, because that meant she would be returning to the Human World, and most importantly, her best friend. Although time passed more quickly in the World of Fairy, it seemed to be dragging by, day by boring day, for Fatima. She and Aunt Fantastica had already come up with a marvelous plan, and now they were merely waiting for spring vacation, so they could put their plan in motion.

The plan involved Fantastica asking Fatima's parents if their youngest daughter could accompany her on a month long trip during her spring break. Fantastica was traveling to several of the other countries in the World of Fairy, to visit some elves and dwarves who were long time friends she had made in her youth. Each year or two, they all took turns visiting each other, and this year it was Fantastica's turn to visit them.

Besides having fun and keeping her aunt company, the two schemers had also told Fatima's parents that she would be writing a special report for school; detailing their travels and describing the different countries and cultures they'd be seeing. Her parents could hardly say no to that, and so they agreed to allow Fatima to travel with her aunt. Obviously, Fatima had no intention of going on a trip with her aunt. Instead, she would be using that time to travel to the Human World, and help Hannah by fulfilling her wish.

Of course, Fatima thought that Fantastica would be going on her little trip without her, but you and I know the truth – Fantastica would be secretly tailing her niece to ensure that she didn't get herself into any serious trouble. But what Fatima didn't know, certainly wouldn't hurt her.

Finally, the long month was over, and Fatima's spring vacation was actually starting. She continued the ruse that she and her aunt had concocted, and packed enough belongings for an entire month. She then kissed her mother and father good-bye; after her father's long-winded lecture on how she was to behave perfectly, make him proud, do everything her aunt asked her to, etc., etc., and flew off to her aunt's apartment. Once she arrived, she was forced to endure another lecture by her aunt, although hers was mercifully shorter, before she was given the magic button which would accompany her once again.

Fantastica then walked with her over to the nearby gateway, sprinkled her magic fairy dust over her, and sent her on her way. Finally, Fatima thought to herself, I'm on my way and nothing's going to stop me from fulfilling Hannah's wish this time; especially since I should have at least a week to get everything done.

In a flash of light and seven nanoseconds later, Fatima arrived at the portal in the woods, already invisible and with all her parts intact. She flew off to Hannah's house, sneaking through the screen of Patrick's window, exactly as she had done on her previous visit. As she flew through his room, she noticed that all of the books were back in the bookcase, and the posters were back on the wall. Remembering her enjoyable antics in this room on her last visit, she couldn't help the mischievous smile that darted across her face. Fatima scooted under Hannah's door and looked around the room. Hannah obviously wasn't there, so she would either be at Darlene's, or over at Ritchie's. Suddenly, an idea popped into her little head, and she excitedly flew over to Hannah's window.

Sure enough, the walkie-talkie was lying on the window sill where Hannah had left it that morning, after discussing with Darlene what clothes they should wear to school that day. Fatima hopped up and down on the "talk" button until it finally clicked on, and then leaned over to speak into the receiver. "Red Racer to Blue Streak; Red Racer to Blue Streak! Are you there, Darlene?" She stepped off of the "talk" button, and waited for a reply. Not getting an answer, she went through the same sequence once again. There was still no answer from Darlene. By this time, Fatima was a bit worn out from all the calisthenics required for her to use the walkie-talkie; not to mention completely out of patience.

Maybe they're both over at Ritchie's, she thought to herself. I'll head over there and see. She flew back through Patrick's room, out the window, and then zoomed down the street to Ritchie's house. Peering through the grime at one of the basement windows, she saw her three friends standing over a workshop table, exactly like the last time.

Fatima flew around the house, located the cracked window with the hole, and squeezed through it. Recognizing that she had an opportunity for a bit of mischievous fun, she decided to scope out the room before she became visible and announced her presence to the kids. Hannah, Darlene, and Ritchie were all standing around a little metal robot, looking quite pleased with themselves. Fatima went over to the robot, and landed right behind it. In her deepest voice, she began talking, while at the same time she grabbed the arms of the robot and began moving them around. "Greetings, Earthlings. I come from a planet far away! My people intend to take over your earth, and make you all our slaves."

The kids' reaction was everything Fatima had hoped it would be, and more. Hannah and Darlene let out piercing screams, before practically jumping into each others arms, and Ritchie let out a large squawk, while tripping and falling over backwards in his haste to get away from the table. Fatima started laughing so hard she thought she'd explode, and ended up dropping Twinkle, before rolling around on top of the table with gleeful abandon. When she finally stopped to catch her breath, she glanced up to find three angry (and somewhat embarrassed) faces glaring down at her. Her laughter ended abruptly, as she looked down at herself and realized that dropping Twinkle had resulted in her becoming visible once again.

"Uh, hey guys," she said slowly, "I'm back." Getting nothing but angry stares in return, she took a deep breath and tried again. "C'mon guys, it was just a little joke. I had no idea it would frighten you all so much. I was just trying to have a little fun. Besides, you have to admit it was kind of funny, right?" she asked in a pleading tone.

The kids' glares slowly melted away, as they looked at each other and then thoughtfully back at Fatima. Hannah was the first to speak. "Okay, Fatima, you had your little joke; at our expense, I might add. Now, we're trying to get some work done. The Science Fair is tomorrow night, and we've finally finished our project."

Fatima stood up and brushed herself off. Picking up Twinkle, she began walking around the robot, examining it with a critical eye. Finally, she stopped and placed her hands on her hips.

"What is it, and what's it supposed to do?" she asked pointedly.

Ritchie looked at the girls, and then let out a deep sigh. "I'll tell you what, Fatima; I'll explain it all and give you a personal demonstration, if you promise to never ever scare us like that again."

Fatima, who actually managed to look somewhat contrite, humbly apologized once again, before giving her solemn promise that she would restrain herself from frightening them in the future. After giving them her promise, a pouting expression replaced her usual grin.

"Aren't you guys even glad to see me again? I've been counting down the hours of this extremely long month, because I missed you guys so much, and couldn't wait to see you again."

The kids exchanged guilty looks, before Hannah replied. "We've missed you too, Fatima, even though it's only been two weeks for us. I'm sorry we got angry at you. It's just that you scared the daylights out of us. But, we're all very happy that you're back again, aren't we guys?"

Darlene and Ritchie both nodded their heads vigorously. Ritchie then eagerly explained their science project to the little sprite. Apparently, the kids had built their own miniature robot, which they affectionately referred to as Robby. They had designed and built it all by themselves, without any help from their parents or older siblings.

The robot was about twelve inches tall and was made completely out of scrap metal. They had mostly used polished tin for the head and extremities, and a lightweight steel alloy for the body. The metal parts were held together with copper bolts, and included a compartment in the back, as well as a hinged jaw which actually moved when the robot talked. It had blue pegs, which would light up when it was turned on, for eyes; and the arms and legs were also hinged, allowing it to walk and move its arms around. A small speaker sat inside the mouth, and that was where the voice came from.

A metal plate on its back could be opened up, revealing a small compartment with a computer microchip inside. The microchip was the finishing touch, and it represented the true genius of their invention. Ritchie had programmed a computer software program into the microchip, so that when instructions were entered on a laptop computer, the robot would then move and talk, according to those programmed commands. After this detailed explanation, which mainly resulted in the furrowing of the sprite's brow, Ritchie decided to give Fatima a demonstration. Motioning her over to the laptop, Ritchie typed in the following command: say "Hello, Fatima," and offer her your right hand to shake.

Fatima returned her focus to the robot. Suddenly, its eyes lit up and the jaws began moving. "Hello, Fatima," a mechanical-sounding voice said. The robot then gave a whirring sound, while it lifted up its right arm and extended its right hand toward the little sprite. Fatima took a few surprised steps backward, and stared at the robot suspiciously. Ritchie typed in another command: say "Welcome to the planet earth," take four steps forward, and then bow at the waist. Once again, the voice came through the speaker as the robot's jaw moved. "Welcome to the planet earth," it said, and then whirred and creaked as it took four steps toward Fatima, and then bowed at the waist. This time Fatima was no longer apprehensive, and instead clapped her little hands together with delight. Her excitement increased when she suddenly thought of an idea.

"This is great guys, but you know what would be even better?"

"What?" they all said in unison, looking worriedly at each other.

"Well, it would be totally awesome if Twinkle and I made a few magical adjustments to make this thing even cooler. Like we could make it spit flames when it talks, or fly around the room over people's heads, or lots of different stuff. I have tons of spells that I could try on it. What do you guys think?" Fatima stared at them with a cocky tilt of her eyebrows.

The kids glanced at her, and then quickly looked away, seeking anything else in the room to focus upon. As the minutes passed silently by, Fatima's confident expression began to wilt, and she looked questioningly at each of the kids. Finally, Ritchie cleared his throat, searching for the right words to say. He certainly didn't want to hurt the sprite's feelings, but neither did he want his creation, on which he'd spent over a month of hard work, ruined by one of Fatima's screwed up spells. Suddenly, his face lit up and he began to speak, feeling relieved that he had come up with a reasonable explanation.

"Uh, Fatima," he started, "we would all love to have you help us out, but the rules of the competition state that we have to do all of the work ourselves. If we allow any outside help, then we would be breaking the rules, and we want to win the grand prize fair and square. Besides, your magic would create such fantastic changes, that no one would believe that we had done it all by ourselves. Surely you understand now, why we can't accept your gracious offer."

Fatima appeared somewhat mollified by Ritchie's carefully orchestrated explanation. However, she still felt a little hurt that they wouldn't let her participate at all.

"Fine," she sniffed haughtily, "if you don't want my help, then I certainly won't force it on you." She looked down at the ground sadly, although she was secretly watching them from the corner of her eye in case they showed any signs of weakening. Unfortunately, she could tell by their facial expressions that they were all in firm agreement regarding this decision. Fatima stalked over to a piece of scrap wood, and sat down with a pouting look on her face.

"Well, thanks for understanding," Ritchie replied. Fatima turned away, fluttering a tiny hand in the air as if to say, whatever.

"Okay," Ritchie said to the girls, "I think this baby is ready to fly." Fatima's head jerked in his direction, and she started to lift Twinkle off her lap. "No, no, no," Ritchie replied quickly. "I don't mean literally fly; I mean that everything's ready for the Science Fair tomorrow night."

"Humph," Fatima said, disgusted by yet another missed opportunity.

At that point, the kids decided to call it a night. They discussed the following day's schedule with Fatima, who was still obviously a bit put out with their unanimous decision to decline any magical adjustments. After they finished, she informed them that she wouldn't be going to school with them the next day, because she needed to put the finishing touches on her plan to fulfill Hannah's wish. Hannah, Darlene, and Ritchie were secretly relieved by her decision, but they were very careful to keep this from Fatima.

After quick good-byes, the kids split up and retired to their own bedrooms. They all slept extremely well, now that the stress of completing their project was behind them. For her part, Fatima didn't sleep quite as well. This was mainly because she was still harboring some hurt feelings and resentment towards her friends, but that too would come to pass.

The next morning, Hannah said a quick farewell to Fatima (along with an admonishment to stay out of trouble), and hurried off to school. In all likelihood, Fatima was going to do nothing more than sit in Hannah's bedroom and sulk all day, but there was no way she was going to let Hannah know that. At least Hannah had promised her that they all wanted her to accompany them to the Science Fair tomorrow night. If she didn't die of boredom before then, she thought bitterly.

School that morning was typically uneventful, although there was a small undercurrent of excitement running through the school, because a lot of the students were anxiously awaiting the Science Fair tomorrow evening. At lunchtime, Hannah, Darlene, and Ritchie found themselves at their usual table, discussing their chances of winning the grand prize. It would be difficult to know for sure, until they saw the other kids' projects, but Ritchie was unfailingly optimistic about their chances of winning.

As the three friends continued their discussion, Hannah noticed movement out of the corner of her eye. Turning her head in that direction, she was greeted by the sight of Tony Parsons and his usual band of lunkheads stalking towards them. Hannah's first thought was, oh no, not this again, as she watched their approach.

Lately, Tony had been harassing Ritchie almost daily. Like most bullies, Tony had a knack for discovering his opponent's weaknesses, and baiting Ritchie about the Science Fair had resulted in hours of fun for Tony and his cronies. Tony was sincerely disappointed that tomorrow was the day of the Science Fair, because then this avenue of torture would no longer be available to him. Ritchie's eyebrows rose and his mouth drew into a thin line of displeasure, as soon as he noticed Tony's presence.

"Hey, four eyes, how ya doin' today?" Tony asked nonchalantly. Ritchie studiously ignored him, while he concentrated on eating his sandwich.

"It's too bad the Science Fair's tomorrow, because I'm betting it's gonna turn out to be the worst day of your life. You know, with me winning the grand prize and all." Tony glanced around at his friends' faces, basking in the limelight of their obvious admiration. Ritchie still managed to keep his mouth shut, but the strain of doing so began to show, as a thin sheen of sweat broke out on his brow and his eyes glittered dangerously.

Unfortunately, Tony was just getting started. He intended to continue haranguing Ritchie until the little nerd lost it completely. He apparently felt very confident that his science project would easily beat out anything Ritchie and a couple of girls could come up with. He, of course, would have been no where near as cocky if his project had actually been designed and built solely by him. The truth was that his dad had badgered one of the electrical engineers who had built the props for his last movie production into making something cool that his son could enter into this year's Science Fair.

Tony's project, which he intended to take full credit for, was a large metal sphere that was actually an electromagnetic device which could create static electricity. When the device was turned on, you could rest your hands on the sphere, and the static electricity created would cause all of your hair to stand up on end. Tony had absolutely no idea how the device worked, but he was confident that it was awesome enough to win him the grand prize. To be perfectly honest, Tony had no real interest in going to the Pacific Science Center. As Ritchie suspected, he merely wanted to win the prize so that Ritchie couldn't.

"Boy," Tony continued, "I'm kind of interested in seeing the piece of crap you came up with. Let me guess, it's about the lifecycle of the earthworm. No wait, I know, it's about how to make malt balls out of rabbit turds, and you're going to be munching on the finished product." Tony's friends all started laughing and Tony pounded his thigh, blown away by his own incredible stroke of genius. Ritchie, who had been handling things pretty well up until that point, totally lost his temper.

"Tony, I'm surprised you're even participating in the Science Fair, because I wasn't aware that you had ever even passed a science class. I had you pegged as more likely being the poster child for Morons Are Us. I mean it's hard to think up a science project when you have the brain capacity of a Neanderthal. My entry will obviously be vastly superior to yours, because unlike you, my IQ is larger than my shoe size."

When Ritchie finished, Tony just stood there with his mouth hanging open in disbelief. Although he hadn't completely understood everything Ritchie said, it was obvious that the little pipsqueak was trying to make him look stupid. Because Ritchie was supremely pissed off, he had practically shouted his response, and most of the cafeteria had overheard him. Quite a few of the kids were laughing at this point, which made Tony even angrier.

Surrounded by all the other kids, as well as quite a few teachers, there wasn't a whole lot Tony could do to Ritchie at the moment. Tony, red-faced, and with his teeth clenched together hard enough to chip a tooth, leaned over and whispered something in Ritchie's ear. Then he straightened up, and stomped out of the cafeteria; his friends following right behind him, like lemmings running blindly over a cliff.

Ritchie sat there white-faced with his fingers clenched around his half-eaten sandwich. Hannah and Darlene watched him worriedly, until Hannah finally cleared her throat to speak.

"Ritchie, are you okay? What did that jerk say to you?"

Ritchie put his sandwich down, and stared at Hannah for a moment. Finally, he gulped and answered her. "He said he would make sure I didn't win the trip to the Science Fair. Also, as soon as he gets the chance, he's going to beat me to a bloody pulp." Ritchie gave the girls a sickly smile, then gathered up the rest of his lunch, and threw it into a nearby trash can.

"Don't worry," Hannah said fiercely, "he's not going to get the chance to do either of those things. Darlene and I will stick by you for the rest of the day, and tomorrow we'll have Fatima with us. If he tries anything then, she'll fix him for sure."

Ritchie brightened up a little after hearing that bit of encouragement. His face regained some of its color, and he even returned Hannah's reassuring smile. But in spite of her promise, he spent the rest of the day peeking over his shoulder, half-expecting Tony Parsons to appear at any moment, ready to beat the crap out of him. Whether Tony never got his chance or lady luck was on Ritchie's side that day, he never knew; but Ritchie made it home that day in one piece.

His sleep was fitful that night, although he told himself it was due to his excitement that the day of the Science Fair had finally arrived, rather than his fear of Tony Parsons. Hannah slept much better than Ritchie, and even Fatima had a more restful sleep than the previous night. Hannah had informed her of Tony's threat when she returned home from school, and Fatima was planning to keep a careful eye on Tony Parsons and his group of trouble makers tomorrow.

The next morning, Hannah and Fatima rose bright and early. The day of the Science Fair was finally here. Hannah's dad had agreed to give the kids a ride to school, so they wouldn't have to carry the parts of their project while they walked. Participants were supposed to set up their entries in the gymnasium before classes began, which meant they needed to be there fairly early. By 7:00, Ritchie and Darlene had arrived at the Flannigan house with the robot and computer in tow. Fatima was already invisible and in her usual spot on Hannah's right shoulder. Tom loaded the kids and their stuff into his truck, and dropped them off in front of the school by 7:15. Ritchie's eyes darted around nervously, worried that Tony would appear at any moment.

However, in spite of his apprehension, the morning went smoothly, and they had no trouble arranging their project in preparation for the fair that evening. The gym was then closed and locked, and the students all wandered off to their 1st period classes. Ritchie was immensely relieved that everything had turned out just fine, and he gently chided himself for worrying so much for nothing. He sauntered down the hall towards his Advanced Algebra class, whistling a jaunty tune as he walked along. Chuckling under his breath, he thought to himself, it looks like everything's going to be okay after all; if only poor Ritchie had known what the day still held in store for him.

Tony Parsons sat slumped in his seat, barely paying attention to his first two classes of the morning. Third period finally found him in his Basic Reading class, which was taught by Coach Harris. Fortunately for Tony, the Coach spent most of the period going over the football plays he would use for that week's game, and paid little or no attention to the class. Everyone was expected to bring a book of their own choosing and spend the entire class reading it.

Most of the students used that time to catch up on their other homework, or to take a snooze. Coach Harris didn't really care what they did with their time, as long as they were quiet and well-behaved. The other bonus, and the most crucial part of Tony's plan, was that Coach Harris always carried a key to the gymnasium. With this fact in mind, Tony approached the Coach as soon as the final bell for class rang.

"Coach Harris, I left the book I'm reading in the gym when I was setting up my science project. Can I use your key and run down there to grab it?"

The Coach peered at him over the top of his play book with a quizzical expression. "Tony, do you mean to tell me you're actually reading a book?"

"Yeah, and I was just getting to the good part, so I'd really like your permission to get it real quick."

The Coach heaved a big sigh, before reaching down to grab the keychain which hung below his huge belly. He selected a key, and handed it to Tony. "Get your butt back here in five minutes, and don't be messing around," he said, not unkindly.

Tony thanked him with an angelic smile on his face, as he grabbed the key and ran down the hall. Once he reached the door to the gym, he looked around carefully to make sure there was no one else in the area. Satisfied that he was all alone, he quickly unlocked the door, and then pulled it closed behind him. Searching the various tables, he found the one where Ritchie and the girls had set up their entry, and quickly read the signboard that described how the robot functioned. He had already heard through the school grapevine all about their robot, and how it supposedly worked. That was when he'd gotten the idea for his little adjustment.

Tony reached into his back pocket and pulled out a small screwdriver. Working as fast as he could, he removed the metal plate from the back of the robot, and took out the small microchip inside. Locating the switch which activated the chip, he hooked a small tape recorder up to it. Now, when Ritchie hit the command key on the laptop, the switch would be activating Tony's tape recorder, instead of Ritchie's microchip. Tony rubbed his hands together with malicious glee. This was going to be awesome. He refastened the metal plate, and let himself out of the gym, carefully locking the door behind him.

Tony hurried back to Coach Harris's class without anyone catching a glimpse of him. As he entered the classroom, he noticed with relief that the Coach's face was still buried in his playbook. Walking past his desk, he deftly grabbed his book, which had been in his backpack the entire time. He stood beside Coach Harris's desk, waiting to be noticed. After several minutes, he cleared his throat loudly, and the Coach finally looked up. Tony gave him a huge smile, holding the key out in one hand, while his other hand held up the book. Coach Harris merely grunted, as he grabbed the key from Tony, and hooked it back on his belt. Tony sat down at his desk pretending to read, but secretly he was gloating over the fact that he had set up a wonderful surprise for Ritchie Pearson – one that Ritchie was definitely not going to appreciate.

That evening after dinner, Ritchie, Hannah, and Darlene met at the Science Fair and gathered around their project. As people began trickling in, a large group of them surrounded the robot and waited for the initial demonstration. Hannah and Darlene took turns explaining how the robot worked, and then turned the production over to Ritchie. Grinning broadly, he began typing some simple commands into the laptop. All eyes turned towards the robot, as he punched the command key, and waited for it to respond. Almost immediately, its blue eyes lit up and the jaw began to open. But instead of the greeting which Ritchie had programmed it to say, a voice which sounded suspiciously like Tony Parsons loudly said, "Science sucks!"

Everyone began to laugh, assuming Ritchie was playing a little joke on them. Ritchie and the girls were not laughing, however, as Ritchie bent over the laptop, and furiously entered in new instructions. But no matter what Ritchie programmed the robot to do, it just stood there every time, repeating the same statement, "Science sucks, science sucks!" Losing interest, the crowd dispersed to view the other science projects.

Ritchie was almost to the point of tears, as he whispered angrily to Hannah, "Someone sabotaged our robot, and I bet I know who." Removing the metal plate from the robot's back, the kids peered inside. Sure enough, instead of the complicated microchip, there was a tape recorder hooked up to the activating switch. Ritchie grabbed the tape recorder and practically ripped it out, his actions fueled by pure anger. He handed it to Hannah as proof, and she and Darlene rewound the tape and played it for themselves.

After listening to the tape for a full five minutes, Hannah and Darlene looked up at each other and nodded grimly. Although it would be almost impossible to prove, they were both certain that the voice on the tape belonged to Tony Parsons. During the entire five minutes of tape they had listened to, the only thing it had said was the short phrase "Science sucks," over and over again.

Meanwhile, their computer microchip was nowhere to be found, and all of them were certain that they knew exactly where the missing chip was. "Tony has it," Ritchie hissed angrily between gritted teeth. "And I'm going to get it back right this minute," he said determinedly.

"But Ritchie," Hannah pleaded, "he's just going to deny everything, and then what are you going to do?" Ritchie suddenly looked like a deflated balloon, as he realized that Hannah was right.

While Hannah, Darlene, and Ritchie stood paralyzed by indecision, Ritchie heard a tiny whisper in his ear. "Don't worry, Ritchie, I promise you that your robot will be as good as new in a matter of minutes; you can count on me!" Then the voice was gone. Sharing this news with the girls, Ritchie put up a sign which read "Temporarily Out Of Order." Then they waited to see what would happen next.

Meanwhile, on the other side of the gym, Tony was about to display his project. His father had explained to him how the machine worked, but Tony had only listened long enough to figure out how to turn it on, as he found the whole thing to be rather boring. Talking in a loud voice to attract as much attention as possible, he invited Mr. Andrews and Ms. Peterson to place their hands on the giant sphere for his first demonstration. After both of the Principals had done so, he moved over to the control box, and switched on the machine. Everyone waited for several moments, keeping their eyes on Mr. Andrews and Ms. Peterson, but it quickly became obvious that absolutely nothing was happening.

Completely bewildered, Tony turned the machine off, and then flipped the switch to the "on" position again. However, there was still no evidence of any static electricity, and Tony was beginning to get angry. Reassuring the spectators that it was just a minor glitch, he bent over the control box and attempted to make some minor adjustments. Secretly, he was wishing that he had paid a bit more attention to his father's explanation, because he honestly had no idea how the stupid thing worked.

The reality of the situation was that even if Tony had completely understood how the electromagnetic device worked, it wouldn't have helped him in the least, because it had been altered by Fatima and Twinkle's sprite magic. Determined to show what the machine could do, Tony placed both hands firmly on the sphere and ordered one of his friends to flip the switch. Barely a second had passed, when suddenly Tony's hair sprang straight up off of his head, and then began to turn a bright shade of the most unnatural blue.

Feeling the effects of the static electricity coursing through his hair, Tony allowed a big grin of triumph to spread across his face. Finally, the dang thing was working, and with Ritchie's robot being a complete bust, he was sure to win the grand prize. Oh man, he could hardly wait to see the look of shock and disappointment on the little nerd's face when he realized that Tony had beat him. While these thoughts were running through his mind, Tony's hair began to crackle and smoke.

The people crowded around him, immediately began to back away, several of them screaming at the sight. Smelling smoke and feeling the heat which had enveloped his head, Tony finally realized what was happening. A high-pitched shriek escaped his mouth, as he panicked and began beating at his hair ineffectively.

Quickly deciding that dunking his head in water was the only answer, Tony bolted through the crowds of people, straight for the nearest boys' bathroom. Racing through the door, he stumbled into the first stall and plunged his entire head into the toilet. Taking advantage of the fact that Tony was more than preoccupied with the whole burning hair situation, Fatima reached into the front pocket of his jeans and retrieved the robot's microchip. Concealing it in the pouch on her belt, so that it too would be invisible, Fatima raced through the gym straight towards her three friends, and deposited the chip into Ritchie's hand. Within half a minute, he had the microchip back in its rightful place, and the robot was working like a charm.

At that moment, Mr. Andrews reentered the gym with Tony Parsons in tow. The feeling of panic which had enveloped the crowd moments before had eventually dissipated, once it became obvious that the electromagnetic device wasn't going to explode or shoot blue flames all over the gym. Everyone looked at Tony Parsons with obvious curiosity and wonderment. Tony's hair was more than half-gone, and what was left was a shade of bright blue and was standing straight up off of his scalp. He had bald patches intermixed with the blue patches, and portions of his head had severely singed patches of hair on it. Several kids in the crowd began laughing at the sight, and before long, most of the gym's occupants had joined in.

When the crowd resumed observing the various projects, large numbers of people gathered in front of the robot to watch Ritchie's impressive demonstration. Before long, the majority of the gym's occupants were gathered by the robot, amazed and delighted by its complex maneuverings. Each demonstration was accompanied by thunderous applause from the crowd, and Ritchie and the girls enjoyed every minute of it.

At the end of the evening, to the delight of all the students, parents, and teachers; Ritchie, Hannah, and Darlene were awarded the grand prize. Staring sullenly from his place beside his fizzled project (which Mr. Andrews had ordered him to unplug and cover with a tarp until it could be safely removed) Tony glared up at Ritchie as he was awarded his prize. Ritchie caught his eye briefly, and even though Tony's hair was still bright blue and standing straight up in the places it hadn't been charred, his look still made Ritchie shiver with fear. He was going to have to avoid Tony Parsons for a very long time, because it was obvious that Tony was not finished with him yet.

CHAPTER 16

HANNAH'S MAGICAL TRANSFORMATION

That night, after the Science Fair was over, everyone gathered at the Flannigan house for a joyous celebration. Ritchie's parents and Darlene's mom were able to attend, but Mr. O'Brien was away on a business trip, and unable to come. However, he did call Darlene to congratulate her and her friends on their victory. The kids would be going to the Pacific Science Center in June during their summer vacation. The six weeks until that time would seem very long indeed, and they would all be counting down the days until it was time to go on their trip.

After they had finished their cake and ice cream, the kids left the adults downstairs talking, while they went up to Hannah's room for a little privacy. Once Hannah's door was closed, they all clamored for Fatima to become visible again. The little sprite appeared immediately, sitting cross-legged on Hannah's desk with an expression of feigned indifference on her face. As soon as her three friends saw her, they surrounded her and began chattering excitedly. Although Fatima had some difficulty understanding them, as they were all talking at the same time, she was finally able to come to the conclusion that they were each expressing their thanks.

For quite awhile, Fatima sat back and allowed them to gush about how wonderful she was, and about how she had rescued their science project by recovering the microchip, and about how they wouldn't have won the grand prize without her help. But after five or ten minutes of this, Fatima finally held up her tiny hand in a gesture which meant that enough was enough. As the kids wound down and became silent, Fatima took a deep breath and spoke.

"Let me start by saying that I'm really happy you guys won the Science Fair, and I'm even happier that I was able to help you do that. I have to admit, though, that at first I was awfully hurt and angry that you refused to let Twinkle and me take part in your project. In fact, I had originally decided not to help out when you guys discovered the microchip was missing, because you had already told me that you didn't want my assistance. But then I realized what that stupid, little brat had done; and it made me so angry, I could spit nails. I knew I couldn't let him get away with it, and besides, I remembered what Hannah and I had talked about on my last visit."

"What was that?" Hannah asked curiously.

"You know, about the value of friendship, and how friendship should be based on truth and honesty. That made me realize I just couldn't let you guys down; after all, you are my best friends," she said with a contented smile.

The kids grinned at each other, and then turned their attention back to Fatima. Hannah was the next one to speak. "Fatima, I'm really sorry that we hurt your feelings. We never meant for that to happen. But I'm so glad that you decided to help us out. You've definitely proven that you're a good friend, and I'm truly sorry if I ever doubted that. Can you find it in your heart to forgive me?"

Fatima beamed at Hannah, as she replied. "Of course I can, that's what friends do, isn't it?" Everyone laughed together, nodding their heads in agreement.

Finally, Ritchie piped up and said, "So Fatima, tell us how you managed to get the microchip back."

Fatima gave him an evil grin, and wiggled her tiny eyebrows up and down. "Actually it was pretty easy, because Tony was a little preoccupied with the fact that half of his hair was on fire. As soon as he dunked his head into the toilet in the boys' bathroom . . ." Here Ritchie interrupted her to ask in disbelief, "He dunked his head in the toilet?"

"Yep," she said in a self-satisfied tone, "and while he was in that rather compromised position, I reached into his front pocket and grabbed the microchip. Then I flew lickity-split back to you guys, and gave the chip back to Ritchie. Boy, did you see the look on his face when you guys were awarded the grand prize? I mean it was hard to take him seriously with half his hair singed off, and the other half bright blue; but if looks could kill, you guys would have dropped dead on the spot!"

Hearing this, all of the blood seemed to drain out of Ritchie's face. Fatima didn't notice, though, as she continued going on and on about how mad Tony had looked. Hannah, however, took a quick glance at Ritchie's face, and immediately began drawing her finger along her neck; a silent gesture intended to shut Fatima up. Unfortunately, Fatima misinterpreted her signal, and instead of shutting up, she just continued on in the same vein. "Oh yes," she said to Hannah, "I certainly agree. I mean it did look like he probably wanted to cut off your heads, or something; especially you, Ritchie," she stated with a mischievous gleam in her eye.

Ritchie took several steps backward and slumped onto Hannah's bed in absolute dejection. "I'm dead meat," he moaned to the girls. "I'm not even going to live long enough to make it to the Science Center. Tony will kill me before then. Gosh, Fatima, why did you have to set his hair on fire! I mean I'm really thankful and all about the whole rescuing the microchip thing, but wasn't it enough to just turn his hair blue?" Ritchie groaned.

"But Ritchie," Darlene interjected, "she had to set his hair on fire, so that he'd have to go put it out. Then, while he was busy with that, she was able to rescue the microchip. It was all part of the plan, right Fatima?" she asked cheerfully.

Fatima glanced at each of them in turn, and then stared down at the pointy shoes on her tiny feet. "Well," she said slowly, "since telling the truth is an important part of friendship," she stopped and looked at Hannah for confirmation.

Hannah nodded her head firmly. "Go on, Fatima," she said supportively.

"Oh, okay, if you really want to know the truth, my spell was only supposed to make his hair stand up straight and turn bright blue. I didn't mean to set it on fire." She paused and looked thoughtful for a moment. "In fact, I'm not really sure exactly how that happened." She pondered that mystery for several seconds, before her expression brightened once again. "But we're darn lucky it did, aren't we? Otherwise everything wouldn't have turned out so perfectly. Besides, I checked his head over carefully before we left, and only his hair was burned. His scalp was just fine – not a single burn or blister on it." She gave the kids a big grin, but Ritchie just stared at her morosely.

"Yeah, I'm lucky all right. Tony Parsons is going to beat the crap out of me, as soon as he catches me. You call that lucky?"

Fatima, Hannah, and Darlene cupped their hands over their mouths to stifle their giggles. "Cheer up, Ritchie, I'll be here for awhile still, and I promise to keep my eye on Tony for you. Now get rid of the glum look, because this is supposed to be a celebration. And can someone please get me a piece of that cake, because it looked delicious." Ritchie finally found himself with a smile back on his face, and he left the room to grab Fatima a piece of cake.

After another hour or so, the party wound down, and the O'Briens and Pearsons said their good-nights and headed home. Hannah waved good-bye to her friends, told her parents she was going to bed, and headed back up to her room. She sprawled back on her bed with a contented smile on her face, happy but exhausted, after her extremely busy day.

Fatima flew over and plopped down beside her friend. They both gave simultaneous sighs, and then grinned at each other. Fatima decided this was the perfect moment to bring up the first part of her plan, which was the initial step in fulfilling Hannah's wish. She had been pondering her first move all day yesterday while the kids were at school, and felt that she had come up with a great idea. She just hoped that Hannah agreed to it. Fatima rolled over onto her stomach, and propped her chin up on both hands. She took a deep breath, and then told Hannah the first part of her plan.

It was actually quite simple. Fatima figured that in order for Hannah to get Sean Adams' full attention, she had to get him to really notice her. With that in mind, Fatima wanted to use Twinkle to give Hannah a glamorous make-over. She planned on using her magic to give Hannah a stylish new hair-do, as well as a brand new, fashionable outfit. She would also use some magically applied make-up to cover Hannah's freckles and to enhance the natural beauty of Hannah's features. Basically, she was going to use her magic to give Hannah a whole new image – one that Sean couldn't possibly ignore.

Hannah thought about it for a few minutes, and then asked Fatima the question that had immediately popped up in her mind. Namely, was Fatima sure that she could successfully use her magic to do exactly as she intended, and nothing more. Fatima tried not to look hurt after her friend's question; because she had to admit that her track record was anything but perfect. After all, Hannah now had some experience observing Fatima's magic spells, and they never seemed to turn out the way she planned.

However, this spell was much easier than the others, and Hannah would be able to observe the results in the safety and privacy of her own room, before they left for school that morning. If there was anything she didn't like about it, Fatima could always change it then.

Hannah immediately saw the wisdom of Fatima's advice, and began to get quite excited about the whole idea. After all, she had never been very fond of the way she looked, and the idea of a new image certainly appealed to her. The two girls began whispering eagerly about their plans for the next morning. Hannah grabbed several fashion magazines out of her hope chest, and started flipping through them. She wanted to find the hairstyle and outfit that she liked the best, so that Fatima would have a picture to work with.

After she had selected the styles she liked the most, she showed them to the sprite, who agreed that her magic was totally capable of producing that look. Planning further, the two decided that Hannah would take the bus to school the next morning. That way she would look as fresh as a daisy when she arrived. More importantly, the school bus let the students out on the north side of the football field where Sean would be practicing. She would be walking along the edge of the field on her way into the school building, and Sean couldn't help but notice her grand entrance.

Satisfied that their plan was perfect, the girls headed off to bed. Hannah was worried that she would be too excited about tomorrow to sleep, but the busy day had exhausted her. She fell asleep as soon as her head hit the pillow, leaving Fatima wide awake with her own uneasiness. She had to pull everything off perfectly tomorrow, or she would be letting her best friend down. The spells seemed simple enough, but her magic so often turned out differently than she planned. Worried, but weary, the tiny sprite eventually fell asleep.

The next morning, the girls woke up in a state of anticipation. Hannah quickly called Darlene on the walkie-talkie to explain their plan, and to tell her that she would be taking the bus to school that morning. Darlene was understandably intrigued by the whole idea, and begged Hannah to let her accompany them. Hannah immediately agreed, secretly glad for the additional support, and Darlene promised to be over within the hour. Now it was time to set their plan in motion.

Fatima carefully studied the pictures of the styles they had decided on last night, while Hannah went to take her shower. When Hannah returned, dripping wet and wrapped in a towel, Fatima was ready to begin. First, Hannah put on her underwear, and then gave Fatima the signal that she was ready. Fatima had Hannah stand before her in the middle of the room, and then grabbed Twinkle, pausing to wipe her sweaty palms on her clothes.

Suddenly, she raised her wand above her head and began waving it around in a circle, mumbling a bunch of words that Hannah couldn't make heads or tails of. Hannah tried not to grin, but the little sprite looked so serious in spite of all her wild gesticulations, that she really couldn't help it. Also, the grin helped dispel her anxiety, because she had to admit that she was still more than a little worried that Fatima's spell would go awry.

Deciding that the best course of action would be to close her eyes, Hannah clamped them tightly shut while Fatima continued. After two or three minutes, Hannah realized that the room had become silent and still. Fatima must be finished, she thought to herself. Daring herself to be brave and open her eyes, she slowly unclenched her eyelids and fastened her gaze on Fatima. The sprite was hovering in the air several feet in front of her face, gaping at Hannah with an awestruck look. Hannah waited for her friend to say something, but Fatima's tongue seemed to be frozen. Mildly irritated by her silence, Hannah brushed past the sprite to stare at her reflection in the mirror over her dresser.

Her first thought was, is that really me? Her next thought was, I hate to sound conceited, but I'm gorgeous. She whirled around, and looked at the anxious little sprite with a huge grin on her face.

"Fatima," she squealed, "you did it! What an incredible transformation. Sean Adams is going to be so surprised. There's no way he won't notice me now. If I wasn't afraid of breaking you, I'd give you a humungous hug!"

Fatima's eyes sparkled, as she flew around Hannah in excited circles. "Man, Sean Adams is going to trip over his tongue when you step off that bus," she said happily.

At that moment, they heard the front door slam, and seconds later there was a clatter of footsteps coming up the stairs. Fatima was sure it was Darlene, but just to be on the safe side she darted back into Hannah's sock drawer, peeking out to see who it was. Sure enough, after a flurry of knocks on the door, Darlene burst into the room, already chattering excitedly about the plan for the day. One look at Hannah, and Darlene suddenly stopped talking. She stared at her best friend in disbelief.

"Oh my goodness, Hannah, you're beautiful," she said, without a hint of jealousy. Hannah blushed, and shook her head uncertainly.

It was true though. Fatima had done a fabulous job. Hannah's gorgeous chestnut brown hair was curled in gentle ringlets, and tied back into a loose ponytail with curls hanging down around her face. Her makeup was mild and understated with a light blush on her cheeks, and a light green eye shadow which brought out the emerald color of her eyes. She had on a light green peasant blouse, and a mid-length skirt with a pattern of bright blue and green diamonds on it, and several lacy frills at the bottom. A rawhide belt with a wide bronze buckle finished the outfit, and she had soft brown leather boots on her feet, which reached to just above her ankles.

Hannah clapped her hands in delight, as she twirled around in circles for her admirerers. Fatima had popped back out of the sock drawer when Darlene arrived, and was more than happy to bask in the glory, as she accepted her friends' congratulations on a job well done. At that point, it was nearly time for them to catch the bus, so they grabbed their backpacks and headed out the door. Hannah was thankful that Patrick and her parents had already left, because she didn't want to have to explain her new look to them at this point. Fatima had resumed her invisible state, and was in her customary position on Hannah's right shoulder when the school bus pulled up to their stop. Hannah and Darlene were the first ones on the bus, and they hurried to a seat in the very back to attract as little attention as possible at this point.

Hannah became more and more nervous as the bus approached their school. What if Sean didn't even notice her new look, or even worse, what if he didn't like it. Hannah gently bit her bottom lip, agonizing over these possibilities. The bus was only two or three blocks away from the junior high, when Darlene suddenly realized that Fatima had forgotten all about Hannah's glasses. As soon as she mentioned it (in a hushed whisper so no one else would overhear), Fatima closed her eyes and slapped her tiny forehead in disgust. She had been so excited about the magical transformation, that she had completely overlooked the fact she had meant to change the glasses into contacts.

Whispering her intention into Hannah's ear, she quickly waved Twinkle in the air and muttered a few words of magic. With remarkable speed, Hannah's glasses vanished into thin air, to be replaced by a pair of contact lens. Luckily, no one but Darlene had been staring at Hannah when this occurred, because even though Darlene knew what had happened, she still did a double take in surprise. Hannah blinked her eyes several times, and then looked around. Everything was fuzzy and blurry, so she blinked several more times, before gently rubbing her eyes and opening them back up again. Unfortunately, there was no improvement in her vision, even after trying those maneuvers several more times. Oh no, she thought worriedly, I can't see a darn thing. She was just about to open her mouth and say so, when the school bus pulled up beside the football field to let the kids out.

As the students lined up in the aisle and began piling off the bus, Hannah stood up and followed Darlene. At least she thought it was Darlene. Things were so fuzzy she couldn't tell for sure; but with all the kids surrounding them, not to mention the noise level from all the yelling and talking, she didn't have an opportunity to explain her predicament to her friend. To make matters even worse, Darlene hopped off the bus ahead of her and rushed across the football field with the other kids, intending to give Hannah a chance to walk across the field by herself to fully capture Sean's attention.

Hannah stumbled off the bus and looked around anxiously, trying to orient herself so that she could figure out which way to go. In spite of her blurry vision, she was at least able to spot the school in the distance, and she began walking in that direction. Out of the corner of her eye, she noticed a bunch of colorful blurry shapes moving around in a group. Assuming it was the group of kids who had just exited the bus, she turned in that direction, feeling a bit more confident. If she could only catch up to Darlene, she could finally explain what had happened, and then allow Darlene to lead her the rest of the way. Then they could find a spot with some privacy so that Fatima could fix her mistake.

Unluckily for Hannah, the group of kids she was approaching wasn't the kids who had just gotten off the bus with her. It was actually the cheerleaders, who were out on the edge of the football field practicing some of their routines. Hannah continued walking determinedly, drawing closer and closer to Erika and her friends. The cheerleaders had just assembled themselves into a human pyramid, which marked the first occasion that they had actually been successful at this maneuver, following numerous failed attempts. One of the girls was getting ready to take a picture of their triumph, which the entire football team had finally noticed. As the boys began applauding wildly, Hannah, distracted by the noise and commotion, looked away from her careful path, and stumbled on an empty water bucket.

Looking back later, it seemed impossible that the tragic events which followed could all be blamed on something as innocent as an empty bucket. Earlier that morning, the bucket had been full of water, along with several others. Their purpose was to keep the boys on the football team well hydrated, as they ran around sweating on that unseasonably hot spring morning. Once the water had been drunk, the empty bucket had been cast aside. The equipment manager intended to pick it up after practice, along with the others, and place them back in the equipment shed. Unfortunately for Hannah, football practice hadn't ended yet, and so the empty water bucket lay on its side, directly in her path.

From the moment Hannah stumbled, everything seemed to happen in slow motion. In reality, however, it actually happened way too fast for anyone, Fatima included, to react. As Hannah tripped over the bucket, she went sprawling on the ground face-first. The morning dew hadn't fully evaporated yet, making the grass itself more slippery than a greased pig. Hannah skidded along on her stomach for several feet, before her momentum was finally stopped by one of the cheerleaders kneeling on the ground on her hands and knees. This cheerleader formed one of the corners of the pyramid, and therefore had several other girls balanced on top of her, as well as a row of girls beside her.

Following one of the laws of physics, Hannah's momentum was immediately transferred to the girl she struck. In simpler terms, this resulted in that girl being knocked into the girl kneeling beside her, which caused a chain reaction like a row of dominoes tumbling down together. As the football team watched in amazement, the entire formation of cheerleaders fell to the ground amidst a noisy background of screams and yells. For a brief moment nothing could be identified except a jumble of arms and legs, until Erika's head finally poked itself out of the writhing pile. Her shriek sliced through the morning air, causing Hannah to reflexively clap her hands to her ears. Although none of the girls were actually hurt, the injury to their pride was severe, and Erika's wrathful gaze was already looking around for someone to blame.

In less than five seconds, her glare fixed on the hapless Hannah, still lying on her stomach in the wet grass blinking her eyes like a blind turtle, completely unaware of the damage she had caused. At that point all heck broke loose. Screaming at Hannah at the top of her lungs, in order to be heard over the raucous laughter of the football team, Erika proceeded to tell her exactly what she thought of her little stunt, which she bitterly assumed was purposeful. It didn't take long before Annika and the other cheerleaders joined in; and before Hannah could even pick herself up off the ground, she found herself surrounded by a screeching mob. Trying her best to hold back her tears, Hannah whispered "Fatima, help me."

The words had no sooner left her mouth, when several things began happening at once. With a howling roar, a huge wind suddenly appeared out of nowhere, gusting across the football field and everything in its path. The cheerleaders staggered around from the force, and their skirts flew up around their waists, and their pom-poms were ripped from their hands. Suddenly, large black clouds roiled across the sky, covering the sun, which had shone bright and warm just moments before. Hailstones the size of walnuts began pelting down, caroming off the heads of cheerleaders and football players alike. Amidst the havoc, no one noticed that Hannah seemed to have an invisible shield around her, as neither the wind nor the hail touched her in the least.

The football players quickly put their helmets back on, and huddled on the field in a large group, trying to use each other for protection against the freak storm. The cheerleaders' outfits were no match for the wind and hail, so they ran screaming towards the school in an attempt to find shelter. Now that everyone's attention had been drawn away from her, Hannah used the opportunity to make good her escape. She picked herself up off the ground, and began running blindly in the other direction. Hot tears of embarrassment and frustration ran down her face as she raced away, trying to put as much distance as possible between her and the chaos she had accidentally caused. Sean Adams was the only boy on the team who lifted his head from the huddle at that moment, and witnessed her escape. As he watched her run away in shame, he had a sympathetic expression on his face. Unfortunately, even if Hannah had taken the time to look his way, she wouldn't have been able to see his expression, because her vision was still way too blurry.

By the time she was halfway home, Fatima was finally able to coax Hannah into explaining to her exactly what had happened. As soon as she understood the mistake she had made, she immediately replaced the useless contacts with Hannah's own glasses. But by that time, of course, the damage had already been done. Hannah had nearly reached her house when she glimpsed Ritchie, pedaling along on the newly repaired Ritchiemobile. She slowed down as he pulled up beside her with a concerned look on his face. Hannah sat down on the curb and told Ritchie the whole story, wiping away the new tears which sprung up as she talked. When she finished, he solemnly reached into his pocket and offered her his handkerchief. Otherwise, he just sat there helplessly, unable to think of the right words to comfort her.

Fatima appeared, and sat down on the curb beside her friend. In a trembling voice, she offered Hannah yet another apology. Feeling terrible, she took a deep breath, and then stated that she was going home. As Hannah glanced over at her in surprise, Fatima explained further. She had decided that she was going to release Hannah from their pact of friendship. That pact had been based on the fact that Fatima needed to repay Hannah's kindness by granting her a wish, so that she could fulfill the sprite code of honor. But, obviously, Fatima wasn't magically proficient enough to maintain her side of the bargain. Also, she had ended up bringing her friend nothing but grief; so she was going home, because Hannah's life would be much better without her in it. Fatima hung her head, and waited for her friend's response. She didn't have to wait for long.

"Fatima, I am shocked that you would even say such a thing," Hannah began. "What happened today was just a mistake, pure and simple. Even though I'm angry and embarrassed, I'm not mad at you, because I know you only had the best of intentions. I'm going to go up to my room, and clean myself up, and when I get back I expect you to still be sitting right where you are. We're best friends, you silly little nitwit, and that's never going to change. Besides, your magical storm saved the day, because otherwise I wouldn't have been able to escape from that mob of cheerleaders. That was truly fantastic! Now wait right here with Ritchie, and I'll be back in a flash."

The little sprite's eyes lit up, and a happy smile wreathed her face. "You mean it?" she asked hopefully.

"Of course I do," Hannah said, as she walked up to her front door. Then she disappeared inside the house. Fatima was overjoyed that her best friend had already forgiven her, and she was determined to do a better job with her next bout of magical assistance. However, there was one thing about the whole morning that was still bothering her – where the heck had that storm come from?

CHAPTER 17

THE RETURN OF THE RITCHIEMOBILE

While Hannah was inside changing out of her muddy, wet clothes and brushing her bedraggled hair, Fatima and Ritchie waited for her out on the curb. Since they had some extra time, Fatima asked Ritchie to tell her all about the Ritchiemobile and how it worked. Ritchie was happy to oblige, and cheerfully explained the functions of all the buttons and switches, including the nitrous oxide. When he had finished, Fatima sat there for a moment with a thoughtful expression on her face. Recognizing that look, Ritchie hastily added, "Well that's the Ritchiemobile, and it's exactly the way I want it." The gleam in Fatima's eyes slowly winked out.

"Well," she said hesitantly, "I don't suppose you would want to consider any magical adjustments, would you, because I was just thinking of a few things that could be added? Hannah told me all about the accident you had a couple of weeks ago."

"Oh, that's totally fixed now. I just had to add some extra braking power to make up for the additional speed the nitrous oxide provided. It's in perfect working condition now."

Fatima looked up at Ritchie with a disappointed expression. "I suppose the real reason you don't want me messing with it is because I completely screwed up Hannah's magical transformation today. Well, I can't say I blame you," she finished with a heartfelt sigh.

"Fatima, that's not it at all," Ritchie protested. "It's just that everything's working perfectly now, so I have it exactly how I want it."

At that moment, Ritchie was saved from further argument because Hannah walked out her front door, ready to return to school. She gave her two friends a brave grin when she reached the curb, and announced she was ready to go. She had changed into a pair of blue jeans and a white button-down shirt, with a blue bandana wrapped around her ponytail. Ritchie secretly thought that she still looked beautiful, but he wasn't about to voice his opinion out loud. Fatima smiled brightly at her best friend, as she flew up to her shoulder and promptly disappeared. Ritchie also gave Hannah a big grin, as he strapped his helmet back on, and lowered himself into the Ritchiemobile's seat. He reached into his backpack strapped behind the seat, and produced an extra bicycle helmet. Offering it to Hannah, he announced with a small bow and a flourish of his hand, "Your chariot awaits, Miss Flannigan." Hannah giggled, and then gave the Ritchiemobile a dubious look.

"Uh, Ritchie, I don't want to offend you or anything, but remember the last time you rode this? I think that one accident a day is my limit."

Ritchie nodded his head in agreement, before he replied. "Don't worry; I'm not even going to switch on the motor. You can sit on the box behind the seat, and I'll just pedal us both to school." He glanced at the watch on his wrist before adding, "But we better get a move on if we're going to make it in time for 1st period."

Hannah, looking quite relieved at his promise not to turn on the motor, hopped on behind him, and they hurried off to school. She was not at all looking forward to facing Erika and Annika in her first class, but she really didn't have a choice in the matter. At least Darlene, who was probably wondering where Hannah had disappeared to, would be there for support. She only hoped that Sean had been so busy with football practice, that he hadn't noticed her clumsy accident. But given the level of chaos and destruction she'd caused, that probably wasn't going to be the case. Oh well, she sighed to herself, she would just have to deal with it.

Ritchie and Hannah arrived at the junior high just as the first bell of the day rang. That gave them five minutes to get to first period, which should be plenty of time. Ritchie had just locked up the Ritchiemobile at the bike rack and placed his helmet in his backpack, when he glanced up to find Tony Parsons glaring at him from the other side of the bike rack. Apparently, Tony and his group of friends had also just arrived, because they were all busy locking up their bikes, too. With a mean sneer on his face, Tony walked over and checked out the Ritchiemobile.

"Where did you get that piece of crap, Pearson?" he asked.

Ritchie stood there paralyzed with fright, his brain trying to coax his mouth into answering.

"I asked you a question, nerd," Tony growled with menace.

Ritchie continued to stare helplessly at him, totally petrified, and unable to answer even the simplest of questions. He did notice, however, that Tony had a whole new look; although it was nowhere near as flattering as Hannah's new image had been. His entire head was now shaved, but Ritchie could still see areas where the stubble was a bright blue. Thankfully, his instinct for self-preservation was still strong enough that he didn't allow his glance to linger on Tony's head for very long. Finally, his tongue loosened up enough to answer Tony's initial question.

"Uh, actually I built it myself," he said, in a voice only slightly louder than a whisper.

"I should have guessed. It looks like something a four-eyed, geek would build. I bet you think you're pretty fast on it, don't ya moron?"

"Well, actually it does go pretty fast, because it has a . . ." Ritchie was about to explain that it had a motor and everything, when Tony interrupted him.

"Well, I'll tell you what nerd breath. You're gonna have a chance to show me how fast it goes, because as soon as school's out today, me and my buddies are gonna meet you right here. We'll give you a ten second head start, before we start chasing you on our bikes. And when we catch you, which we will cuz lamebrain geeks are slow, we're gonna beat the crap out of you. See ya after school, nerd." Tony walked off with his friends in tow, laughing and giving each other high fives.

Ritchie stood by the bicycle rack, trembling with fear, while his mind raced to think of some kind of plan that would save him from a beating by Tony and his gang. Still thinking about his dilemma, he turned towards the school, and began walking towards his locker. Hannah fell in beside him, and he looked over at her in surprise. He had been concentrating so hard on Tony and his friends that he had completely forgotten about Hannah. He tried to smile at her, but barely managed to lift the corners of his mouth.

"Hey," he said meekly, "I suppose you heard all of that."

"Yeah, I was standing right behind you, and I overheard the whole thing."

"I'm dead," Ritchie said bluntly. "They're going to catch me after school, and do some serious damage to my body."

"But, Ritchie," Hannah commented, "all you have to do is get the motor running, and then you should be able to outrun them without a problem."

"Yeah, but you heard what Tony said. They're only going to give me a ten second head start, and knowing Tony, he's probably even lying about that."

"Ritchie, if I was able to hear the whole conversation then you-know-who did, too. I'll bet that she'll make sure that she's here to help you after school. So quit worrying, and let's get to class before we're tardy."

Ritchie reluctantly agreed, and they hurried off to their 1st period classes. Morning classes went by quickly, and in no time at all it was lunchtime. The three friends met at their usual table in the cafeteria. Ritchie looked totally miserable, stealing glances over his shoulder every minute or two, obviously worried that Tony would come over to remind him of their after-school meeting. However, for once Tony and his friends didn't make a lunchtime appearance at their table. As the noon hour drew to a close though, Ritchie looked anything but relieved. He kept sighing heavily, while he stared glassily at his mostly uneaten lunch. He looked like a death row prisoner who had just been told that today was the day of his execution.

Hannah and Darlene had been attempting to draw him into their conversation, but he had yet to utter anything but one word responses. Darlene had already spent the morning comforting Hannah about the debacle on the football field. Now, she had her hands full trying to comfort Ritchie about his promised beating at the hands of Tony and his gang. While Darlene was busy with Ritchie, Hannah excused herself to go to the bathroom. She returned five minutes later, and motioned Ritchie closer so she could talk to him without the risk of being overheard.

"Listen, I talked it all over with Fatima, and she said to tell you not to worry. She's going to make sure everything's taken care of, and she's going to meet you at the bike rack as soon as school's out. You won't be able to see her, of course, but she promises that she'll be there to help you. So cheer up and quit worrying," Hannah said with a reassuring smile.

Ritchie nodded his head grimly, and tried to give the girls a courageous smile. At that moment, the bell for 5th period rang, and the three friends said their good-byes, before hurrying off to their classes. All through his afternoon classes, Ritchie struggled to concentrate on his teachers and the material he was supposed to be learning; but it was no use. He just couldn't get Tony Parsons and his threat out of his mind. The anticipation was practically driving him crazy, and he found himself wishing that the final bell would ring, so he could just get the whole thing done and over with. However, when the bell finally did ring, his heart started racing, and his stomach jumped up into his throat, and he decided that the last thing he wanted to do was walk out to that bike rack. Unfortunately, he didn't have any other choice.

With a heavy heart and his head hung low between slumped shoulders, Ritchie walked outside and headed over to where the Ritchiemobile was parked. Sure enough, Tony and his gang were already waiting for him; bikes mounted and ready to go with the gleam of promised bloodshed in their eyes. Ritchie's pulse rate jumped even higher, and his breathing increased dramatically. Small black spots began dancing across his vision, and he suddenly realized that he was coming close to actually fainting.

Get a grip, he told himself, as he deliberately tried to slow down his breathing. He clenched and unclenched his hands several times, before willing his heart beat to slow down to a more reasonable rate. Unzipping his backpack, he pulled out his bicycle helmet and strapped it on his head. Then he unlocked the Ritchiemobile from the bike rack and fastened his backpack behind the seat. He didn't see any evidence that Fatima was there, but he trusted her to keep her promise.

His daydreaming was rudely interrupted by Tony's shout – the countdown was beginning! Tony began counting backwards, starting at ten. His counting seemed way too fast to Ritchie, who was feverishly trying to get the Ritchiemobile turned around, so that he could start pedaling. He finally freed it from the rack when Tony reached six, and at that moment, he leaped onto the seat and began pedaling for his life.

As he raced out onto the street which ran in front of the school, his eyes lingered on the red button for the nitrous oxide. If he'd only had the opportunity to turn on the motor first, he would be able to push that button now, and leave those knuckleheads eating his dust. But that wasn't a possibility now he thought, shaking his head grimly, and there was no way he'd be able to outrun eight of them.

While he was thinking those less than happy thoughts, he finally noticed that there was more than one button beside the steering wheel. Now, besides the red button for the nitrous oxide, there were three other buttons there as well – a blue one, a black one, and an orange one. Where the heck did those come from, he thought to himself, and more importantly, what the heck did they do? Pondering the answers to those questions, he realized that his pedaling had slowed, and he quickly increased his speed as he took a quick glance behind him. What he saw made his eyes open wider and his blood run cold. Three of Tony's friends were right on his tail. At this rate they would catch up to him before he even made it to the end of the street. As he turned back around, he noticed a familiar figure sitting on top of the steering wheel.

"Fatima," he gasped in relief, "you did show up."

"Of course I did," she replied in a cocky tone. "I told you I wouldn't let you down. Didn't you trust me?"

"Yes," Ritchie gasped, "I was just starting to get a little worried. What do we do now? Those goons are right behind us."

"That's exactly where we want them," Fatima answered confidently. "Did you notice the extra buttons I added? I know you told me not to touch it, but I figured we'd need a few more weapons at our disposal to get away from those morons. But," she added quickly, "I can remove them right now if you want me to."

"Gosh, no!" Ritchie cried. "Just tell me what to do."

Fatima gave him a particularly evil grin, before moving over to the panel where the buttons were located. She lifted up a tiny finger and then held it over the black button for a second, before pushing it with a squeal of anticipation. Ritchie cranked his head around to look behind him. Even in his current state of terror, he couldn't help but be curious about the results. As he watched expectantly, a huge gout of inky black oil shot out from the back of the Ritchiemobile, completely covering the street directly behind him in its slippery black goo.

The three boys who were directly behind Ritchie, widened their eyes in surprise, while their faces formed expressions of disbelief. As soon as their bicycle tires hit the pool of oil, they immediately began sliding and skidding around, completely out of control. Two of them slid towards the curb on their left, and their bicycles caromed off of it, ejecting the occupants onto the yard facing the street. The other boy was slightly less fortunate, as he slid towards the right side of the street, coming in contact with a nearby garbage can. Ritchie let out a whoop of exhilaration, as he caught sight of the boy lying on the curb covered in a huge pile of trash. He turned around and gave Fatima a high five with his index finger, and they both started laughing together.

Fatima looked behind them, noticing that Tony and four of his friends had managed to escape the path of the gooey oil, and were closing the gap between them quickly. Ritchie saw the expression on her face, and turned around to check their progress. He immediately whirled back around, and concentrated on pedaling faster.

"What do we do now?" he gasped between breaths.

Fatima grinned, looking totally unconcerned, as she leaned back over the panel of buttons and selected the blue button next. Giving Ritchie a mischievous smile, she pushed the blue button with her tiny hand. They both turned around simultaneously, anxious to see the effect on their pursuers. As

Ritchie watched in amazement, hundreds of shiny marbles began pouring out the back of the Ritchiemobile. The looks on the faces of Tony and his friends was one of horror, rather than amazement. Tony's friends started weaving and swerving in an effort to miss the marbles, but there were way too many of them. Once again, bikes and boys were sliding towards the curbs, and spilling off onto the grass lining the sides of the street.

By the time the Ritchiemobile reached the end of the block, Tony himself was the only one still upright on his bike. He had fallen way behind in his effort to dodge the marbles, but the look of determination on his angry face proved that he still intended to catch up to Ritchie, and pay him back for the whole Science Fair fiasco. Ritchie turned back towards Fatima with a worried expression, and turned right at the end of the block, pedaling furiously in an attempt to reach his house before Tony caught him. Now, there was only one button left.

"Fatima, what do I do now?" he yelled.

"Now, we wait until he's right behind you. Then, when he thinks that he's got you in his clutches, we use our final weapon."

"What will it do?"

"You'll find out soon," she said cheerfully.

Half-way down the block, Ritchie noticed that Tony had made up most of the ground he had previously lost. He was only ten feet away, and gaining fast. Ritchie took a second or two to close his eyes, and heartily hope that this was one of Fatima's magic spells that didn't backfire in the end. But, whatever his apprehension, he had no choice except to trust that she'd gotten everything right this time. Fatima watched and waited until Tony was only four or five feet away. She hovered over the orange button, and then suddenly dropped down, both feet landing square on the button. Ritchie immediately turned around to see what was going to happen.

All of a sudden, Ritchie heard a huge roar and a magnificent gout of smoke and flames gushed out of the back of the Ritchiemobile. Tony was instantly engulfed in a thick cloud of black smoke, and the Ritchiemobile surged forward like a racehorse out of the starting gate. The last glimpse he had of Tony Parsons was of a soot-covered shape straddling his bike in the middle of the road, coughing and hacking from the smoke which still surrounded him.

Ritchie and Fatima, on the other hand, rocketed down the street traveling at least 30 mph. Ritchie gave a huge yell of triumph, and then concentrated on keeping the vehicle under control. In less than two minutes, he was already on

Sycamore Street, and when he finally used the new braking system it brought them to a gentle stop right in front of the Pearson house.

Ritchie removed his helmet, and looked at the little sprite with eyes that were glowing with excitement and exhilaration.

"Fatima," he shouted at the top of his lungs, "you did it! That was supremely awesome. Did you get a look at Tony? He's going to have to take about fourteen showers to get all of that soot off of him. I mean, those guys didn't have the slightest chance of catching us. We left them in the dust, man."

Fatima grinned at him, obviously enjoying their awesome victory. Ritchie faced her as a look of realization crossed his face.

"I can't wait until Hannah and Darlene get home. They're never going to believe this, but you know what I just realized?"

Fatima shook her head in confusion.

"You cast the perfect magic spell. Everything happened exactly like it was supposed to, without any surprises. The girls are going to be so proud of you! C'mon, let's go sit on the stairs of Hannah's house and wait for them."

Fatima flew right behind Ritchie, as he ran across the street. All in all, the whole adventure had been an awful lot of fun. There was only one thing that she didn't understand. Why in the heck hadn't the darn thing started flying after she pushed the orange button, like it was supposed to? Oh well, she thought to herself, the kids don't need to know about that part; and she cheerfully sat down beside Ritchie to wait for the girls to come home.

CHAPTER 18

FATIMA'S MASTER PLAN

Not more than ten minutes later, Ritchie spotted Hannah and Darlene jogging down the street. By the time they made it to the front steps of the Flannigan house, they were both sweating freely and were completely out of breath. Hunched over with their hands on their knees, gasping for air, Hannah and Darlene stared at Ritchie and Fatima in amazement and disbelief. They kept glancing over at the fully intact Ritchiemobile, and then back at the obviously uninjured Ritchie with questioning expressions. Finally, Hannah was able to ask the most important question, in between gasps for air.

"Ritchie, how did you manage to escape from Tony Parsons and all seven of his friends?"

Ritchie just grinned at the girls, and then he and Fatima exchanged knowing looks. Irritated by their continued silence, Darlene piped up next. "Yeah, and why did we just run past and notice that all of them were either lying around nursing various injuries, or trying to push their mangled bikes down the street?"

Hannah nodded in agreement, before she suddenly remembered to ask one other question. "Oh yeah, and why was Tony Parsons completely covered in what looked like soot and motor exhaust?"

The last question resulted in Ritchie and Fatima finally ending their annoying silence. All of a sudden, they both started laughing uproariously, until tears streamed from their eyes and their stomach muscles began to ache. When their laughter eventually tapered off, Hannah and Darlene sat down on the steps beside them, and Ritchie generously allowed Fatima to tell them exactly what had happened. When she finished telling the girls about their grand adventure, Hannah and Darlene could only stare at her in awe and amazement. Darlene was the first one to break the silence.

"That is absolutely the most awesome story I've ever heard. It even beats the stories your dad's always telling about leprechauns and stuff," she said, turning to Hannah. Her best friend nodded her head vigorously, before adding a few comments of her own.

"Yeah, but you could have made it even better by changing the last part to something like, a dragon appeared and blew its fiery breath at Tony Parsons charring him blacker than a charcoal briquette, or something like that."

Ritchie and Fatima stared at each other with expressions of total confusion.

"What in the heck are you guys talking about?" Ritchie asked slowly. "Don't you believe us?"

"Well, guys," Hannah said seriously, "we just ran home the same way you went on the Ritchiemobile, and we certainly didn't see any evidence of oil slicks or thousands of marble. Although," she added thoughtfully, "it's obvious that you guys did something to Tony and his moronic friends, because they were in pretty bad shape. You and Fatima, on the other hand, don't have a single scratch on you. So c'mon, tell us the truth. What really happened?"

Ritchie just stared at her in disbelief, but Fatima clapped both hands over her mouth and started to giggle. Her tiny wings fluttered violently in an effort to suppress them, but she wasn't very successful. Ritchie turned his attention to the tiny sprite.

"What are you laughing at now?" he asked, obviously peeved. "It's not funny! They don't even believe us," he added in a tone of righteous indignation.

Fatima finally stopped giggling long enough to answer. "You guys forgot about one little thing."

"What?" they all asked in unison.

"You forgot the fact that all of those things were created by sprite magic. As soon as the oil and marbles served their purpose, they disappeared exactly like they're supposed to. I mean, gosh," she said with a snort of indignation, "how did you think we were going to explain a huge pool of oil or thousands of marbles appearing out of nowhere on the street in broad daylight? I mean, don't you think people might have been just a little suspicious? No way am I that stupid! Besides, this way Tony and his friends are going to be babbling about something that no one else saw, and that no one in their right mind is ever going to believe. They're going to look like a bunch of idiots. And I'll bet you a million bucks that they're going to be giving Ritchie a wide berth from now on," she finished, wiggling her eyebrows up and down mischievously.

Hannah stared at the chortling sprite, as realization dawned on her face. "You mean that whole story was true? That is so awesome! I'm just sorry we missed all of the excitement. But I guess you guys couldn't really wait for us, since you had eight bullies on your tail."

Hannah walked down to the curb and checked out the Ritchiemobile. Sure enough, right beside the red button on the little panel there were blue, black, and orange buttons also. The others had joined her down at the curb, and Ritchie was grinning proudly, as he stared at the Ritchiemobile.

"See," he said cockily," I told you Fatima made a few magical adjustments."

While the kids watched, the extra buttons suddenly disappeared, leaving the red button all by itself again. Ritchie blinked his eyes several times rapidly, and then turned to Fatima questioningly.

"Fatima, what happened to the other buttons?"

Fatima smiled sweetly at him before answering. "I'm afraid that I had to take them away, now that they've served their purpose."

"But I thought I'd get to keep them," Ritchie protested.

"Oh, no!" the sprite said quickly. "Sprite magic can only be used by a sprite, and while you're cute and all, you're certainly no sprite."

Ritchie's cheeks turned bright red after that statement.

"Besides, like you said yourself, the Ritchiemobile is already perfect and exactly the way you want."

Ritchie groaned, hearing his own words coming back to haunt him, and Fatima and the girls started laughing. Ritchie good-naturedly joined them. When they finished, Hannah asked the most important question of the day.

"Well, Fatima, what do we do now? I mean, what's the next part of your plan?"

Fatima grinned as she replied, "I'm glad you asked, because we all need to get working on it right away."

The kids formed a circle around her, and she carefully outlined the next phase of the plan she had designed to increase Hannah's popularity. Fatima had noticed all of the posters plastered up in the hallways at school, encouraging students to enter the upcoming elections. The positions available for 9th graders included class president, vice president, secretary, and treasurer. Fatima wasn't messing around with the small stuff anymore – she wanted Hannah to run for 9th grade Class President.

Hannah's immediate reaction was to say, no way; but after ten or fifteen minutes of persuasion, Fatima, Ritchie, and Darlene had finally talked her into it. Although Hannah still seemed somewhat reluctant, she gradually thawed to the idea, and eventually threw herself whole-heartedly into the planning. But they were going to have to move quickly, because the candidates had to give their initial speeches explaining why they were entering the race, on Friday at the Homecoming assembly; and that was only two days away.

Moving upstairs to Hannah's room, the little group had hammered out a solid plan by the time they were each called away to dinner. Darlene and Ritchie's job would be to make and display the campaign posters and buttons for the election. Hannah's duty was to write her campaign speech, which had to be awesome in order to persuade as many students as possible to vote for her. Finally, Fatima promised to use her magic to start increasing Hannah's popularity, before the election even took place. Unfortunately, that was all she'd reveal to the kids at this point. They would just have to be patient and wait to see how she was going to do that.

There was one more part of Fatima's plan, and that involved the 8th grade creative writing contest. Fatima had remembered Hannah mentioning the contest during her last visit to the Human World, and the deadline was now just around the corner. In fact, the entries for the contest were all due tomorrow, and Mr. McKenzie and the other two English teachers would be the judges. They would select a winner from the 8th grade boys, and a winner from the 8th grade girls. The winning papers would be read by Mr. McKenzie during the Homecoming assembly, and Fatima figured that the extra exposure could only improve Hannah's chances of becoming Class President next year.

Hannah had already finished her paper, which was entitled "The Magic of Friendship," and she just needed to check through it one more time that evening. Unfortunately, she was supposed to baby-sit Sean Adam's little sisters that evening, but she figured she should have some time that night to get that done. Fatima read through the paper while Hannah was eating dinner, and proclaimed it an outstanding paper that was sure to win the contest.

After dinner, Hannah put the paper into her backpack, along with the rest of her homework, and went downstairs to get her bike out of the garage. Fatima used Twinkle to become invisible once again, and then climbed into Hannah's backpack for the ride over to the Adams' house. When they got there, Mr. Adams was getting ready to head off to his evening job. He handed

Hannah ten dollars, and told her that Sean should be back from football practice around 9:00 PM. The team was having an extra long practice that day, as well as the next day, to get ready for the Homecoming game on Friday night. The Roseveldt Pirates needed to win that game in order to go to the State Championships.

Hannah pocketed the money, and then she and the girls waved good-bye to Mr. Adams. Sean's little sisters were Bethany, who was eight years old, and Charity, who was six years old. They were good little kids, but they were very energetic, and by the time she was able to put them to bed at 8PM, she was fairly exhausted. At least now she had an hour to put the finishing touches on her paper, and complete the rest of her homework. While Hannah was totally engrossed in that, Fatima took the opportunity to snoop around Sean's room. Her goal was to discover similarities between Sean and Hannah, and use that information to prove to them how compatible they would be together. What she found was even better.

While searching through Sean's desk, she discovered a paper he had written recently. A note scribbled on the front page written by Sean himself, seemed to indicate that Sean had written the paper intending to turn it in for the creative writing contest, but had then decided not to; probably because of a mixture of self-doubt and embarrassment.

Fatima quickly read through the paper and absolutely loved it. It was all about the importance of family and friends, and it used some beautiful metaphors as well as numerous quaint quotations from famous figures in history. After she finished reading it, she knew in her heart that his paper would easily win the creative writing contest for the 8th grade boys. There was no way she was going to let Sean miss out on this opportunity. Besides, she truly believed that if he and Hannah both won the writing contest, Sean would start to see how much they had in common. Then he might dump that stupid, snotty cheerleader.

Waving Twinkle over the paper, she made it invisible and then shrunk it down so that it fit in the pouch on her belt. When Hannah turned in her paper tomorrow, Fatima would slip Sean's paper underneath it so that his would be turned in, also. Hearing voices below, Fatima flew downstairs and discovered that Sean had returned home. He and Hannah were talking about the upcoming Homecoming game and assembly. After they had finished talking, Hannah said good-bye, and she and Fatima headed back home on her bike. When they got back to the Flannigan home, Hannah hurriedly finished her remaining homework, and then they got ready for bed. As the girls relaxed in their beds, they talked again about their plans for the next couple days.

Tomorrow at school, Hannah would be turning in her paper for the creative writing contest, and would also be turning in her application to run for Class President. Then, that afternoon and evening, she would be writing her candidate's speech for the assembly the next day, while Darlene and Ritchie would be making the posters and buttons for her campaign. On the next day, Friday, there would be the announcement of the winners of the creative writing contest, and then the speeches for the class election would be given at the Homecoming assembly. Friday night would be the Homecoming football game, and the kids (along with Fatima) would definitely be going to that.

The next morning Hannah felt as if a circus of butterflies were performing somersaults in her stomach. She wasn't at all sure that she wanted to go through with the whole running for class president thing, but Darlene and Ritchie managed to successfully persuade her to follow through with their original plan. Everything almost came to a crashing halt, though, when Hannah went to pick up the application in the school office, and discovered whom she would be running against.

Of course, she should have guessed that Erika Scott would be running for president. But when she discovered that fact, she felt her heart drop into her stomach, and she almost refused to complete the application right then and there. Luckily, Darlene and Ritchie presented a strong front of support, and the tiny voice of encouragement in her right ear certainly helped, too. With renewed resolve, she decided to continue following their plan, but it was obviously going to be much harder than she had originally anticipated. But what did she have to lose? Just the whole election, she thought miserably, when Darlene posed the question to her.

At the beginning of their English Literature class, Hannah walked up to the front and turned in her entry for the creative writing contest. Mr. McKenzie gave her a big smile, which she promptly returned, and then whispered good luck to her before she returned to her seat. Little did she know that underneath her paper, Fatima had placed the paper of Sean's that she had "borrowed" the night before. When class ended, Mr. McKenzie reminded everyone that their papers would be judged that afternoon, and the winners would be announced during the next day's class. The winners' papers would then be read by him at the Homecoming assembly.

The rest of the school day passed uneventfully, and immediately after school the three friends gathered in Hannah's bedroom to complete their assigned duties. Ritchie and Darlene spread their materials out on the floor, and set to work making the campaign posters and buttons for Hannah's presidential run. Hannah sat at her desk, writing out the campaign speech she would be giving during the next day's assembly.

All three of them were quiet, intently concentrated on their tasks, and Fatima found herself growing quickly bored. Rummaging around in Hannah's backpack for a piece of paper to write down some plans of her own, she happened upon the miniature tape recorder that Tony Parsons had used to sabotage their robot. After playing around with it for awhile, she managed to figure out exactly how it worked. Suddenly, a devious plan began to form in the little sprite's brain.

Looking around the room, she confirmed that her friends were deeply absorbed in their own projects, and thus wouldn't be paying the slightest bit of attention to her. Fatima grabbed the tape recorder and flew into Hannah's parents' bedroom. Noticing the phone and phone book sitting on the table beside their bed, she settled down and got to work. First, she looked up Justine Bateman's number, and then dialed it carefully. When Justine answered the phone, Fatima quickly punched the "record" button on the tape recorder. Pretending that she had gotten the wrong number, she was able to capture Justine's voice on the tape, before she hung up. After playing back the short conversation, and listening to it very carefully, she was able to use Twinkle to change her own voice into an exact duplication of Justine's.

Satisfied that she sounded exactly like the friendly cheerleader, she looked up Erika Scott's phone number, and then proceeded to dial it. While she waited for someone to answer, she rewound the tape back to the beginning so she would be ready to record the ensuing conversation. As luck would have it, Erika answered the phone almost immediately. Using Justine's voice, Fatima began what would turn out to be a long, and particularly revealing, conversation. Erika fell for the trick; hook, line, and sinker. By copying Justine's voice, Fatima was able to ask Erika numerous leading questions which encouraged her to vent about a lot of her so-called friends, as well as a bunch of the other kids at school.

The telephone conversation ended up lasting for an entire thirty minutes, and Erika did most of the talking. While I can't repeat the conversation word for word, I can tell you that Erika managed to make numerous offensive comments about an awful lot of the students in the 8th grade class. Just a few examples included her calling Annika a copycat and a show-off; calling the other cheerleaders untalented idiots who couldn't get a single cheer routine right; calling Tony Parsons a rich snob who looked ridiculous with his shaved head; and calling most of the other 8th graders stupid little sheep who would do whatever she told them to do.

But perhaps the most surprising were her comments about Sean Adams, whom she had been dating for almost six months now. When Justine (a.k.a. Fatima) asked how their relationship was going, Erika's answer was that she was getting quite bored with him, because he spent too much time on his homework; and wasted a lot of time playing with his younger sisters, instead of spending time with her. She finished by stating that if he spoke to Hannah at school one more time, she was going to dump him right on the spot.

Finally, Erika said she had to get off the phone because her mother was taking her shopping for new clothes, yet again. Fatima hung up the phone, and then pushed the "stop" button on the tape recorder. She rewound the tape and played it back to make sure the recording had been successful. After listening to the entire conversation, she erased or edited out the parts that were either too boring or not mean enough. The result was a lovely fifteen minute rant by Erika, in which she managed to criticize or put down over half of the 8th graders at school. Fatima had big plans for the tape. She intended to play it over the PA system at school some time in the next few days. When the other students heard what Erika really thought of them, they would definitely not be voting for her as Class President. In fact, the tape would virtually guarantee that Hannah would be winning the election by a landslide.

The only problem that remained would be talking Hannah into letting her use the tape. From past experience, Fatima knew that Hannah considered truth and honesty to be very important. It was going to be a challenge, but Fatima figured that she would eventually be able to persuade Hannah to allow her to play the tape at school; once she explained how devastating it would be to Erika's run for president.

But just in case, she was going to make an extra copy of the tape with Twinkle's assistance. That way if Hannah made her give up the tape, she'd still have a backup. Fatima flew back to Hannah's room, where the kids were still busily working on their individual projects. Landing on the desk beside Hannah, Fatima asked Darlene and Ritchie to gather around them. She then explained where she had been for the last hour, and what she'd been doing.

Following her explanation, she placed the tape recorder on the desk in front of them, and proceeded to play the tape. She watched their faces as they listened to Erika's mean spirited tirade. Their expressions changed from disbelief to horror to downright anger by the time the recording had finished. Hannah looked at Fatima with obvious concern, while Fatima explained her devious plan. Her reaction was exactly what Fatima had been worried it would be.

Basically, she refused, under any circumstances, to allow Fatima to play that tape at school. She felt it was a dirty trick that would result in a lot of hurt feelings, and she had no intention of being part of something so petty and spiteful. At the end of her speech (after fully detailing for Fatima, once again, how she expected her actions to be guided by truthfulness and honesty), she held out her hand, and waited patiently for Fatima to give her the tape. Fatima, realizing it was a lost cause, reluctantly surrendered the tape and murmured a somewhat insincere apology.

The little sprite then retired to the sock drawer, where she ended up pouting for the rest of the evening. The kids cheerfully ignored her, however, and finished their projects right on time. After Ritchie and Darlene left for the evening, with the posters and buttons finished and ready to be distributed the next day, Hannah attempted to draw Fatima out of her little funk.

Fatima, however, refused to be comforted, and the girls went to bed that night with a frosty silence between them. But by the time the sun rose the next morning, the sprite seemed to have recovered her usual cheerful demeanor. Being careful not to mention the incident with the tape recorder the night before, Hannah happily accepted the fact that her friend seemed to have forgiven her. With their friendship back on track, they hurried off to school.

Today was going to be a very busy day. Darlene and Ritchie plastered the school's hallways with the posters they had made the night before, and handed out the campaign buttons urging everyone to vote for Hannah for Class President. Erika Scott took one look at their posters, and stomped off down the hall. But not before she loudly voiced her opinion on whom the obvious choice for president should be. Hannah was feeling extremely nervous about her upcoming speech at the assembly that afternoon. Her anxiety was temporarily forgotten, however, when Mr. McKenzie announced the winners of the creative writing contest during their 2nd period class. Hannah had won first place for the 8th grade girls, and Sean Adams had won first place for the 8th grade boys.

As soon as he heard the announcement, Sean looked up at Mr. McKenzie with a look of disbelief written all over his face. In reality, Sean was both stunned and confused. He hadn't even turned in his paper, because he was too worried about what his girlfriend and the other jocks would think about him entering a sissy writing contest. But as Mr. McKenzie moved around the classroom handing back the papers, he stopped at Sean's desk and laid his paper in front of him.

It was obviously the same paper that Sean had written last week, and later hid in his desk at home. But how in the world had it ended up in Mr. McKenzie's hands? Sean shook his head in complete bewilderment, as Mr. McKenzie offered him a smile of approval and a hearty congratulation. Apparently, he had made copies of the winning papers, and would be reading them both in front of the entire student body at the assembly later that day.

Sean closed his eyes in misery and sank down further in his chair. Dang! He was going to be teased about this for a long time to come. Opening his eyes and glancing about the room to see how the other students were reacting to the news, Sean's eyes happened to light upon Hannah. She was staring proudly down at the paper in front of her, and when she looked up, she caught his eye and gave him a huge glowing smile and a "thumbs up" sign. Sean returned the smile, and suddenly realized that he also felt a sense of pride.

Who cared what anyone else thought! He had written a good paper, and even if he didn't have any idea how Mr. McKenzie had gotten it, he should still be proud of his work. After all, he did want to be an author someday, and this was certainly a good start. He pushed himself up in his chair, and nodded his appreciation and thanks to several of the other students who offered their congratulations. As soon as the dismissal bell rang, he walked over to Hannah and congratulated her on her winning paper.

Sean walked out of the room with a feeling of pride, which lasted until lunchtime when Erika heard the news. As she flounced over to the table where he was sitting with his best friends, Shane and Paul, Sean could already tell by her expression what her response was going to be. She sat down beside him, and wound one of her blond curls around her finger.

"So, I heard you won some stupid writing contest. Why would you even care about something like that? I mean, you should be concentrating on football right now anyway, because if we lose tonight, we're out of the championship game; and that's much more important."

Sean couldn't help the irritation he immediately felt surge through him in response to her comments. "Why do you care about a football game? Usually you just gripe about how much time I spend on the field."

"Honestly, Sean, are you a total moron? The championships are televised, which means that the girls and I will be on TV, too. I've spent a lot of time coming up with some spectacular cheers, and I want the chance to perform them for someone besides the stupid kids who come to the games."

"Seems like you think there's a lot of stupid things around here," he said, gathering up his half-eaten lunch.

"Whatever," she said, as she tossed her hair back. "I just hope that it doesn't take too long for Mr. McKenzie to read your paper and the nerd's paper at the assembly, because I need to have enough time to give my speech for Class President."

"Actually," Sean said as he prepared to stalk off, "I think people will be a lot more interested in hearing Hannah's paper, than your speech." Then he was gone.

Erika just sat there in stunned silence, with her chin dropped down to her chest. She gave Shane and Paul, who were obviously trying very hard not to laugh, an icy stare before she flounced off again. As soon as she was gone, Paul gave Shane a high-five, and then they walked off to find Sean.

At 2:00 that afternoon the bell rang, and everyone rushed off to the auditorium for the Homecoming Assembly. Like always, Coach Harris was the first to speak. He spent five minutes rambling on about school spirit and how important that night's game was, before the microphone was taken over by Mr. McKenzie. Once again he announced the winners of the 8th grade creative writing contest; although by that time the news had already spread around the entire school.

First, he read Sean's paper. At the end there was general clapping, as well as some loud support from the jocks, who added a bunch of whoops and yells. Then he read Hannah's paper out loud to the group of students. For several seconds after he had finished, there was total silence in the auditorium. It was so quiet that you could have heard a pin drop. Hannah looked around nervously, before bending her head down to stare at her hands clenched in her lap. It was exactly what she had feared – everyone hated her story; and now she was going to have to go up there and give a stupid speech on top of everything else.

Hannah had just squeezed her eyes shut in total misery, when she began to hear some scattered clapping around the auditorium. Several seconds later, the clapping swelled to a roar. Hannah opened her eyes to peek around, and discovered that almost everyone in the room was standing up and clapping. Apparently, her paper had been a big hit! Hannah couldn't believe her ears; it sounded like everyone loved her paper. Maybe she had a shot at winning the election after all! While Mr. McKenzie waited for the applause to die down, he looked down at Hannah and Sean with a proud smile.

When the noise level had finally calmed down, he announced that it was time for the students running for class offices to speak. The applicants for secretary and treasurer would go first, followed by the students running for Vice President, and lastly, those running for President. Hannah felt her nervousness begin to increase, once again. She had never spoken in front of the entire school before, and didn't really relish the idea of starting now.

But if she was elected to the office of Class President, she'd be doing this kind of thing a lot, so she might as well try to get used to it. She filed up towards the front of the auditorium with the other candidates, who all lined up by the steps leading up to the stage. Sean, Shane, and Paul were sitting towards the front of the room, and she found herself standing right beside their seats. In spite of the fact that Erika was standing only a few feet away from them, Sean leaned over to whisper to Hannah.

"Hey, Hannah, congratulations once again on winning the writing contest. Your paper was truly awesome."

Hannah tried not to blush as she replied. "Thanks, Sean, you're paper was really good, too. You definitely deserved to win."

Sean broke into a easy grin, as he accepted her congratulations with a humble grace. "Good luck with your speech," he added sincerely.

"Yeah," Paul Andrews broke in, "maybe we'll be voting for you." He gave Hannah a cocky wink, totally oblivious to the frosty glares Erika was directing their way. "Hey, you look kind of nervous," Paul added. "Here you go; chew on a piece of gum for awhile to calm your nerves," he said thoughtfully.

Hannah accepted his offer gratefully. She popped the piece of gum in her mouth and chomped away. Surprisingly, it did seem to calm her nerves. She continued chewing until it was almost time for her speech. Then she quickly spit the gum out into her hand, as there was nowhere else to put it at the moment. Hearing her name called by Mr. McKenzie, she walked up to the podium and arranged her notes in front of her. She was concentrating so hard on the task at hand, that she didn't notice the few snickers breaking out from the students sitting directly in front of her.

Taking a deep breath to steady her nerves, she began speaking; glancing at her notes occasionally to make sure she was staying on track. She also reminded herself to glance up often while she was talking, and to remember to smile frequently. She had barely gotten a third of the way through her speech, when she began to notice that a large number of the students were snickering or laughing openly.

Thoroughly confused, she searched the auditorium until she found the spot where Darlene and Ritchie were sitting. Darlene had a desperate look on her face, as she kept pointing at her mouth, and then at Hannah. Attempting to continue her speech, she racked her brain for an explanation for Darlene's behavior. To make up for the lapse in her concentration, she gave the room a big smile and reshuffled her notes.

At that point, it seemed as if everyone in the auditorium was laughing and pointing up at the stage. Looking for support, Hannah turned towards Mr. McKenzie with a questioning look on her face. Mr. McKenzie stood up and walked over to the podium. Stepping away from the microphone, Hannah happened to glance over towards Sean. Paul and Shane were laughing hysterically, punching each other on the shoulder and sneaking glances in Hannah's direction. Sean, on the other hand, was sitting with his arms crossed over his chest, a stormy look on his face. As Hannah watched him, he leaned over and said something to Paul and Shane. They immediately stopped laughing, and Paul looked up and gave Hannah an apologetic glance along with a shrug of his shoulders.

At that point, Hannah suddenly had an inkling of what might be happening. She unclenched her hand, and looked at the piece of gum she had just spit out. The gum was coal black, and her hand had numerous black smudges from holding on to it. Paul, ever the practical jokester, had given her a piece of trick gum – the kind that turned black once you chewed it; making your teeth, mouth, and lips black, too. That was what all the laughing was about. No one had even been listening to her speech because they were too busy laughing at her black smile. Honestly, she thought to herself, how did I manage to fall for that? Hannah looked behind her where Erika Scott was standing, waiting for her turn to speak. Erika gave her a huge grin with a look of pure triumph in her eyes.

Hannah allowed Mr. McKenzie to lead her away from the podium. She was desperately trying to hold back the tears which threatened to spill down her face. As she walked by Sean and his friends on her way out of the auditorium, Sean slipped out of his seat and followed her out into the hallway. As soon as the door to the auditorium had closed behind them, Sean caught up to her and begged her to wait until he had a chance to explain. Hannah stopped walking and turned around to face him. Sean was momentarily distracted by the look of anguish on her face, but he took a deep breath, and began to speak.

"Hannah, I'm really sorry about what happened in there. I had no idea that the piece of gum Paul gave you wasn't just a regular piece of gum. I'm going to rip his arms off for doing that to you; I can promise you that. He always has to be the practical joker, and it's time he realized that his jokes can really hurt people. He asked me to apologize to you for him, but I think that's something he needs to do himself. It's probably not any consolation, but just so you know, he admitted that Erika was the one who put him up to it. I'm really sorry."

Hannah looked into his eyes, and saw the honesty behind his words. She lifted her head up high and squared her shoulders before answering.

"That's okay, Sean. I know it wasn't your fault. Besides, it was just a joke. Don't worry, I'll get over it," she said with a brave smile.

Sean smiled uncertainly, and then hesitated before adding one more thing. "Just so you know, I'm going to be voting for you."

Hannah gave him a radiant smile, until she remembered that her teeth were black at the moment. She quickly put her hand over her mouth, and nodded her thanks to him. Then she turned around, and gave him a wave over her shoulder. Heading into the girls' bathroom, she stood in front of the sink and began rinsing out her mouth, attempting to wash the black color off of her teeth and lips.

When she raised her head to look in the mirror, Fatima suddenly appeared in the mirror's reflection standing on her shoulder, giving Hannah a shock at her abrupt appearance. The little sprite looked very angry, and Hannah immediately began trying to calm her down. After a spirited tirade, Fatima finally wound down and the ranting and raving eventually ended, giving Hannah cause to sigh in relief. She explained to Fatima that as soon as she finished at the sink, they could head home and put this whole incident behind them.

However, as Fatima watched her best friend calmly go about her business, the anger she felt deep in the pit of her stomach began to intensify. Nobody was going to treat her best friend like that and get away with it. Inside her little head, her brain was feverishly working on a plan for revenge – Paul Andrews and Erika Scott were going to pay for their behavior; and the price was going to be quite high.

CHAPTER 19

REVENGE OF THE SPRITE

By the time Hannah had finished scrubbing all traces of the gum from her lips and teeth, the dismissal bell had already rung. Hannah locked herself in one of the bathroom stalls, and waited there for ten or fifteen minutes. She was hoping to escape from the school without being seen by any of the other students, and hiding out in the bathroom for awhile would be her best chance of doing that.

Hopefully, Darlene and Ritchie would wait outside for her, because she really didn't want to walk home all by herself today. Originally, they had planned on going to the Homecoming football game tonight, but after her experience today, she wasn't sure that she wanted to go to an event that most of the school would be attending. Oh well, she thought to herself, I'll have to face them all again sooner or later, so I might as well get it over with tonight. Besides, she didn't want to miss an opportunity to watch Sean play.

After fifteen minutes of waiting, Fatima was beginning to show signs of impatience, so Hannah decided that they could finally head home. Leaving the girls' restroom, with an invisible Fatima back in her customary place, Hannah peeked out the door and glanced both ways. The school hallways were pretty much empty. No kid in their right mind would hang around school any longer than they had to; especially on a Friday afternoon.

Hannah snuck out of the bathroom and ran down the hall to exit out the door on the side of the building. She hurried across the front lawn at an angle, so she could reach the street running by the front of the school in as little time as possible. Thankfully, there were only a few students still present on the school grounds, and none of them seemed to notice her. Hunching her shoulders in a protective gesture, she kept her eyes cast down at the toes of her shoes, and walked as quickly as she could without drawing attention to herself. The only creature that noticed her hasty departure was a chubby gray squirrel that chattered noisily at her, irritated that she had disturbed its spring foraging for discarded acorns. In spite of the hectic afternoon she'd just experienced, she couldn't prevent the smile which sprang to her lips from watching the squirrel's noisy display.

Once Hannah reached the street in front of the school, she jogged down it for two blocks, and then turned right on Sycamore Street. From there it was a straight shot to her house, and she only had four more blocks to go. Feeling much safer once she reached her own street, she slowed down to a fast walk. Ritchie and Darlene had either grown tired of waiting for her, or they had decided that she had already headed home.

Sure enough, as she got closer to her house she could see that they were both sitting down on her front steps waiting for her. They stood up as she walked towards them, and she immediately noticed the worried expressions on their faces. She flashed them a smile to reassure them that she was just fine, and their expressions immediately changed to ones of relief.

Hannah swung her backpack off her left shoulder before sitting down on her front steps. Ritchie and Darlene promptly joined her, watching her face carefully, while they waited for her to speak. Hannah let out a big sigh, wracking her brain for something to say. There just wasn't a way to get around the fact that she'd made a fool of herself in front of the entire school. Finally, she opened her mouth and just let the first words that came to mind spill out.

"Well, that was certainly an embarrassing experience. I think that my chances of winning the election for Class President might be somewhat affected by my performance at the assembly. I'm probably not going to get 100% of the votes anymore," she said, in an attempt to inject some humor into the situation.

Neither Darlene nor Ritchie seemed to find the situation very funny, however. Hannah tried again.

"It's okay, guys! It's not that big of a deal in the first place. I never thought for a minute that I seriously had a chance of beating Erika Scott anyway."

Darlene and Ritchie both opened their mouths to speak at the same time, when Fatima suddenly appeared between them. The little sprite was obviously still angry about the incident at the assembly, and she let them all know it in no uncertain terms.

"That stupid prank is going to come back to haunt them both! Erika Scott and Paul Andrews are on my black list now, and they're going to pay for their little stunt. I sure hope it was worth it," she seethed.

Looking somewhat alarmed, Hannah quickly interrupted before Fatima could continue her rant.

"Fatima, I already told you that we need to put this behind us and move on. We just need to come up with a new plan now. We still have plenty of time before you need to return to Fairy Town, so let's use that time wisely, and not get sidetracked by attempting to plot some type of revenge. Besides, if we start thinking like that, then we'll only be bringing ourselves down to their level. And that's something we are definitely NOT going to do!"

Hannah continued staring at Fatima, even after she had finished her little speech. She wanted the sprite to know that she was completely serious about letting this go without any sort of retaliation. Fatima glared back at her for several minutes. Ultimately, it was Fatima who broke eye contact, as she looked over at Darlene and Ritchie for support. They both looked away quickly, and she realized that she was on her own. Putting an apologetic expression on her face, she glanced back at Hannah and nodded her head mutely. If her best friend wanted her to drop it, then she would for now. But if Hannah expected her to forgive and forget, then she was going to be in for a bit of a surprise later. Until that time, Fatima could pretend to go along with the plan.

Satisfied that she had successfully made her point, Hannah smiled at her friends, and then clapped her hands together briskly several times.

"Well, what are we waiting for? We have a football game to go to later. Let's get changed and eat, and then we'll head over to the football field on our bikes." Her friends readily agreed, and headed off to their own houses to get ready.

Two hours later, they all met back at Hannah's house. The game would start in about half an hour. Patrick was going with some of his friends, and Brian Adams had already stopped by to pick him up. Hannah's parents were going too, and Tom offered to give the kids a ride to the field, but they politely declined. Instead, they mounted their bikes and rode off towards the school.

Although football had never been one of Hannah's favorite sports, she was actually eagerly anticipating tonight's game. Sean would be quarterbacking, and she was always thrilled to watch him play. Plus, if they won tonight's game, they would advance to the state championships, and that hadn't happened for the last six years. They just had to win this game!

By the time the kids reached the football field, the stands were almost full. The excitement in the air was palpable and contagious, and it seemed as if the whole town had decided to attend this game. In spite of the fact that the day had been sunny and unseasonably warm, a chill had arrived as the sun descended, and everyone was bundled up in bright jackets and sweaters. Looking around the field, it appeared that every color in a large box of crayons was represented.

Squeezing through the crowd, the kids managed to find three seats together at the top of the students section of the bleachers. The Pirates were just finishing their warm-ups, and Hannah was easily able to locate Sean down on the field. The three friends were so excited about the upcoming game that they had completely forgotten about their little friend. Hannah had even neglected to admonish Fatima to be on her best behavior and stay out of trouble; a fact which would come back to haunt her later. While the kids waited for the game to start, they had absolutely no idea that Fatima was no longer in their company.

The truth was that as soon as her friends had taken their seats, Fatima had flown down to the sidelines to do a little investigating. The football players had finished their warm-up drills, and were gathered around Coach Harris for his pre-game speech. All of the boys had removed their helmets so that they would have no trouble hearing their coach's words. Fatima had no difficulty finding Paul Andrews, and figuring this would be her best opportunity to put her devious plan into action, she hovered over his helmet and waved Twinkle around. Satisfied that her magic spell was in place, she flew over to the Pirate's bench, sat down, and waited for the game to start.

Several minutes later, the head referee blew his piercing whistle, and the fight for the football began. Meanwhile, up in the bleachers, Hannah and her friends had run into Patrick and Brian. Talking briefly to them, Hannah learned from Brian that Paul had already received his punishment from his father regarding the incident at the assembly. Being the Vice Principal, Mr. Andrews had been an eyewitness to the prank, and he had no trouble discovering who the culprit was. Paul had better enjoy the game tonight, because he wasn't going to be enjoying much else for awhile.

Apparently, he had been given a weeks detention at school, as well as additional punishments at home, which included being grounded for two weeks and losing his allowance for an entire month. Mr. Andrews also expected him to publicly apologize to Hannah at school on Monday. After hearing this news, Hannah almost felt sorry for Paul, and she personally felt that he had been punished more than enough. She intended to accept his apology gracefully next week, and assure him that there weren't any hard feelings.

Down on the field, the Kootenai Tigers were driving towards the end zone with remarkable ease. The defensive players for the Pirates seemed nervous and tight, and the Tigers were having no problem running the ball down the field. But just when it seemed that a touchdown was inevitable, one of the Pirates was able to intercept a pass and run it back halfway down the field. Now it was Sean and the offenses' turn. With Sean at quarterback, Shane as the top receiver, and Paul as the star tight end, the Pirates had the #1 passing offense in the league. It was time for them to show the Tigers what they were up against. Sean began tossing passes right and left, and Shane and the other receivers made catch after awesome catch until the Pirates were down on the 5-yard line, ready to score.

In these situations, Sean usually faked a hand-off to the running back, and then threw a short pass to Paul in the end zone for a touchdown. Everything went as planned, until Paul dropped the pass which had been thrown perfectly to him. The Pirates tried to run the ball into the end zone, but they were stopped at the two-yard line. Planning another throw to their tight end, they ran the play which usually guaranteed them six points. Unfortunately, the pass was supposed to be to Paul on the right side of the end zone, and Paul had run over to the left side of the end zone instead. Sean couldn't get the ball to him over there, and ended up being sacked for a loss of five yards. Instead of a touchdown, the Pirates had to settle for a field goal, which gave them a 3-0 lead.

As the offense came off the field, Sean jogged over to Paul for an explanation.

"Why didn't you run the right route?' he asked his tight end, obviously irritated.

"Because someone kept yelling at me to go left, and I got confused. It's like there's a voice in my helmet or something. That's why I dropped that first pass. Just as the ball got to me, someone screamed in my ears. It scared me so badly, that I dropped the dang ball." After finishing that statement, he removed his football helmet and peered inside with a perplexed look on his face. Sean was staring at him, wondering if his friend was going crazy.

"What are you talking about? Are you going looney tunes on me? There's nothing in your helmet, Paul. Now get your mind on the game, or we're going to lose!"

Sean slapped him on the shoulder pads, and then walked over to Coach Harris to get his instructions for the next offensive series. Paul shook his head back and forth, continuing to examine the inside of his helmet. He really hadn't expected Sean to understand, because he didn't know what was going on himself. Every time he tried to run a route or catch a pass, a voice would start yelling in his ear, and then he'd lose his concentration. It sounded like it was coming from inside his helmet, but that was impossible.

Several feet away, an invisible sprite sat with a devious grin on her face. Her spell was working perfectly. The voice that Paul was hearing in his helmet was hers, of course. She intended to make sure that Paul didn't catch a single pass that night. Then, when the Pirates ended up losing, the entire team and all of the other students would blame him. That should teach him not to play practical jokes on other people, she thought angrily.

The rest of the first half of the game was virtually identical to the first offensive series. Paul continued to run the wrong routes, and when Sean was able to throw a pass to him, in spite of him being in the wrong place, he dropped the ball every time. With only two minutes to go until half-time, the Pirates were behind 24-6. They desperately needed to score a touchdown before the game clock ran down. So far they had only managed to score two fieldgoals.

Coach Harris called Paul out of the game with their next time out. Pointing at the bench behind him with his thumb, he took Paul out of the game and replaced him with another boy. Paul hunched his shoulders in shame, as he walked over to the bench and sat down heavily. Once again he removed his helmet, and peered inside with a sense of desperation. What in the world was going on?

Suddenly a roar of applause came from the bleachers behind him. The Pirates had finally scored a touchdown. Yeah, Paul thought bitterly, they just needed to get me off the field. Swinging his helmet down beside him, he headed towards the tunnel which led to their locker room. He needed to settle down and get his act together, or the coach was going to bench him for the rest of the game. Hearing his name called, he looked up into the stands and spotted Sean's brother, Brian. Paul spent so much time over at the Adams' house that Brian was almost like a big brother to him.

"What's going on with you?" Brian called to him.

Paul walked up to the railing where he could talk a little more privately. "Something's wrong with my helmet. I know this is going to sound crazy, but it's yelling at me," he said helplessly.

Brian arched his eyebrows in disbelief, but before he could reply, the Coach's bellow broke into their conversation.

"Andrews, get your butt back to that locker room now!" he boomed. Paul gave Brian a look of pure misery, and then trotted into the tunnel. Brian shook his head slowly as he headed back towards his seat by Patrick.

"Well, what's going on with him?" Patrick asked as soon as Brian sat back down.

"I don't know, dude. He said something about a voice in his helmet. I think he's losing his mind, man," Brian exclaimed, twirling his finger around his ear.

From their seats right behind the boys, Hannah, Darlene, and Ritchie managed to overhear the entire conversation. Hannah mulled their words over in her mind, curious about Paul's weird explanation. All of a sudden, she sat bolt upright as a possibility occurred to her. Turning to face her two friends, she noticed that they also had looks of comprehension slowly appearing on their faces.

"Fatima," they all said in unison. Hannah carefully reached up to her right shoulder and felt around. Her hand discovered nothing but empty air.

"She's gone," she replied, in answer to her friends' questioning expressions. "Let's go find her," she stated, and they all got up and filed out of the bleachers.

"Okay, here's the plan, guys. We're going to start calling her name, and if anyone asks us what we're doing, then we say we're looking for my dog that ran off." Hannah looked at Darlene and Ritchie expectantly. "Okay," they both said together, "let's go."

The kids began wandering around the field calling Fatima's name. You can only imagine Fatima's surprise when she heard her name floating by on the evening's gentle breeze. Quickly locating her friends, she flew over and landed on Hannah's shoulder. Feeling the sudden weight, Hannah quit yelling and motioned for Darlene and Ritchie to come back. When they were all together again, the kids walked to a spot behind the bleachers, where they could safely question the little sprite. Hannah handled the interrogation.

"Fatima, where have you been?" she whispered.

"I was just looking around," Fatima said in an innocent tone.

"Something is going on with Paul Andrews, and I think you know what it is."

"What are you talking about?" Fatima asked. "I haven't even been near him."

Hannah just stood there in silence, while the sprite began fidgeting nervously. Finally she spoke again. "Remember our talk about the importance of truth and honesty in a friendship?" Hannah waited for her comment to sink in before she spoke again. "Well, I guess you really don't know what's going on, because I know you wouldn't lie to me."

After hearing these words from her best friend, Fatima finally broke down. "Okay, I confess. I bewitched Paul's helmet so that I could yell stuff at him while he's playing. I'm the reason he's been doing so poorly. I just wanted to teach him a lesson after what he did to you today," she said in a pleading tone.

"I knew you were involved," Hannah whispered accusingly between clenched teeth. "Well I hope you're proud of yourself, because now we're probably going to lose this game, and miss out on going to the playoffs. In order to get back at Paul for a stupid, little joke, you've managed to punish the rest of the football team, as well as the whole school. I sure hope you're happy with your decision," Hannah said frostily, crossing her arms over her chest.

Fatima felt totally ashamed of herself. "I'm sorry," she whispered into Hannah's ear. "I promise to fix everything; you'll see." And with those words, the sprite was gone.

Hannah shook her head in disgust, and then passed Fatima's admission on to Ritchie and Darlene, both of whom mimicked her response. The little group then trudged back up towards their seats at the top of the bleachers. Half-time was nearly over, and the Pirates were just running back onto the field for the second half of play. Hannah winced as she watched Coach Harris grab Paul Andrew's face mask, while yelling and waving his other arm around. In spite of his obvious frustration with his star tight end, it looked like the coach was going to give Paul a chance to redeem himself, and Hannah sighed in relief. Fatima better fix everything like she promised, she thought grimly.

As it turned out, she didn't need to worry about that after all. The team that walked out onto the field in the second half looked nothing like the team that had fumbled their way through the first half. It became obvious after several minutes of play that the Roseveldt Pirates were themselves once again. As Sean completed pass after pass, the Tigers tried everything they could to stop the Pirates from scoring, but were woefully unsuccessful. The final score was the Pirates 27 and the Tigers 24. The Roseveldt Pirates would be heading to the playoffs for the first time in six years, and the players and students were celebrating wildly. Paul had played a spectacular 2nd half, and ended up scoring both of their 2nd half touchdowns.

Coach Harris patted himself on the back for getting through to his tight end with his half-time speech. Actually, Fatima's reversal of the spell she had placed on his helmet was the real reason Paul's playing had improved so dramatically, but no one besides Hannah and her friends needed to know that. The kids ended up staying for the post-game bonfire celebration, and then rode their bikes home for the night.

The mood in Hannah's bedroom that night was somber. Hannah quietly got ready for bed, while Fatima sat in the sock drawer watching her friend anxiously. Hannah hadn't spoken a single word to her since their heated discussion at half-time, and Fatima was close to tears. Hannah had already gotten into bed and switched off the light, before Fatima had screwed up her courage enough to speak.

"Hannah," she said in a quavering voice, "are you still mad at me?" She heard a heavy sigh from the other side of the room, and waited in agonizing silence for her friend's answer.

Finally, Hannah replied. "No, I'm not angry anymore, but I am very disappointed in you." Fatima winced when she heard those words, recalling her father saying the same thing to her on numerous occasions. "I want you to promise me that you won't do anything like that ever again. Being a good friend means being truthful and honest to each other, and if you're doing stuff like that behind my back, then you're not being a good friend."

Fatima took a moment to digest Hannah's words before she replied. "I understand, and I promise to be a much better friend in the future," she said quietly.

When Hannah answered, the warmth had returned to her voice. "Okay, but I'm going to hold you to that promise forever – or at least until you're 300 years old." The girls giggled together, their friendship intact once again. Both of them slept well that night, and the next morning the sunlight streaming through the blinds guaranteed a beautiful spring day. Hannah decided that they needed to put all of the planning aside for the next two days, and just concentrate on enjoying the weekend; and their restored friendship. When Darlene and Ritchie came over later that morning, she told them her idea and they both agreed it was a good one.

After an hour or so of brainstorming, they decided that the entire weekend should be spent entertaining Fatima by showing her all the fun things there were to do in the Human World. The sprite had only been to their world on three occasions, and each time she had been focusing on fulfilling Hannah's wish in order to complete her obligation as a sprite. Now it was time for her to have a little bit of fun. It didn't require much persuasion to get Fatima to agree, and the rest of that weekend was filled with fun and laughter.

The kids took Fatima to play miniature golf, which she won; although they suspected she cheated by using Twinkle more than her golf club, and they also took her to the movie theater. She loved the movie, which was about a boy witch named Harry Potter, but ended up eating way too much popcorn. Saturday ended with a giant-sized tummy ache for the little sprite, but all in all the day was wonderfully enjoyable.

The next day was sunny and warm once again, and the kids took their guest to a picnic at a little park in their neighborhood. When no one else was around, they took turns pushing her on one of the swings. It was a blast to watch because once they had pushed the swing as high as it would go, Fatima would sail off and then glide down for a safe landing. They ate peanut butter sandwiches, fruit, and cookies, and then played tag on the monkey bars. Fatima was hardly ever it because as soon as one of the kids got close enough to tag her, she'd just fly away.

That afternoon they took her down to the lake, and although it wasn't yet warm enough to swim, they built sand castles by the water and allowed Fatima to pretend that she was the fairy queen of the castle. Near sunset, they rented a paddleboat and pedaled it around the lake. In spite of the fact that she lived in the spectacular World of Fairy, Fatima had to admit that the Human World possessed a beauty of its own, and she was glad she had gotten to share it with her best friends.

On their way home that evening, they finally discussed what their plan would be for the upcoming week at school. Although the whole gum incident had been extremely embarrassing, Fatima was still of the opinion that Hannah should continue the race for 9th grade Class President, and Ritchie and Darlene readily agreed with her. Hannah was still feeling rather hesitant and reluctant about the whole thing, but she eventually allowed her friends to talk her into it.

The candidate's next round of speeches would be on Wednesday, and the election would then be held on Friday. Fatima wasn't at all sure that she would still be around by then, because her vacation could be ending at almost any time now. However, if she did have to leave before the election results were released, she promised to sneak back afterwards to find out who had won.

Winning the election would virtually assure Hannah of an increase in her popularity, and Fatima felt that Sean Adams was really starting to like Hannah. In fact, Fatima's ultimate goal was that the two of them would be chosen as the prince and princess for the 8th graders at the Prom held at the end of the school year. Hannah scoffed at that announcement. If Sean and Erika weren't chosen as this year's prince and princess, then the world would probably fall off it axis and quit spinning.

At any rate, running for Class President seemed like enough of a challenge at this point, and Hannah just wanted to make it through the week without another disaster. They all agreed that would be a major accomplishment. With plans to meet in front of Hannah's house the next morning, Darlene and Ritchie headed home.

Hannah spent the hour or two until bedtime, finishing up the homework she had cheerfully neglected all weekend. It had definitely been worth it though, because they had all had a blast the last two days. Hannah fell asleep instantly that night, pleasantly exhausted from the whirlwind of activity that weekend. Fatima, however, lay awake well into the night. She still had an important decision to make, and she was no closer to figuring it out than she'd been when she first went to bed. On one hand, she felt that if she played the tape she'd made of Erika's conversation, Hannah would be guaranteed to win the election. On the other hand, Hannah had specifically asked her not to, and she had promised not to go behind Hannah's back anymore. Fatima heaved a great big sigh, desperately wishing that her Aunt Fantastica was here to help her with her decision. In the end, she decided that she would simply have to follow her heart in this matter – and that is just what she did.

CHAPTER 20

A BROKEN FRIENDSHIP

The next morning Hannah woke up to face her least favorite day of the week – Monday. Hannah hated Mondays with a passion, and it was her firm opinion that nothing good ever happened on a Monday. This day would prove to be no exception. Hannah noticed that Fatima seemed quiet and withdrawn that morning, rather than her usual cheerful and bubbly self. When Hannah questioned her, Fatima told her friend that she hadn't slept very well the night before. This was a truthful enough statement, because the sprite had tossed and turned for most of the night, while she attempted to make a decision regarding the tape.

There had been numerous instances during that long and sleepless night when Fatima had wished that she had never recorded the tape in the first place. If that had been the case, she wouldn't have been faced with the difficult decision she had wrestled with all night. But unfortunately, she had recorded the tape, and now she had to decide what to do with it. She could either destroy the tape, and pretend that it had never existed, or she could trick her best friend and play the tape over the school's PA system like she had originally planned.

Fatima felt that Erika certainly deserved to have her spiteful words reach the ears of the other students. She would equally deserve the bitter reactions that would certainly follow from the students she had made negative comments about. Hopefully, the result would be that a lot of the students would no longer be voting for her in the upcoming election, and maybe Sean would even break up with her.

Thus, in one fell swoop, Fatima could fulfill Hannah's wish and successfully achieve her obligation as dictated by the Sprite Code of Honor. The one downside to this decision was that she would be breaking her promise to Hannah. She fully realized how much importance Hannah placed on truth and honesty, and by playing the tape she would be willfully ignoring that. But if she didn't play the tape, she had absolutely no idea how she was supposed to fulfill Hannah's wish. Even with her magic to fall back on, she had completely run out of other ideas. And she was determined to do this on her own, without asking her Aunt Fantastica for assistance.

With that thought in mind, Fatima finally decided on her course of action. She was going to play that tape today, with or without Hannah's permission. Hannah obviously felt that playing the tape was disgraceful and underhanded, but Fatima disagreed. Erika had volunteered all the information on that tape of her own free will. It was Fatima's firm opinion that it didn't matter that Erika hadn't known the conversation was being recorded. Besides, once Hannah saw the results playing the tape for everyone produced, she would surely change her mind.

What mattered in the long run was the goal you ultimately achieved, not the methods you used to achieve it. Fatima smiled to herself, and nodded her head with determination. Her best friend would understand afterwards why she had to break her promise, and she would forgive her once she saw how important it was in achieving their goal.

When Hannah returned from showering, she noticed that Fatima seemed to be in a much better mood. In fact, the little sprite was back to being her usual boisterous self. Flitting back and forth around the room, she was singing a cheerful little tune and turning somersaults in midair. Hannah immediately started giggling at the sprite's silly antics, and Fatima responded by bouncing up and down on Hannah's bed, contorting her tiny face into various hysterical expressions. Hannah laughed until the ruckus caused Patrick to knock on her door and ask what the heck was going on. After Fatima dove into the sock drawer, Hannah opened the door to her brother's repeated knocking.

"What are you doing in there?" Patrick asked, as soon as she answered the door.

"None of your business," Hannah responded.

Patrick looked around the room suspiciously, but didn't notice anything out of the ordinary that would explain Hannah's behavior. He shook his head disgustedly and walked back to his room, muttering under his breath about girls and how unstable they were. Hannah just giggled and slammed the door shut. Fatima immediately popped her head out of the drawer with an evil grin on her face, which almost caused Hannah to lose it once again.

Almost late for school, the two girls raced downstairs and out the door to meet Ritchie and Darlene outside. The little group hurried towards the junior high, talking and laughing while they discussed the fun activities they had indulged in over the weekend. Forgotten for the moment were the whole gum incident, the upcoming elections, Erika and her friends, and the near loss at the football game. Fatima basked in the attention, happy and contented with the strong bonds of friendship she had forged over the last few weeks. This was definitely something she would cherish forever.

When they reached the school there was barely enough time for them to sprint to their lockers to put their jackets and backpacks away, before the 1st period bell rang. Darlene and Hannah rushed into the Home Economics classroom and slid into their chairs with about a minute to spare. Mrs. Oglivie clapped her hands together to get the class's attention, the moment the final bell rang. Instructing the students to hurry and copy down the morning assignment, which she had already written out on the blackboard, she sat down at her desk and waited for the morning announcements to begin. After several minutes, Ms. Peterson's voice came over the PA system, outlining the activities which would take place at school that week. She then reminded the students when each of the clubs would be meeting, and finished up with a few miscellaneous announcements. As soon as the PA system went silent, Mrs. Oglivie rose from her desk to start that morning's class.

Today was the day they would be learning how to bake bagels, an announcement which caused a chorus of groans from the students. Bagels were incredibly boring to make, and were nowhere near as tasty as the treats they usually baked in Home Economics. What a perfect assignment for a Monday, Hannah thought, as she and Darlene pulled out the ingredients listed on the blackboard.

The girls had barely started measuring out their flour, when the PA system crackled to life once again. Everybody stopped what they were doing, and looked around with expressions of surprise. Usually, after morning announcements, the PA system was quiet for the rest of the day. Occasionally after lunch, Mr. Andrews would announce the time of an afternoon assembly, but there were no assemblies planned until Wednesday, when the candidates for the 8th grade election would be giving their final speeches. Otherwise, the PA system was only used in the case of an emergency.

With that fact in mind, the kids all stopped what they were doing, and waited to hear what was going on. After several seconds of complete silence, they heard a loud click and then Erika Scott's voice came booming out of the speaker. Turning around in her seat, Erika stared at the classroom speaker with a surprised expression on her face. It was quickly transformed into a proud smile of acknowledgement, however, when she made the mistaken assumption that someone in the office was broadcasting the speech she had given during the assembly last Friday. Her mistake became evident though, as the recording continued.

Hannah and Darlene listened in horror as Erika's voice began to describe all the people she disliked and exactly why she disliked them. The smile on Erika's face froze into a mask of shock, as she listened to herself ridicule Annika and the other cheerleaders. Annika turned to face her supposed best friend with tears in her eyes, while she listened to Erika recite all of the things she disliked about her, including all of the things Annika did that bugged her.

By the time Erika's rant had moved on to ridicule the other students, Annika had already run out of the classroom, sobbing into her hands which were clasped to her face. Erika started to stand up to go after her, but then thought better of it and flopped back into her seat. Her voice continued to boom from the room's speaker, and the list of verbally attacked students grew with each passing minute.

Currently the tape was at the part where Erika had listed all of her boyfriend's faults, and Sean was glaring at her with a fierce expression that became darker as the recording continued. Even Mrs. Oglivie, whose face registered the same look of shock and surprise as most of the other students, wasn't immune from the attack; because now the recording was to the part where Erika made fun of her teacher's weight and the horrible recipes she tried to make in class.

By this point, Erika had sunk so low in her seat that only her eyes were visible above the surface of her desk. Everyone in the class, with the exception of Hannah and Darlene, was now glaring at the hapless cheerleader. Hannah and Darlene, however, were staring at each other with identical expressions of disbelief. Thankfully, everyone else's attention was still on the unfortunate Erika, so no one else noticed the short exchange that took place between them.

"Oh my goodness!" Hannah said breathlessly. "How is this happening? I mean it's impossible, right?" she said to Darlene, without waiting for an answer. "She gave me that tape, and I destroyed it. You even saw her put it in my hand."

Darlene only had a chance to nod briefly, before Hannah continued.

"Besides, I specifically told her she wasn't to play that tape under any circumstances, and she agreed. Actually, she did more than that. She promised me!"

Hannah stood up so fast that her chair tipped over backwards and crashed to the floor. The amazing thing was that everyone was still so mesmerized by the recording, which was still playing over the PA system, that no one even noticed the minor distraction. Even Mrs. Oglivie failed to notice that Hannah had gotten out of her seat, and was now sprinting across the room and out the door.

As she raced down the hallway towards the office, she happened to glance into several of the other classrooms that she passed. It was obvious that the response Mrs. Oglivie's classroom had to the tape recording was universal. Every student that she saw during her mad dash down the hall seemed equally hypnotized by Erika's voice droning on and on in her snotty tirade against her peers.

Turning the final corner of the hallway, Hannah practically slid into the office at full speed. She glanced wildly around the room, and quickly located the microphone to the PA system. Lying beside it was the miniature tape recorder Tony had left in their robot, the wheels of the recorder continuing to turn as the tape reached its conclusion. Hannah grabbed the recorder in one hand, and reached out with the other hand to flip the switch on the microphone off.

Silence suddenly descended upon the building, and at that exact moment Ms. Peterson stepped into the office, obviously out of breath from the jaunt she had just made. She had been in the gymnasium on the other side of the school when the recording had started, and had just now made it back to the office. Her surprise at finding Hannah in her office, with the tape recorder in one hand and the PA microphone in the other, was evident by the expression on her face.

Watching the Principal look from her to the objects in her hands, Hannah's heart sunk as she realized how guilty she must look. Ms. Peterson would surely decide that she was responsible for the morning's disruption, and Hannah couldn't blame her for reaching that conclusion. After all, she was clearly unable to explain what had really happened, because no one was going to listen to an explanation that involved a sprite from Fairy Town.

What made matters even worse was that not only would Ms. Peterson believe that she was responsible for this disgusting act, but she would also most likely think that Hannah had done it to win the election. Given the respect that Hannah had for her Principal, that was almost enough to break her heart.

Hannah stood there with her head hanging down, waiting for Ms. Peterson to say something. There were several moments of silence which seemed to draw out forever, before the Principal finally spoke.

"Hannah, I don't understand. Why would you do something like this? I realize that Erika isn't one of the nicest people, and it's probably tempting at times to reveal what kind of person she really is to those who don't realize it; but to do something like this, where so many people will be hurt so badly, and all this just to win an election. I'm afraid this is something that I would never have thought you were capable of. Do you have anything to say for yourself?"

Hannah shook her head slowly, unable to look her Principal in the eye. Tears were welling up in her eyes, and they would be spilling down her cheeks very soon.

Ms. Peterson sighed, before speaking again. "I guess I don't have to tell you that you're disqualified from the elections now. You're also dismissed for today. I expect you to be in my office at 8AM tomorrow morning to discuss the rest of your punishment. Go home now, please." She started to turn away, but then faced Hannah again. "Hannah," she said in a voice cracking with barely contained emotion, "I'm so disappointed in you. I never thought you were this kind of person." Then she turned around and walked out of the office.

Hannah stood there in the office for several more minutes, willing herself not to start crying yet, because once she started she wasn't certain she'd ever be able to stop. Finally, she regained an element of self-control, and shuffled out of the office. As she walked down the long hallway to her locker, she kept her head down and her gaze focused on the toes of her sneakers. She was totally oblivious to her surroundings, and trudged along on autopilot, neither hearing nor seeing anything around her. Once she reached her locker, she opened it up and removed her backpack. Slipping the offensive tape, still in the recorder, into her backpack, she closed the locker door and hurried outside. The closer she got to her house, the faster she went, and by the time she reached her block, she was practically running.

Bursting through the front door of her house, she ran upstairs to her room. At least Patrick was at school and her parents were at work, so she had the entire house to herself for the rest of the day. By the time they got home, she might be finished crying, she thought bitterly. Of course, then she was going to have to tell them that she had been sent home from school, including an explanation of why. Her parents were going to be even more disappointed in her than Ms. Peterson had been. That thought alone was the straw that broke the camel's back. Throwing herself face down on her bed, she began sobbing so hard that the bed shook beneath her.

After crying for what seemed like an hour, but was actually only ten or fifteen minutes, Hannah lifted her tear-stained face and looked around her room. She had completely forgotten about the little instigator who had caused all of this trouble in the first place. Glancing about, she noticed that her sock drawer, which had been open earlier that morning when she left for school, was now completely shut. Hannah thought that was very suspicious, because if she hadn't closed it, then who had? Patrick and her father had no reason to come into her room when she wasn't there, and if her mom had dropped off her clean laundry, she would have left it folded in a pile on her bed like she usually did. With all the other possibilities exhausted, that left only one other prospect.

Hannah quietly walked over to her dresser and stood in front of it. The tears had dried on her face by now, and her expression was one of steely determination. Reaching down and grabbing the knob on her sock drawer, she suddenly yanked it open. The sight which immediately greeted her was of two tiny legs kicking in the air as Fatima struggled to right herself. Hannah's violent motion had caused her to topple backwards into the mound of socks, and it took a few moments of strenuous exertion before she was able to extract herself from her sock prison. When she finally succeeded in pulling herself upright, so that she could pop her head out, Fatima immediately noticed the angry face glaring at her from only a foot away.

Her first reaction was to attempt an escape by diving back among the socks, but she was thwarted by the hand which had a firm grip on one of her wings. Instead of successfully escaping, she was lifted out of the drawer and unceremoniously dumped onto the surface of the dresser. Sprawled out on top of the dresser, she hurriedly sat up and adjusted her clothes and hair in an attempt to regain some of her dignity. She crossed her tiny legs and laid Twinkle across her lap, before looking up at Hannah with what she hoped was an apologetic expression.

Her friend continued to stare at her with a fierce glare, which was beginning to make the sprite quite uncomfortable. Deciding that perhaps she should be the first to speak, Fatima cleared her throat and frantically searched for the right words to say. She needed to come up with the perfect explanation, because she sensed that she was only going to have one chance to fix the breach in their relationship.

In a voice cracking with emotion, she began speaking. "Hannah, I know you're most likely very angry with me at the moment, and the first thing that I want to say is that I'm very, very sorry. I know I promised you that I wouldn't play that tape, and I obviously broke that promise this morning. I agonized over that choice all through the night, and I truly thought that I had come up with the right decision. I realize it was an awful thing to do, but it was the only way that I could think of to fulfill your wish. You deserve to be the Class President much more than Erika does, and you also deserve to have Sean as your boyfriend, while she doesn't. Playing that tape for everyone at school was the only way I could think of to get you both of those things. So even though you probably still think it was the wrong thing to do, I disagree because I did it for the right reasons."

The little sprite had spoken all of those words with the same breath, and she paused now to catch her breath so that she could finish her explanation. However, before she could even open her mouth to continue, Hannah began talking. Like Fatima, her voice was filled with emotion, but unlike the sprite her words were fueled with anger and disappointment.

"Fatima, I don't care why you played that tape, because no matter how good of a reason you thought of to justify your actions, what you did was wrong. You not only broke your promise to me, you did it by lying to me and deceiving me. I've tried and tried to teach you the true meaning of friendship, and despite that, you have repeatedly lied to me and betrayed me. I offered you a friendship based on truth and honesty, and you've responded with dishonesty and trickery. Your actions today hurt a lot of people and no matter what you were trying to achieve, you were wrong to do it in that manner."

Hannah paused for a moment to take a deep breath, and then continued. "I have given you plenty of chances to change your behavior, yet you continue to ignore the fact that how you accomplish a goal is just as important as achieving the goal itself. Well, this is the last straw! I'm releasing you from your duty as a sprite according to your code. I no longer want you to fulfill my wish, and I no longer want to be your friend. Good-bye, Fatima," she said in a quiet voice. With a sad look on her face, she turned away and walked back over to her bed.

Fatima sat there in complete shock as she watched Hannah walk away. So many things were running through her mind, that she wasn't sure what her response should be. Hannah couldn't mean what she was saying; she was just feeling angry and overwhelmed. She probably just needed a little more time to calm down, and then she would apologize again and everything would be okay. Fatima had almost convinced herself that this was true, when Hannah spoke once again, in a hollow, empty tone.

"Fatima, I'd like you to leave now, and not come back. I'm afraid that I don't ever want to see you again." After speaking those words, Hannah lay down on her bed and curled up on her pillow, with her back to the little sprite.

Fatima tried to swallow the large lump which had formed in her throat, but it wouldn't budge. It slowly began to dawn on her that Hannah was completely serious. Because of her choice that morning, Hannah no longer wanted to be her friend. She had somehow managed to ruin the most important friendship she had ever had. As the reality of the situation became clear, Fatima felt as if her heart would shatter into a million tiny pieces. Trying to fight back the tears which were beginning to run down her cheeks, she slowly stood up and grasped Twinkle tightly in her hand. Murmuring a quiet "good-bye," she flew down the hall to Patrick's room, and let herself out through the torn screen in his window.

Flying towards the meadow, she somehow managed to make it to the hidden portal without running into any of the trees or bushes that grew in the wooded glen. This was almost as miraculous as one of Fatima's magic spells, because her vision was completely clouded and blurred by the tears welling up in her eyes. Reaching the portal unharmed, she reached into her pouch and pressed the magic button as she passed through.

Emerging from the gateway on the other side, she barely even noticed that she was back in the World of Fairy; she was so distraught by the conversation which had just taken place. Her head hanging with shame, she flew right into her Aunt Fantastica without even realizing it. Her aunt enveloped her in her loving embrace, and then wordlessly led her tearful niece back to her apartment.

Settling Fatima on the couch beside her, she held her niece's hand tightly and waited for her to speak. Overwhelmed with feelings of sadness and loss, Fatima began to tell her aunt all about her recent experiences in the Human World. As she continued her story, the words began to spill out faster and faster until, suddenly, she was done. Fantastica sat quietly for several minutes after Fatima had finished. At last, she let out a big sigh and then placed a hand under Fatima's chin. She gently lifted up her niece's head to meet her gaze.

"Fatima, I'm very sorry that things turned out the way they did. I truly believe that you thought you were doing the right thing at the time. But I think that if you look deep down inside your heart, you'll realize that you always knew it was the wrong thing to do. I'm afraid that you let your judgment be clouded by what you hoped to achieve. Now I think you understand what Hannah already knew and tried to teach you. Basically, it all boils down to this—the way you achieve something, is just as important as what you achieve."

"What do you mean, auntie?" Fatima asked quietly.

Her aunt sighed again, before replying. "I mean that if you are dishonest or lying or cheating to try and achieve a noble goal, then the goal itself becomes tainted and it's no longer as noble as it was."

Fatima gazed back at her aunt and a light of understanding began to shine in her eyes.

"That's what Hannah was trying to tell me," she exclaimed, "but I didn't listen to her. I just kept doing things my way, even though I knew what I was doing was wrong. Now I've ruined our friendship, and she's never going to forgive me. She doesn't ever want to see me again."

Fatima resumed her sobbing, and her aunt rocked her back and forth in her arms, attempting to soothe her.

Finally, Fantastica spoke the only words which could probably calm her niece. "Fatima, if you like, I'll go talk to Hannah for you. If I explain exactly how sorry you are for all the trouble you caused, then I think she'll understand. Especially when I tell her how important her friendship is to you, and how you mistakenly allowed your dishonest behavior to override your good intentions."

Fatima looked at her aunt with a gleam of hope in her eyes. "Will you really go talk to her?" she asked excitedly.

"Yes, I will," her aunt replied.

Fatima threw her arms around her aunt's neck and squealed her thanks into the poor woman's ears. When she had settled down, Fantastica instructed her to go straight home, and wait there for her return. As soon as she talked to Hannah, she would come back and tell Fatima what Hannah had said. Fatima raced out of her aunt's apartment, all thoughts of tears forgotten.

As she watched her niece flit away, Fantastica allowed a smile to cross her lips. Her niece had a good heart; she just tended to let herself get carried away by her own impulsiveness. Fantastica had every intention of getting Hannah to understand this, and Fatima was going to be very surprised when she returned. She planned on coming back with much more than mere words – in fact, her plan was to bring Hannah back with her to Fairy Town, so that the girls could heal their friendship together in person.

CHAPTER 21

FATIMA'S KIDNAPPING

Hannah lay on her bed in the same position she had been in for most of the day. It was hours past the time when Fatima had left to return to the World of Fairy, and Hannah didn't think she had ever felt so all alone. Several times during those long, lonely hours, she had wondered if perhaps she hadn't been a little hasty with the sprite. Her bitter words kept coming back to haunt her, causing a renewed cascade of tears on each occasion. Retracting her friendship with Fatima and telling her she never wanted to see her again, seemed both harsh and cruel now that she had settled down and had more time to reconsider. Those words had been spoken in the heat of passion, fueled by feelings of anger and disappointment.

But she had been deeply hurt by Fatima's dishonesty, and had felt extremely betrayed by the sprite's actions that morning. Hannah sighed, and looked at the clock on her bedside table. The time read 3:12 PM, which meant that Darlene would be home from school any time now. Her best friend had piano lessons this afternoon, but Hannah knew that she would check in with her first, just to make sure that she was all right. Sure enough, right on cue, her walkie-talkie crackled to life and Darlene's anxious voice came out of the speaker. She didn't even bother with their code names, which meant that she was truly upset.

Hannah immediately picked up the walkie-talkie and responded to her friend's call. The relief in Darlene's tone upon hearing Hannah's voice was obvious, and Hannah felt a wave of affection for her friend wash over her. At least she could always count on Darlene to be there for her. Hannah quickly summarized the events which had occurred that morning after her mad dash to the office. She included her suspension for the day, as well as the fact that additional punishments would surely follow after her meeting with Ms. Peterson the next morning. Darlene was quite upset about the fact that Hannah was no longer able to participate in the election taking place later that week. But she was the most disappointed to hear that Hannah had sent Fatima back to the World of Fairy; never to return again.

After several moments of sympathetic silence, Darlene recounted the events which had taken place at school that day. Chaos had reigned over every classroom for quite awhile following the playing of the already infamous tape. Poor Erika had been the target of so much anger and hostility, that even Darlene had felt sorry for her. Mrs. Oglivie had fixed her former pet with an icy glare for the rest of the class period, and once she returned from her crying jag, Annika had taken a seat on the other side of the room.

During their lunch break, Erika had sat alone at her usual table, while all the other cheerleaders sat at a different table, far away from her. With only ten minutes left in the lunch period, Sean had approached her table and, by Erika's reaction, had apparently broken up with her. This was later confirmed by both Paul and Shane, both of whom had witnessed Sean's fury after hearing what Erika had said about him on the tape.

At the very end of the school day, Erika had been called into Ms. Peterson's office, but no one knew yet what the results of that meeting had been. Hannah absorbed all of this information, and realized that she also felt a certain amount of sympathy for the unfortunate cheerleader. Well, one thing was certainly clear; Fatima's plan had obviously been successful. Hannah at least had to give her credit for that. Just as the little sprite had intended, Erika was now on the bottom rung of the popularity ladder, and Hannah might have moved up a few notches in everyone's mind. And, of course, Sean had broken up with Erika, which was also part of Fatima's plan. However, Hannah had been correct in her estimation that a lot of people were going to have their feelings hurt by the contents of that tape, and that was exactly what she had been trying to avoid. Hannah sighed heavily, and thanked Darlene for the information.

It was time for Darlene to go to her piano lesson, but she promised Hannah that she would call her back as soon as she returned home. Hannah thanked her again and then signed off. She lay back on her bed and thought about how she was going to break the news of her suspension, and the disciplinary acts soon to follow, to her parents. She squeezed her eyes shut in anguish, thinking about how disappointed they were going to be when they heard about the events of today.

When she opened her eyes, she gave a gasp of surprise and scuttled up to the head of her bed, while her eyes remained glued to the foot of it. At the end of her bed was a small woman about six inches in height dressed in a shimmering pink dress with silver sequins sewn on it, and she had a silver tiara in her golden hair. Hannah blinked her eyes rapidly several times, but the image remained the same. Hannah slowly relaxed, settling herself into a seated position with her back against the wall, and continued to stare at the tiny woman.

Whoever the creature was, she obviously bore Hannah no ill will, as was evidenced by the smile on her face and the gentleness which seemed to cloak her. Hannah offered her a tentative smile, and was further assured by the fact that the woman's own smile grew even broader in response. Hannah was attempting to screw up her courage enough to speak, when the little woman began talking first.

"Hello, my dear! I must apologize for startling you, because that was certainly not my intention. Allow me to properly introduce myself; my name is Fantastica, and as you've probably already guessed, I am Fatima's aunt." The little fairy actually gave a small curtsey after her polite introduction.

Hannah struggled for the right words to say in response, but the friendly fairy saved her the trouble. "You must be Hannah, the wonderful friend my niece has been gushing about for the last couple of months."

Hannah's eyes were downcast as she stated, "Some wonderful friend I turned out to be. I'm afraid I probably ruined any chance of continuing our friendship, because of the careless things I said to Fatima this morning. Knowing how close the two of you are, I imagine that she's already filled you in about our disagreement."

Fantastica nodded her head thoughtfully before she answered. "Yes, she did indeed, and as I pointed out to her, the majority of the blame for that argument could rightfully be laid at her feet. She had no right to do what she did this morning, especially since it involved breaking her promise to you. I'm afraid that my niece is quite impulsive at times, and often acts before she considers the consequences of her actions. You had every right to be angry with her, and she understands and accepts that now. She asked me to come here to give you her sincerest apologies, and I hope that you're willing to forgive her and accept that apology."

"Oh, I do and I am!" Hannah exclaimed. "I told her I didn't ever want to see her again, but I realize now that I didn't mean it. If she's still willing to be my friend, I would be more than happy to continue our friendship. Can you please give her that message for me?" Hannah asked imploringly.

Fantastica giggled as she walked up to Hannah and grasped one of her fingers with her tiny hand. "I have a much better idea, my dear. Why don't you come with me, and you can tell her yourself."

Hannah's face brightened instantly. "You mean she's somewhere nearby?" she asked excitedly. "Oh, that's wonderful! Could you please lead me to her?"

Fatima's aunt laughed her wonderful tinkling laugh again. "Well," she replied, "she's not exactly close by, but I can get you there with just a sprinkling of magic fairy dust."

Hannah's eyebrows rose in disbelief when she finally understood the implication of the fairy's words. "You mean you're going to take me with you to Fairy Town?" she gasped.

Fantastica nodded her head solemnly. "That is, if you're willing to accompany me."

"Oh, you bet I am," Hannah exclaimed, "but I'll need to be back fairly soon, so my parents won't worry about me."

"Don't worry, my dear, we can spend several hours or more in the World of Fairy, while only an hour or two will pass here in your world."

Hannah nodded her head eagerly as she jumped up and prepared to leave. First, she left a note for her parents which said she was studying with Darlene in case they got home before she returned. Then she grabbed her jacket and backpack (to cover her regarding the whole "studying" angle), and they were off. They reached the hidden portal in the woods in no time at all, and Hannah waited with barely contained excitement as Fantastica prepared the way for the magical journey to follow with a sprinkle of magic fairy dust.

Meanwhile, back in Fairy Town, Fatima had been waiting for what seemed like forever for her aunt's return. As the long minutes stretched into hours, she grew more and more anxious. What if Aunt Fantastica hadn't been able to find Hannah? What if she found her, but Hannah refused to accept her apology? What if, in spite of her aunt's explanation, Hannah still wasn't able to forgive her? As the doubts piled up in her mind, Fatima started to get upset all over again. Pretty soon the tears began to stream down her face, and she huddled on her bed with her face in her pillow, sobbing as if her little heart would break.

This was where her dear sister, Fawn, found her when she stopped by for a visit. Her relief at seeing a friendly face, as well as having another sympathetic shoulder to cry on, caused Fatima to break the code of silence she had imposed upon herself since her original journey to the Human World. In between her tears and sobbing, she told Fawn absolutely everything – from her struggles in the spider web to that morning's incident with the tape.

The relief she felt at finally being able to share this knowledge with her beloved sister was incredibly freeing; as if a huge burden had suddenly been lifted from her shoulders. Another positive aspect was her sister's understanding response. Rather than scolding her little sister or acting disappointed in her actions, Fawn was lovingly understanding, and even sympathetic to Fatima's plight. With encouraging words, she was able to coax Fatima into accompanying her back to Fantastica's apartment, where they would wait together for their aunt's return.

Fatima readily agreed, and off they flew to the apartment. As they exited Fatima's room and passed down the long hallway, neither of them noticed the dark shadow which hovered by the bedroom door. Oblivious to the fact that someone had been eavesdropping on their entire conversation, they continued chattering happily to each other as they flew out the front door.

As soon as they had departed the fairy townhouse, the shadow dropped down to the floor and materialized into their oldest sister, Faye. She had just stopped by to retrieve some items of clothing she had forgotten when she moved out the past year. Hearing voices at the end of the hall, she had stood with her ear against the door, overhearing her sisters' entire conversation. With a dark expression of jealousy and anger on her otherwise pretty face, she flew out the front door, and headed downtown.

She had decided to go down to the Liaison Office where she worked, and find her boss, Aristotle Fanconi, to tell him the whole story. Fatima had broken numerous rules and regulations which governed acceptable interactions between humans and fairies, and she needed to be punished for this. Her actions could very well prove dangerous for Fairy Town specifically, and the World of Fairy in general, and it was part of Faye's job to prevent this kind of thing from happening. Of course, as you have probably already guessed, Faye was extremely jealous of Fatima and Fawn's relationship, as well as the special attachment they both had with their Aunt Fantastica.

However, she refused to acknowledge that this played any role in her decision to inform her boss about Fatima's recent activities. The truth of the matter was that she couldn't allow such things to go unreported because of her position in the Liaison Office. Doing anything less would be compromising her position in the office. Besides, as payment for such valuable information, she would certainly be promoted to a more prestigious position. If the cost involved some kind of punishment for her sisters and aunt, she would just have to accept that as a fair and reasonable consequence.

Quieting her conscience with that thought, she entered the front door of the Liaison Office, and flew up the stairs until she reached the top floor where Aristotle's office was located. She knocked timidly on his door, and was greeted by a rough voice bidding her to enter. Faye opened the door and shuffled inside, quickly closing the door behind her. Looking around the office, she noted that Aristotle was sitting behind his desk, while his top aide and confidante, General Mazzarati, lounged on the leather couch which occupied one side of the room.

Aristotle was a small man, tiny even by fairy standards. He was barely the same height as Faye, and her father easily towered a full five or six inches above him. Fastidious about his appearance, and quite sensitive about his short stature, he usually wore a plum colored suit coat with large black boots, that rose above his knees and had three inch soles to make him appear taller.

He had a full head of shaggy black hair and a craggy face, which was partially hidden by a full beard and mustache. The tips of the mustache reached his pointy little ears and were waxed to form curls at their ends. Unfortunately, neither the mustache nor the beard could hide the huge bulbous nose rising from the center of his face like a mountain. In addition to its largeness, his nose was also a hideous shade of bright red, which only added a touch of homeliness to his already ugly features. With his choice of suit color, he most closely resembled a plump little plum.

Faye pulled her eyes away from his face, and instead settled for staring at the General. Her view wasn't much improved by this switch. General Mazzarati was a full six inches taller than the mayor, but was almost as ugly. He was an older fairy whose unattractive face was wreathed with a mass of wrinkles intertwined with jagged scars sustained during the famous Century War. Unlike Aristotle, his shiny head was completely bald and he lacked both a mustache and beard. The only hair on his head was that which composed his hairy black eyebrows, and a few straggling hairs that stuck out of each nostril. His dirty gray eyes were set back far beneath his rough brow, giving him the appearance of a weasel. He smiled at Faye, revealing an irregular line of stained teeth.

Faye barely suppressed a shudder as she turned her attention back to her boss. Aristotle offered her a brief smile, which seemed out of place on his stern features, and then questioned her regarding her rather sudden appearance. Faye swallowed the lump which had gathered in her throat, and informed him that she needed to discuss a matter of grave urgency with him – something which could actually threaten the safety of everyone living here in Fairy Town.

She waited for Aristotle to excuse the General, which would allow them to pursue the conversation in absolute privacy. Flicking a glance at the General first, Aristotle looked back at Faye and gestured for her to continue. She took a deep breath, and then let the entire conversation that she had overheard spill out. She carefully outlined each journey that Fatima had taken to the Human World, thoroughly describing the events which had occurred there.

By the time she had finished she was completely out of breath, and felt both physically and emotionally exhausted. While she had been telling her story, the grim look which usually resided on Aristotle's face had been replaced with a shark-like grin, which had grown wider and wider as Faye continued speaking. Currently, he looked as pleased as a fox in a henhouse, and the General seemed equally contented. Faye glanced back and forth anxiously between the two men, waiting for their response.

Aristotle was the first to speak, and he congratulated her on a job well done. Immediately after offering her his abbreviated praise, he asked her to run along home, and ordered her not to speak to anyone else regarding this grave matter of national security. But before she was excused, he promised her that a promotion would be bestowed upon her shortly, and then warned her that punishments would need to be meted out to her aunt and sisters because of the gravity of their offenses. However, he also promised that he would deal with those issues in a fair manner, and would keep the information to himself so the family name would not be disgraced.

Faye thanked him for his thoughtful consideration and allowed herself to be quickly escorted from the office. As soon as the door had closed behind her, Aristotle looked over at the General with a malicious grin on his hideous face.

"This is exactly the kind of incident we've been waiting for!" he exclaimed. "With this information we can finally put our plan into action. We will kidnap the sprite and direct her aunt to bring the human child to us. Then we will inform the Council about the plotting between them."

The General looked somewhat confused, and so Aristotle added further confirmation.

"You know, the plot they had come up with to help the humans overtake Fairy Town."

"What plot was that again?" the General slowly asked.

Frustration building inside of him, Aristotle raised his voice. "The plot that doesn't really exist, you idiot, but that we will make up. We'll tell the Council that Fatima and this human, with Fantastica's help, are trying to take over the World of Fairy. That will inspire fear and anger within the Council, as well as all of Fairy Town. With their fear of humans at a fevered pitch, the townpeople will then allow us to destroy the Liaison Office, and disband the institution of fairy godmothers. Then we will rule all of Fairy Town, because everyone will be so grateful that we saved them from certain destruction. We will never have to do anything good for humans ever again. In fact, if we play our cards right, everyone will be so scared and angry, that we may eventually be able to convince them to allow us to take over the Human World and use humans as our slaves. We're on the verge of getting everything we've always dreamed of and more!"

Aristotle rubbed his grimy little hands together gleefully. The General allowed a small smile to crease his evil countenance. The two fairies sat back down and huddled together over the Mayor's desk. It was time to put the final steps of their plan in action. The Mayor had been waiting years for this type of situation to arise. His hatred of humans had seethed within him ever since the loss of his only child, Tinkerbell. Finally, he had been given the chance he had been looking for – and it had practically been dumped in his lap.

Unknown to the two men, Faye was still outside the office door in the waiting room. She had hesitated before leaving, uncertain if she shouldn't remind Aristotle once more about his promise to go easy on her family members. Once he'd raised his voice to explain the entire plot to the General to ensure his full comprehension, she'd overheard the rest of the conversation. She hurried down the stairs and out of the Liaison Office, before they had the chance to discover that they'd been overheard.

She sat down on a bench in a nearby park, and covered her face with her hands. Tears streamed down her cheeks, and her heart beat faster than a hummingbirds. What had she done? Not only would she be responsible for the impending arrest of her aunt and two of her sisters, but she may have unwittingly set in motion a plot to destroy any and all interactions between fairies and humans. Also, if Aristotle's plot went as he had planned, the responsibility for the destruction of the entire human race could be laid at her feet. She'd ruined everything; and all because of her own jealousy and feelings of inferiority. She just had to fix the mess she'd made, but she hadn't the faintest idea where to begin.

Suddenly a thought struck her and she lifted her face from her hands, a look of determination replacing her tears. Fawn would know exactly what needed to be done. All she had to do was swallow her pride and inform her sister of the events which had taken place. It would require her to admit that her betrayal had been the instrument which had set their evil plan in motion, but she knew that her good-hearted sister would eventually forgive her. As soon as she came to that conclusion, she stood up from the park bench and flew off; straight to Aunt Fantastica's apartment where she knew her sisters would be waiting for their aunt's return.

Indeed, that is exactly where her sisters had gone. They had been waiting for their aunt's return for over two hours now, and Fatima was beginning to get impatient. She was also quite hungry, because with all of the events which had taken place that day, she had neglected to eat either breakfast or lunch. She scoured Fantastica's apartment, but couldn't find a single thing which sounded good to her. Fawn, being the generous soul that she was, volunteered to run out and get her little sister her favorite food of chocolate-covered strawberries, as a special treat to make up for the horrible day she'd had. Fatima eagerly agreed, and Fawn took off, promising to return soon.

She had only been gone for ten minutes, when Fatima heard a loud knock on the door. Thinking that her sister had returned in record time with her dessert, she pulled the door open wide. Before she even knew what was happening, a sack was thrown over her head, and she was shoved back into the apartment. Overcome by surprise, she froze in terror as Twinkle was wrenched from her grip. The sack was then drawn down over her feet, and she soon found herself imprisoned in its musty darkness. She tried to scream, but the sack was too thick, and her voice was completely muffled. She felt herself rudely thrown over a shoulder and then lifted into the air. Fatima's last thought before she fainted with terror, was that she hoped her sister and aunt would be safe. Then all was darkness.

In the meantime, Fawn had just returned to the apartment building, loaded down with a full dozen of the chocolate-covered strawberries. Just as she reached the front door of the building, she was surprised to see Faye flying straight towards her, yelling and waving her arms to capture Fawn's attention. As soon as Faye reached her sister, she told her all about her meeting with the Mayor and the General. She left nothing out, even when she saw the look of disappointment that crossed Fawn's face upon learning of her role in the matter. When she finished describing the men's reaction, and included their conversation that she had accidentally overheard, the look of disappointment on Fawn's face had transformed into an expression of genuine worry.

Giving her sister a quick hug of forgiveness, they both raced inside the building and flew up to the apartment at breakneck speed. Spying Fantastica's door standing wide open, Fawn's worry turned into frank alarm. The sisters split up and searched the apartment, calling Fatima's name over and over. Unfortunately, she was nowhere to be found. Fearing the worst, they sat down together on the couch in the living room, while they tried to decide what their next move should be. Faye was starting to panic, terrified that her confession in Aristotle's office had resulted in something terrible happening to her youngest sister. Fawn gathered Faye into her arms and attempted to soothe her. All the while her mind was racing in an attempt to think of a plan that would allow them to help their sister.

Hearing a familiar voice, both girls looked up and sighed in relief. Aunt Fantastica was home! Both girls jumped up immediately, and began to shower their aunt with a torrent of words. Fantastica looked back and forth between the two anxious fairies with an expression of confusion that only increased as the girls continued talking. Finally she'd had enough, and held both hands up in a halting gesture and ordered them to be silent. Then, one at a time, she allowed them to explain the predicament they were in. When the girls had finished, Aunt Fantastica's look of confusion had been replaced by a thoughtful expression. After a moment or two, she began to speak.

"Well girls, it looks like we're in a bit of a mess." Faye, looking utterly ashamed of herself, began crying again, and her aunt continued. "There's no reason to assign any blame here, Faye. What's been done is done, and now we all need to work together to fix it. And just in case things aren't complicated enough, I need to introduce you to someone. Hannah, come in here please, my dear."

As the two fairies looked on in amazement, a human walked through the front door of the apartment. Fawn and Faye gasped, as Hannah shyly introduced herself. Neither Fawn nor Faye could speak, they were so awestruck, so Fantastica continued to do the talking.

"This is Hannah, Fatima's best friend in the Human World. I had to use some fairy dust to shrink her down a bit of course, but I wanted to bring her along with me as a surprise for Fatima. Now it looks as if we're the ones who have ended up being surprised. Well, we're just going to have to put our heads together and decide what to do next."

While she had been talking, Hannah had only been half-listening, as she couldn't help looking around the room in wonder. Noticing a piece of paper lying on the table on the other side of the room, she walked over and glanced at it to satisfy her curiosity. As soon as she picked it up and began scanning it, she gave a gasp of surprise and immediately handed the note over to Fantastica. Fantastica quickly read the note, before passing it to Faye and Fawn in turn.

The note had been written by Aristotle, and the message was plain. He and the General had kidnapped Fatima and were holding her at a secret location. Fantastica and Fawn were ordered to kidnap the human child, and bring her to them in order to ensure Fatima's safe return. After reading the note over and over again, the fairies stared at each other in consternation. Remarkably, it was Hannah who came up with a plan, which she quickly explained to the worried fairies. Fantastica nodded her head in agreement, while Hannah went over the finer points of her plot. As she listened to Hannah, her smile grew wider and wider.

"You know," she said when Hannah had finished, "this just might work."

According to the plan, Faye would fly to her parent's house and inform her father, who was on the City Council, about all of the events which had taken place. Then, he would be able to get to the City Council before Aristotle, and defuse their entire plot. Meanwhile, Fawn and Fantastica would take Hannah along with them to the secret meeting place designated in the note. They would then be able to tell Aristotle and the General that their devious plot had been discovered and foiled, guaranteeing Fatima's safe return.

Agreeing that the plan was a good one, they each readied themselves for their specific task. While Faye flew off to their fairy townhouse, Aunt Fantastica replenished her supply of magic fairy dust. Then Hannah grabbed her backpack, and allowed Fawn and Fantastica to sprinkle her with their fairy dust. They each clutched one of her hands, and then they were off – to rescue Fatima.

CHAPTER 22

TRIUMPH OVER EVIL

Flying over Fairy Town, with a fairy holding each of her hands, Hannah couldn't help but marvel at the incredible city stretched out beneath her. She had never seen such an array of bright colors and fantastic structures, and in spite of the fact that she was about to be used as a pawn to rescue Fatima from two evil fairies, her spirits still soared with wonderment and delight. The brightly colored buildings with their marvelous towers, arches, and spires were a testament to the fairies' architectural abilities endowed to them by their magical fairy dust.

The city was as busy as a beehive, with fairies and sprites zipping around every which way, beautifully illustrating their industrious nature. The luscious green parks and sparkling blue lakes and rivers dotted the landscape at regular intervals. Overwhelmed by the panoramic scene racing by beneath her, Hannah's eyes were wide open with awe and amazement. This was even better than her most vivid dream, and she would have pinched herself to confirm that this was all real, if she could have risked freeing one of her hands from the fairies' tight grip.

The fabulous flight lasted much too briefly as far as Hannah was concerned. It seemed that in no time at all they had reached their destination, a large craggy mountain rising high in the air, almost looming over the city at the northern edge of its boundaries. The steep hillside was covered with forest green trees and bushes, along with irregular rock formations, at least one of which hid the entrance to a dark cave. Spying a bright red bush halfway up the side of the mountain, the two fairies dropped down from their path just beneath the clouds, and gracefully landed by the bush which had been referred to in the note left by Aristotle. Somewhere nearby should be the mouth of the cave where Fatima was being held.

Hannah discovered it first, and called to Fawn and Fantastica, eager to show them her observation. As the three of them made their way carefully through the jagged rocks piled by the cave's opening, Hannah felt her excitement leach away, to be replaced by the first tendrils of fear. Somewhere inside that cave was one of her best friends in the whole world (or worlds Hannah thought with a nervous giggle), and she was being held prisoner by two decidedly evil fairies. Furthermore, if their plan didn't work out the way they intended, she might end up being their prisoner too. Hannah gulped, and glanced around the cave nervously. Shifting her backpack to a more comfortable position, she ventured further into the cave. She had just turned the corner and was peering down a long gloomy passageway, when she heard Fantastica anxiously calling her back.

As she turned around quickly, the toe of her right sneaker collided with a large rock in her path, causing her to trip. Falling headfirst towards the ground, Hannah reached out and grabbed for anything that could stop her fall. Her left hand closed around a stony projection, and she grasped it with all her strength. Fortunately, this saved her from doing a face plant on the sharp rocks beneath her feet. The unfortunate aspect was that the rock she grabbed was apparently part of a spring mechanism which released a trap door directly underneath Hannah's feet.

Without any warning, Hannah plummeted down through the trap door and slid along a smooth tunnel which descended sharply downwards. The air around her was damp and frigid, and the space was so dark that Hannah couldn't have seen her hand even if she had held it directly in front of her face. The tunnel seemed to stretch on for miles, but finally Hannah was dumped out the end, landing on a hard floor which knocked the wind right out of her.

When she was finally able to catch her breath, she glanced wildly around the enclosed space, almost frightened out of her mind. She found herself in a room with stone walls on three sides, and a fourth side which featured thick iron bars set closely together. A small light bulb hung from the ceiling, so that Hannah could at least see her immediate surroundings, which were illuminated by its weak light.

Although Hannah had no idea where she was, and didn't recognize anything around her, the reader will of course recognize this prison cell from the very beginning of our tale. So much has happened since then, and it was so many pages ago, that you may need to take a moment and refer back to that very first page. However, it's altogether more likely that you remember that moment very well, and have been patiently waiting since then to find out what will happen to our unlucky heroine. Thus, I won't waste anymore of your time, and we will continue where we left off.

Hannah shivered uncontrollably as she wrapped her arms around her chest and rubbed her hands briskly up and down her arms. Her light spring jacket afforded her little warmth within the cold damp confines of this stone fortress. She wondered what had become of Fawn and Fantastica. Had they realized yet that she had disappeared? Would they be able to figure out what had happened to her, and if so, how long would it take them to find her? Hannah sat down and leaned her back against one of the rocky walls. Her only hope for escape was that the two fairies would locate her quickly and use their magic to free her from this prison.

However, even that small hope was cruelly dashed to bits a moment later when she glimpsed movement through the bars of her cell. Leaping up, she scrambled over to the cell door and wrapped each hand around an iron bar, pressing her face to the opening between the bars for a better look. What she saw made her heart sink into her stomach, and an overwhelming feeling of despair washed over her. Fantastica and Fawn were shackled together in chains with a male fairy on either side of them. The men were leading them back towards Hannah's prison. Both of the female fairies appeared frightened and disheveled, and Hannah immediately noticed that they were both missing the pouches which usually hung from the belts at their waists – pouches which contained their magic fairy dust. Hannah instantly guessed that their male captors must be the infamous Aristotle Fanconi and General Mazzarati; the very same fairies responsible for Fatima's kidnapping.

Hannah looked around the cavernous space in front of her, wondering where Fatima could be. She didn't have to wonder for long, because as Fantastica and Fawn were led closer, Hannah heard a familiar voice call out to them. It was Fatima, and Hannah was immensely relieved to know that the little sprite was alive and well. Or, she quickly amended, at least as well as she could be in this horrible situation. As the group of fairies drew nearer and nearer to Hannah's cell, Fantastica finally noticed Hannah staring silently at them from her prison. A look of pure relief washed quickly over her face, as she glanced at Hannah and then over to the other side of the cavern.

Hannah strained to crane her neck around the iron bars so that she could get a glimpse of whatever Fantastica was staring at that was diagonally across from her. Her efforts were eventually rewarded when she was able to see another cell which appeared identical to hers. The only difference between the two cells was their occupants, because the other cell held her best friend in this world.

"Fatima," she cried out joyfully, "you're okay!"

Fatima's pointy little ears perked up at the sound of Hannah's voice. "Oh my goodness, Hannah! Whatever are you doing in the World of Fairy? Now you're in more trouble than you were this morning. Hannah, I'm so sorry about this whole mess. It's entirely my fault!"

Before she could continue, Hannah firmly interrupted her. "No, it's not, Fatima. I came here with your aunt to tell you that I'm sorry for the way I treated you, and I was hoping you would forgive me, so that we could continue our friendship."

Fatima's eyes sparkled in the dimly lit cave. "Of course I forgive you, silly. But I'm the one who needs to apologize. Not only for what I did in your world, but for all of this, too."

Their heartfelt conversation was rudely interrupted by the arrival of their captors. Aristotle looked at each of his prisoners in turn with a greedy smile. He rubbed his hands together eagerly, and chuckled at their plight.

"I hate to interrupt this touching little reunion," he said in a nasty voice, "but we have business to attend to. You ladies have been very, very naughty, and it's my job to see that you're all properly punished."

Fantastica stared at him with a look of disdain and disgust, before she opened her mouth to spit out a caustic response. "Aristotle, for your information, Fatima only broke a few relatively minor rules, while Fawn and I have done nothing wrong. And the rules which Fatima did break are ancient and out-dated, and shouldn't even exist in this day and age. But anyways, it's up to her father and the rest of the City Council to determine what her punishment should be. You and your lapdog, the General, have no grounds for kidnapping us, relieving us of our magic fairy dust, and putting us in chains. I intend to see to it that the City Council properly punishes you both for the rules you've broken, too."

When Fantastica finished her heated remarks, she expected the two men to at least offer up their apologies, if not release them right away. To her surprise, Aristotle and the General began laughing uproariously at her little speech. Finally, stopping to catch their breath, they each grabbed a fairy and hustled them over to Fatima's cell. Aristotle removed a key from his belt and unlocked the door of the cell. Fantastica and Fawn were yanked inside, where each of their chains were fastened to a large iron ring embedded in the stone floor. Once they were both secured in the same fashion as Fatima, the men exited the cell and relocked the door. Still shaking their heads and grinning broadly at Fantastica's outburst, they marched back through the cavern and were soon lost from sight.

Stunned and frightened, Hannah stood frozen in place as she watched their retreat. When she came back to her senses several minutes later, she heard quiet murmurings from the cell across the way. Thankful that at least she had some company now, she called out to her friends.

"Guys, what do we do now?"

Everything was silent for a moment, and then Fantastica's voice came drifting across the cavern.

"Hannah, that's what we were just discussing, and I'm afraid that we haven't yet come up with an answer. On the way down here, Aristotle informed us that he had already called all of the members of the City Council – everyone except for Fawn and Fatima's father that is. Aristotle apparently warned them about the plot he had discovered and asked them to call an emergency town meeting at the park square by City Hall. He and the General then told all the council members that they would join them as soon as they had captured the human spy. Unfortunately, he is referring to you. I think he's planning on using Faye's information to accuse us of being spies who were caught plotting with you on how to take over the World of Fairy."

Hannah slowly digested all of this information, before she replied. "But nobody's going to believe him, right? I mean it's just their word against ours, and besides, Farthing will tell everyone what really happened; just like we planned. That's what they're going to believe, right?" she added in a hopeful tone.

Hannah easily heard Fantastica's sigh echo off the walls of the surrounding cavern. She bit her bottom lip in frustration, as she waited anxiously for the fairy's reply. Finally, Fantastica spoke again, and even Hannah recognized the resignation in her voice.

"I'm afraid that things don't look very good for us right now. The fairy people have a lot of respect for both Aristotle and the General. Plus, there is the fact that Fatima has been visiting you in the Human World, and that I brought a human back with me to our world. Those actions alone may frighten and anger a lot of people. And I'm sure those two thugs are counting on that and will be using it to their advantage." She sighed again before she finished. "I think that we should all put our brains to work to see if we can come up with something that can help prove our case; or some evidence that can prove they're lying."

Hannah's shoulders slumped and she felt a wave of dejection run through her. She unclenched her fingers from the iron bars of her cell and shuffled over to the rock wall which looked the driest. Sitting down and leaning back against it, she raised her knees up to her chest and laid her arms across them. Thoughts of her family and friends back in her world threatened to overwhelm her, and she put her head down on her crossed arms, trying her hardest not to cry.

While she sat there, wondering how long it would take her family to realize she was missing and recognizing the fact that they would never be able to find her, she suddenly realized that she could hear the murmur of voices. These weren't the voices of her friends, either. For one thing, they came from the opposite direction of the fairies' cell, and for another, they were male voices.

Lifting her head up off her arms, Hannah glanced around her cell. The voices were coming from the wall opposite her, and she studied it intently in an effort to solve this little mystery. Getting to her feet, she walked over to the wall and began examining it carefully all along its length. When she reached the middle, she realized that the voices were becoming clearer and more distinct.

Glancing up, she saw a crevice in between some rocks that she hadn't noticed during her initial inspection of her cell. She lifted a hand up and held it in front of the crevice. Sure enough, a draft of air washed over her fingers. The crevice must form a natural connection between her cell and a room deeper in the mountain. A room that Aristotle and the General clearly occupied, because it was definitely their voices that she heard.

Hannah scrutinized the base of the wall until she found exactly what she was looking for. In several places, the natural formation of the rocks created various handholds and toeholds that she could use to climb further up the rock face. She carefully climbed halfway up the wall, until the drafty crevice was at a level even with her head. From that position, she could easily hear the entire conversation taking place between her evil captors. Apparently, the rock surfaces combined with the central cavern to create an excellent acoustical sounding board.

As Hannah listened to the crystal clear conversation, it became readily apparent that Aristotle was reviewing their entire plot one more time for the more slow-witted General. Hannah shifted to a more comfortable position, and in the process almost lost her footing when her backpack also shifted, causing a rapid redistribution of its weight.

Whew, Hannah thought to herself, that was a close one. I don't need to add a broken bone or two to my list of problems. I should probably just ditch the stupid backpack because all it has in it are my school books, and I may not need those ever again. After Hannah finished that morbid thought, her eyes suddenly lit up and her forehead wrinkled, illustrating that she was deep in thought. You see, she had suddenly remembered that there was one more thing in her backpack. Something she had placed there earlier that morning, which seemed like a lifetime and another world ago now. It was something she had completely forgotten about until this very moment.

She reached behind her back carefully, and unzipped the small pocket on the side of her backpack. Reaching inside, she drew out the small tape recorder which had caused her such grief on more than one occasion. Perhaps that stupid little tape recorder was ultimately going to be her salvation. Hannah closed her eyes tightly and shook her head back and forth, not at all amused by the irony of the situation. She pressed the small eject button to verify that the tape remained inside the recorder. Once she had established that fact, she rewound the tape to its beginning. I sure hope this works, she thought, as she pressed down the record button and held the recorder up to the entrance of the crevice.

Hannah had absolutely no idea how long she stood there, clutching the rock wall with one hand, while holding the tape recorder aloft with the other. What she did know, however, was that in just a short period of time every muscle in her body screamed in agony, and her arms and legs began to shake with fatigue. But she continued to stand there, not moving an inch, as Aristotle and the General continued their conversation. Luckily, Aristotle was so proud of his wicked plot that he persisted in gloating about it, loudly and thoroughly, until Hannah had managed to record everything that would be needed to prove that his case was built entirely on lies and deception.

She smiled grimly as she pushed the stop button on the recorder, and gently eased her way back down to the stony floor. Moving as quickly as her sore muscles and joints would allow, she walked over to the iron bars of her cell and called out to her friends across the cavern. Fantastica answered immediately, asking what Hannah had been doing during her long, drawn-out silence. Apparently, Hannah had been concentrating so hard on the task at hand, that she hadn't even heard her friends calling to her at various intervals during the time she had been perched up on that rocky wall.

In a voice filled with excitement and hope, she told them all about her opportunity to record the entire plot their captors had concocted – and now it was captured on tape in their very own words. She clicked the play button on the recorder and turned the volume up as far as it would go. Holding it up between the bars of her cell in the direction of her friends, she allowed them to hear a small part of the incriminating tape. Turning off the recorder, she placed it safely in one of the zippered pockets of her jacket, and waited for their response. She didn't have to wait very long before she heard Fatima's familiar squeal.

"Oh, Hannah, you're wonderful! I knew you would think of something. You don't even need a magic wand or a bag full of fairy dust, because your brain alone is magical!"

Hannah felt a warm blush climb up her cheeks, and despite her surroundings, she couldn't help but giggle at her tiny friend's response. Fantastica, always the voice of reason, warned the girls not to get too excited just yet. Yes, they had the tape, and it would certainly go a long way towards persuading the people of Fairy Town, along with the City Council, that Aristotle and the General were the ones guilty of evil plotting and kidnapping. But several problems still remained, the main one being how they were going to get the evidence on the tape from Hannah's prison cell to the emergency town meeting.

Hannah felt her shoulders slump in disappointment, and she blew a puff of air up towards her bangs in frustration. Suddenly she had an idea. If she could just get the tape over to her friends' cell, either Fantastica or Fawn could hide it in their pouch, and then they could secretly pass it to Farthing when they were drug out to face the council at the meeting.

It was a beautiful plan, and it probably would have worked, except for one tiny problem – when Aristotle and the General had apprehended the fairies, they had removed their pouches so they wouldn't be able to use their magic fairy dust to escape. They all hung their heads in dejection when they realized that Hannah's super plan had no chance of succeeding.

As Fatima stared down at the pointed toes of her shoes, her glance lingered for a moment on the pouch at her belt. She stared at it for a moment in stunned disbelief. She had a pouch! Not for magic fairy dust, because she was just a sprite, but to hold the magic button that Fantastica had ordered her to carry on her trips to the Human World. Thank goodness she had actually listened and obeyed someone for once in her life. Everything had been so hectic since she had returned home, that she had completely forgotten to take it off. Furthermore, when she had been kidnapped, they had taken away her magic wand, but ignored the pouch, because they knew a sprite wouldn't have any magic fairy dust.

The little group's optimism had suddenly been restored, and they quickly came up with a plan they hoped would work. They knew that their captors intended to leave Hannah in her cell for the time being. She would be dealt with after the City Council was fooled into accepting Aristotle's lies, at which time he could ensure her proper punishment. Fatima, Fawn, and Fantastica, however, would be taken to the emergency town meeting as their prisoners, so they could be judged for their supposed crimes.

When Aristotle and the General came to take them away, Fatima would cry and plead for one last chance to give her best friend a hug and say good-bye. At that time, Hannah would secretly pass the tape to Fatima, who would then hide it in her pouch. Everyone agreed that it was a good plan, or at least the best they could come up with in their current situation with such limited time.

After waiting for what seemed like hours, Hannah finally heard the sounds which signaled their captors' return. The two men were talking and laughing heartily, apparently buoyed by their expected victory. As they walked past Hannah's cell, she thrust her hands into the front pockets of her jeans and glared at them as they walked by. Neither of the men noticed her, however, because their attention was focused on the other prisoners. From the pocket of his purple suit coat, Aristotle produced the key to the fairies' cell. He opened it carefully, and then he and the General stepped inside and closed the door firmly behind them. They were obviously taking no chances with their captives.

Moving quickly and efficiently, they unlocked the fairies' chains from the iron rings in the floor, and fastened them onto large steel rings that had been added to their belts. The captured fairies would be allowed to fly, but their arms and legs would remain shackled and their chains would be fastened to their captors, thus eliminating any chance of escape. As a further precaution against anyone meddling with his plan, Aristotle withdrew some fairy dust from his own pouch, which he intended to use to cast a spell that would keep his prisoners mute during the entire proceedings at the town square. After all, he planned on doing all of the talking.

Using the spell on Fantastica and Fawn first, he then turned to Fatima. But before he could cast the spell on her, she began pleading with him for the chance to say good-bye Hannah. Aristotle pondered the request for a moment, before he spoke.

"Well, I don't see a problem with that. After all I suppose I should grant you one last request before you face your punishment."

Fatima allowed a look of relief to cross her face, and although she would much rather have scratched out his piggy, little eyes; she managed to utter a quiet "thank-you" instead. Leading Fatima and the others by their chains, he unlocked the door and led them out of the cell. The General followed close behind, his eyes watching them carefully lest they foolishly attempt to escape. Aristotle stopped when they drew abreast of Hannah's cell, and flicked his hand impatiently at Fatima, indicating she could go over and tell her friend good-bye.

Fatima flew over to Hannah's cell, concentrating on the secret exchange they had planned earlier. However, she was still four or five feet away from the bars where Hannah stood waiting, when she was suddenly jerked to a stop by the end of her chain. Glancing back at Aristotle with a look of confusion, she immediately noticed the large grin which stretched across his ugly face. She felt a flash of fury surge through her as she realized that he had never intended to keep his promise.

Wincing as the grating sound of his harsh laughter filling the cavern, she whirled around, intending to tell him exactly what she thought of him. As she opened her mouth preparing to do just that, a sudden idea popped into her mind. Although she couldn't get the tape from Hannah right now like they had originally planned, there was still a glimmer of hope remaining. If she could just keep her mouth shut, and ignore her impulsive nature for once, Aristotle might forget that he hadn't yet cast the spell to make her mute. Then, if she had a chance at the meeting, she could whisper to her father or Faye about the presence and location of the tape – their last hope at salvation.

Fatima bit her bottom lip so hard that it bled, fighting to keep her mouth shut, even as she glanced furiously at the obviously amused Aristotle. At the moment he was bent over double, pounding one knee with a tiny fist, as he howled with laughter at Fatima's plight. Finally, the braying laughter tapered off, and he stared at Fatima with a malicious gleam in his eyes.

"I'm so sorry! I entirely forgot that your chain doesn't reach that far. Oh well, we really must be on our way. Everyone's waiting for us, you know, so just wave good-bye to your little friend. Who knows, maybe you'll see her again real soon. After all, in no time at all she'll be banished to the realm between the worlds, and the same fate will most likely be yours, too. I doubt that even your wonderful father can save you now," he said in a sarcastic tone. He looked around and noticed that the fairies and the sprite all had wide-open eyes which stared at him fearfully. Even Hannah appeared to be shocked by his words.

Aristotle chuckled evilly at their reaction, and then without another word, he took flight, dragging Hannah's friends in chains behind him. Just before she was whisked out of sight, Fatima turned back towards Hannah and said in a hoarse whisper, "I promise to rescue you." Then, in two shakes of a dog's tail, Hannah was all alone once again. Mulling over the Mayor's last words, she tried to quell the terror which threatened to engulf her in its sinewy tendrils. She concentrated on slowing the rapid beating of her heart, taking slow, deep breaths to banish the dark pinwheels floating at the edge of her vision. In spite of these outward signs of calmness, her mind raced fitfully, with question after question boomeranging through her brain, like shiny metal balls in a pinball machine.

When would her parents realize she was missing?

How would they ever find her?

Would Ritchie and Darlene be able to figure out what had happened to her?

Why hadn't she told anyone where she was going?

Would anyone be able to save her now?

And the most important question of all: what, exactly, was the realm between the worlds?

Hannah suddenly gave her head a firm shake and a look of fierce determination appeared on her face. Unzipping the pocket of her jacket, she removed the tiny tape recorder with the evidence still inside. Somehow, some way, they would get this to the meeting in time so that all of Fairy Town could hear the truth. Before she left, Fatima had given Hannah a determined look and a promise. Hannah just had to trust her to do the right thing. That was Hannah's only hope right now – she would just have to put her faith in the little sprite, because this time she knew that Fatima wouldn't let her down.

Meanwhile, Fatima, along with her aunt and older sister, had been flown down off of the mountain and into the center of Fairy Town. As they neared the town square where the meeting was to be held, they couldn't help but notice the huge crowd which had already gathered. It looked like every sprite and fairy who lived in the town itself, as well as the surrounding regions, had gathered to hear the important news that Aristotle, their mayor, had promised to deliver. Fatima gulped nervously when she saw the huge crowd. How was she ever going to get everyone to believe her, a no-name sprite, instead of their respected mayor? Remembering the tape, which contained his admitted lies and deception, she felt a steely resolve strengthen her for the confrontation that lay ahead.

At the very front of the town square stood the courthouse, which held the office of the Mayor, as well as the offices of each of the City Council members. On the stairs in front of the building, a huge stage had been erected, with a podium in front and chairs for all of the council members in a ring behind that. Aristotle and the General landed on the stage with their prisoners in tow. When the crowd saw the two fairies and the sprite in chains, there was a collective gasp of disbelief. So the rumors must be true! As Aristotle strode towards the podium, the crowd noise swelled, with everyone talking and asking questions of each other all at once.

The Mayor held up his hands and waited for silence to descend upon the crowd. As soon as he had everyone's attention, he began to speak. I will not record his words of lies and deception on these pages, because I refuse to give him even that small amount of attention or respect. Suffice it to say that he told all of the despicable lies that he had promised the General he would. He informed those that had gathered that the prisoners standing there in shackles and chains had conspired with a human to bring about the destruction of Fairy Town and all of its inhabitants. He further informed them that the accused had brought this human to the World of Fairy to spy upon them, in order to bring their plot closer to fruition.

As the words spilled from his lips, the crowd grew more and more outraged at the list of crimes attributed to this group of spies. Before long, the noise had become so deafening that Aristotle was forced to end his accusatory speech. When Farthing then rushed to the podium to try to denounce the Mayor and his words, he was immediately booed, and his words were drowned out before he could barely even begin his defense of his daughters and sister. Soon cries of anger demanding severe punishment for the instigators of this horrid plot began to ring throughout the square, and the City Council members readied themselves to cast their votes of conviction and punishment.

Fatima waited in paralyzed silence, her eyes roaming back and forth, searching the empty skies. Searching for what, you might ask? Well, she was searching for a glimpse of her oldest sister. You see, when the prisoners had been led up to the platform to face their accusers and listen to the crimes of which they had been accused, a group of officers from the Liaison Office had been directed to hold their chains, ensuring that escape would not be an option. One of those officers had been Faye, who was still ashamed and overwrought by her participation in this hideous miscarriage of justice.

Fatima, who as you will remember was still capable of speech (as Aristotle had forgotten to cast the spell of silence upon her), had waited for an opportunity and then informed Faye of the existence of the tape and its location. Faye had edged her way off of the platform, and then snuck around the side of the building, before taking flight. She headed straight for the mountain, searching for the small window guarded by iron bars which was part of Hannah's prison cell. Calling Hannah's name over and over, she finally heard an answering reply and located the small window, high up on the wall of the little cell. Using her magical fairy dust, she transformed herself into a tiny bird and flew through the bars of the window.

Holding the tape recorder in her tiny beak, she flew back to Fairy Town as fast as her wings would take her. Nearing the town square, she transformed back into her true self, and landed on the platform beside her father. Quickly whispering in his ear, she explained the nature of the tape, as well as how to use the strange machine. With the recorder firmly in hand, Farthing strode up to the podium and, using his advantage in size, rudely pushed the Mayor out of his way. Before anyone could stop him, he pushed the play button and held the small recorder up to the microphone. As Aristotle's voice boomed out over the speakers, the crowd quickly grew silent once again. No one spoke for the entire fifteen minutes that the tape played.

Several times during the recording, Aristotle attempted to wrest the tape player from Farthing, but he was unsuccessful each time. In fact, by the end of the recording both he and the General had been relieved of their pouches of fairy dust, and were being held by several members of the City Council. Unfortunately for them, the tape spelled out their dastardly plot in each chilling detail. Fantastica, Fawn, and Fatima were immediately released from their chains and shackles, and once their magical elements were restored to them, they flew hurriedly back to the mountain and released Hannah from her prison. The little group then rejoined the gathering in the town's square where Hannah was the object of much friendly scrutiny.

After Fantastica had used the microphone to explain the events which had really taken place between Fatima and Hannah; Hannah was celebrated as a hero, and Fatima was readily forgiven her numerous spritely transgressions. The City Council then met privately within the courthouse to determine a fitting punishment for Aristotle Fanconi and General Mazzarati. I am not at all sorry to inform you that the very punishment the Mayor had threatened

Hannah with was bestowed upon him and his partner in crime. With a unanimous vote by the City Council, both fairies were sentenced to the realm between the worlds. Hannah and Fatima both shuddered when they heard the news, although they agreed that it couldn't have happened to two more deserving fairies.

The party held in the town square that evening was fantastic and grand, even by fairy standards. Hannah didn't think that she had ever had so much fun in one night in her entire life. However, she realized much too soon that she needed to be returning home, before her parents missed her and grew worried. Fantastica agreed to accompany Hannah to the nearest portal and conduct her safely home. Before they left, though, she allowed Fatima and Hannah a few moments of privacy. The girls hugged each other fiercely, both with tears in their eyes, as they said their good-byes. Hannah was the first to speak.

"Fatima, I'm so sorry about the way I treated you in my bedroom this morning. You have my sincerest apology, and I hope that you still want to be my best friend."

"Of course I do, you silly goose, and I'm the one who owes you an apology. All that stuff I did was rotten, and I'm just glad you still want to be my best friend."

Hannah gave her friend a huge smile before she replied. "Well, even if you did mess up some stuff at school, you more than made up for it by saving my life."

Fatima grinned broadly in return. "Yeah, I did do that right at least." Suddenly, her smile faded and was replaced by a gloomy look.

"What's the matter, Fatima?" Hannah asked worriedly.

"Well," Fatima started slowly, "I never did grant your wish and fulfill my duty according to the Sprite Code of Honor."

"Oh, but you certainly tried your best," Hannah replied supportively.

"Yeah, but I didn't finish the job. You know, I could ask Fantastica if I could go back with you so I could try a few more magic spells and see if I can get your wish granted."

"No!" Hannah replied a little too quickly. "I mean that's okay, after everything we've been through, I think we both need a little rest and relaxation. Besides, I think we've both learned that there are a lot of things that are more important than popularity and status; like true friendship and family and all that stuff."

"Well, okay, I guess that's true, but I'll come to visit you as soon as I can. You can count on that."

"Deal," Hannah said happily.

Fantastica flew up to the girls at that moment, and stated that she needed to get Hannah home. The girls hugged each other once again, and then Hannah grabbed on to Fantastica's hand and felt herself lifted into the air. Looking down at the little sprite, she continued waving until Fatima was just a tiny dot on the ground. In no time at all, she found herself back in the wooded glen by her house with the little fairy beside her.

"Thank-you for everything," Hannah said solemnly.

"No, thank-you, my dear," Fantastica replied.

"For what?" Hannah asked curiously.

"For being such a good friend to my dear, little niece, and for showing her the true meaning of friendship. I predict the two of you will have a long and happy friendship, filled with many more adventures."

Hannah grinned happily, and replied, "I bet you're right, but I wouldn't mind having at least a week or two of boredom and monotony. If you know what I mean," she said with a wink.

Fantastica giggled and then, in a flash of light, she was gone. Hannah turned toward home and began walking through the wooded glen. Pretty soon she was skipping, and eventually she broke into a run. Wait until Darlene and Ritchie hear about this, she thought; they're never going to believe it! And off she ran.

EPILOGUE

ONE MONTH LATER

No one likes it when they reach the end of a story. This is especially true when it's a really good story, which I hope you have found this one to be. However, even a good story must come to an end at some point. Therefore, I have chosen this point as the end of our story. But don't be dismayed, because I will be updating you on the lives of Hannah and Fatima in the very near future. The girls have continued to maintain their unique friendship, and have also continued to have further adventures which I think you will find both interesting and entertaining.

The responsibility for deciding at which point to end this story, and where to begin the next story, has fallen squarely upon my shoulders. My only hope is that you, the reader, agree with my decision (which I can assure you was a difficult one). Just in case you feel that there are still too many questions that remain unanswered, I am going to fill you in on several things which occurred during the month following Hannah's rescue. Hopefully, this information will sustain you until I am able to provide you with the next installment regarding the lives of Fatima and Hannah.

After Hannah's departure from Fairy Town, the grand celebration which took place in the town square continued well into the night. By that evening's end, Fatima had been promoted to the level of Senior Sprite, and Farthing had been elected to fill the vacant position of Mayor of Fairy Town. Over the next several weeks, he worked hard to select and promote individual fairies to various positions in the Liaison Office. He selected fairies who would ensure continued prosperity in human-fairy interactions, and with this goal in mind, he appointed Fawn and Faye as co-leaders of the Liaison Office.

Their job would be to continue to promote good relations between the fairy godmothers and their human assignments. They would also be responsible for researching and investigating other ways that fairies could help humans with the difficulties they often encountered in their world. Unlike his predecessor, Farthing intended to sustain, and even increase, the good works and deeds that fairies could provide for the Human World.

Several weeks after the whole kidnapping experience, Fantastica allowed Fatima to accompany her on a quick trip back to the Human World to see how Hannah was doing. They arrived on the night of the Junior Prom, which would seem to be incredibly lucky, but was actually due to Fantastica's careful planning. She had already made several trips to the Human World in the intervening weeks, and was happy to fill Fatima in on the events which had taken place in Hannah's life.

The morning after she returned from Fairy Town, Hannah had arrived at Ms. Peterson's office promptly at 8AM, as requested. At that meeting, Ms. Peterson showed Hannah an anonymous letter she had received just that morning. The author of the letter stated that Hannah had known about the tape's existence and content, but had requested that the tape not be played over the PA system, and in fact, had demanded that it be destroyed. Unfortunately, Hannah's directive had been ignored, and the author had played the tape anyway. Hannah's appearance in the office, where she was discovered with the incriminating tape in her hand, was due to her efforts to stop the tape from continuing. Thus, the author of the letter felt that Hannah should be absolved of any and all punishment, as she was definitely not the one who should be blamed for that horrible fiasco.

Although Ms. Peterson had no idea as to the identity of the author of that letter, she believed its contents. Hannah was allowed to resume her campaign for 9th grade Class President, and actually won the election by a landslide, much to Erika's disbelief and embarrassment. Furthermore, Sean Adams ended up asking Hannah to go with him to the Junior Prom, and she happily accepted.

As Fantastica and Fatima hovered over the students, who were dancing and talking and having a marvelous time, they were both scanning the crowd for Hannah and her friends. At that moment, Mr. Andrews took the stage to announce the royalty for the prom. A King and Queen from the 9th grade class had been chosen, along with a Prince and Princess from the 8th grade class, and the 7th grade class.

Fatima clapped her tiny hands together enthusiastically as she heard him announce Sean and Hannah's names. According to tradition, Sean and Hannah walked up to the stage with the 7th and 9th grade royalty to accept their crowns. As they took their place on the dance floor with the other two couples, the music began to play. Joining their hands together, Sean and Hannah began to dance, staring into each other's eyes. Watching from her invisible perch, Fatima immediately noticed the looks they gave each other – looks full of happiness and promise.

Dancing contentedly in Sean's arms, Hannah thought she heard a small voice whisper "congratulations," but when she looked around there was no one to be seen. She thought nothing more of it, until the end of that magical evening. Hannah was talking to her best friends, Ritchie and Darlene, when she suddenly became aware of a note in the pocket of her prom dress. The note was bright blue in color, and when she opened it there was a message written in sparkling red letters.

The note contained just two sentences, which she read aloud to her friends. The first sentence simply read, "Your wish really did come true." The second line stated, "I'll be back in time for the trip to the Science Center!" As soon as she finished uttering the words the note contained, it promptly vanished into thin air. The three friends looked at each other with expressions that were a mixture of excitement and nervousness. Then, they started laughing together; already looking forward to their next magical adventure.

Printed in the United States
57443LVS00002B/172-183

9 781424 139170